# THE NORFOLK MYSTERY

**Also by Ian Sansom**

**The Mobile Library Mystery Series**
*The Case of the Missing Books*
*Mr. Dixon Disappears*
*The Book Stops Here*
*The Bad Book Affair*

**Other Works**
*The Truth About Babies*
*Ring Road*
*The Enthusiast Almanack* (with David Herd)
*The Enthusiast Field Guide to Poetry* (with David Herd)
*Paper: An Elegy*

# THE NORFOLK MYSTERY

## A COUNTY GUIDES MYSTERY

### IAN SANSOM

**WITNESS**
**IMPULSE**

*An Imprint of HarperCollinsPublishers*

This book was originally published in 2013 by Fourth Estate, an Imprint of HarperCollins Publishers Ltd.

EPub Edition NOVEMBER 2013 ISBN: 9780062320803

Print Edition ISBN: 9780062320810

10 9 8 7 6 5 4 3 2

*For my parents*

For my parents

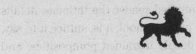

# CHAPTER ONE

REMINISCENCES, of course, make for sad, depressing literature.

Nonetheless. Some stories must be told.

In the year 1932 I came down from Cambridge with my poor degree in English, a Third – what my supervisor disapprovingly referred to as 'the poet's degree'. I had spent my time at college in jaunty self-indulgence, rising late, cutting lectures, wandering round wisteria-clad college quadrangles drinking and carousing, occasionally playing sport, and attempting – and failing – to write poetry in imitation of my great heroes, Eliot, Pound and Yeats. I had grand ambitions and high ideals, and absolutely no notion of exactly how I might achieve them.

I certainly had no intention of becoming involved in the exploits and adventures that I am about to relate.

By late August of 1932, recovering at last from the long hangover of my childhood and adolescence, and quite unable, as it turned out, to find employment suited to my ambitions and dreams, I put down my name on the books of Messrs Gabbitas and Thring, the famous scholastic agency, and so began my brief and undistinguished career as a schoolmaster.

I shall spare the uninitiated reader the intimate details of the life of the English public school: it is, suffice it to say, a world of absurd and deeply ingrained pomposities, and attracts more than its fair share of eccentrics, hysterics, malcontents and ne'er-do-wells. At Cambridge I had been disappointed not to meet more geniuses and intellectuals: I had foolishly assumed the place would be full to the brim with the brightest and the best. As a lowly schoolmaster in some of the more minor of the minor public schools, I now found myself among those I considered to be little better than semi-imbeciles and fools. After grim stints at Arnold House, Llandullas and at the Oratory in Sunning – institutions distinguished, it seemed to me, only by their ability to render both their poor pupils and their odious staff ever more insensitive and insensible – I eventually found myself, by the autumn of 1935, in a safe berth at the Hawthorns School in Hayes. This position, though carrying with it all the usual and tiresome responsibilities, was, by virtue of the school's location on the outskirts of London, much more congenial to me and afforded me the opportunity to reacquaint myself with old friends from my Cambridge days. Some had drifted into teaching or tutoring; some had found work with the BBC, or with newspapers; a lucky few had begun to make their mark in the literary and artistic realms. Those around me, it seemed, were flourishing: they rose, and rose.

I was sinking.

After leaving Cambridge I had, frankly, lost all direction, purpose and motivation. At school I had been prepared for varsity: I had not been prepared for life. After Cambridge I had given up on my poetry and became lazier than ever in my mental habits, frequenting the cinema most often to enjoy only the most vulgar and the gaudiest of its productions: *The Black Cat*, *The Scarlet Pimpernel*, *Tarzan and His Mate*. Where once I had immortal longings my dreams now were mostly of Claudette Colbert. I had also become something of an addict of the more lurid work of the detective novelists – a compensation, no doubt, for the banalities of my everyday existence. The air in the pubs around Fitzrovia in the mid-1930s, however, was thick with talk of Marx and Freud and so – if only to impress my friends and to try to keep up – I gradually found myself returning to more serious reading. I read Mr Huxley, for example – his *Brave New World*. And Ortega y Gasset's *The Revolt of the Masses*. Strachey's *The Coming Struggle for Power*. Malraux's *La Condition Humaine*. These were books in ferment, as we were: these were the writers who were dreaming *our* wild and fantastic dreams. I began to attend meetings in the evenings. I distributed pamphlets. I frequented Hyde Park Corner. I read the *Daily Worker*. I came under the sway of, first, Aneurin Bevan and, then, Harry Pollitt.

I joined the Communist Party.

In the party I had found, I believed, an outlet and a home. I devoured Marx and Engels – slowly, and in English. I was particularly struck by a phrase from the *Communist Manifesto*, which I carefully copied out by hand and taped above my shaving mirror, the better to excite and affront myself each morning: 'Finally, as the class struggle nears its decisive stage, disintegration of the ruling class and the older order of society becomes so active, so acute, that a small part of the ruling class breaks away to make common cause with the revolutionary class, the class which holds the future in its hands.' After years as a pathetic Mr Chips, conducting games, leading prayers and encouraging the work of the OTC, I was desperate to hold the future, any future, in my hands.

And so, in October 1936 I left England and the Hawthorns for Barcelona and the war.

I arrived in Spain in what I now recognise as a kind of fever of idealism. I eventually returned to England almost twelve months later in turmoil, confusion and in shock. Although I had read of the great movement of masses and the coming revolution, in Spain I saw it for myself. I had long taught my pupils the stories of the great battles and the triumphs of the kings and queens of England, the tales of the Christian martyrs, and the epic poetry of Homer, the tragedies of Shakespeare. I now faced their frightful reality.

Even now I find I am able to recall incidents from the war as if they happened yesterday, though they remain strangely disconnected in my mind, like cinematic images, or fragments of what Freud calls the dreamwork. From the first interview at the party offices on King Street – 'So you want to be a hero?' 'No.' 'Good. Because we don't need bloody heroes.' 'So are you a spy?' 'No.' 'Are you a pawn of Stalin?' 'No.' 'What are you then?' 'I am a communist' – to arriving in Paris, en route, early in the morning, sick, hung over, shitting myself with excitement in the station toilets, shaking and laughing at the absurdity of it. And then the first winter in Spain, shell holes filled to the brink with a freezing crimson liquid, like a vast jelly – blood and water mixed together. And in summer, coming across a farm where there were wooden wine vats, and climbing in and bathing in the cool wine, while the grimy, fat, terrified farmer offered his teenage daughters to us in exchange for our not murdering them all. In a wood somewhere, in the bitter cold spring of 1937, staring at irises and crocuses poking through the dark mud, and thinking absurdly of Wordsworth, the echoing sound of gunfire all around, wounded men passing by, strapped to the back of mules. The taste of water drunk from old petrol tins. The smell of excreta and urine. Olive oil. Thyme. Candle grease. Cordite. Endless sleeplessness Lice. The howling winds. The sizzling of the fat as we make an omelette in a large, black pan over an open fire, cutting it apart with our knives. Gorging on a field of ripe tomatoes. The Spanish rain. The hauling of the ancient Vickers machine guns over rocky ground.

And, of course, the dead. Everywhere the dead. Corpses laid out at the side of the road, the sight and smell of them like the mould on jam, maggots alive everywhere on their bodies. Corpses with their teeth knocked out – with the passing knock of a rifle butt. Corpses with their eyes pecked out. Corpses stripped. Corpses disembowelled. Corpses wounded, desecrated and disfigured.

In a year of fighting I was myself responsible for the murder of perhaps a dozen men, many of them killed during an attack using trench mortars on a retreating convoy along the Jaca road in March, May 1937? There was one survivor of this atrocity who lay in the long grass by the road, calling out for someone to finish him off. He had lost both his legs in the blast, and his face had been wiped away with shrapnel; he was nothing but flesh. A fellow volunteer hesitated, and then refused, but for some reason I felt no such compunction. I acted neither out of compassion nor in rage – it was simply what happened. I shot the poor soul at point-blank range with my revolver, my *mousqueton*, the short little Mauser that I had assembled and reassembled from the parts of other guns, my time with the OTC at the Hawthorns School having stood me in good stead. To my shame, I must admit not only that I found the killing easy, but that I enjoyed it: it sickened me, but I enjoyed it; it made me walk tall. I felt for the first time since leaving college that I had a purpose and a role. I felt strong and invincible. I had achieved, I believed, the ultimate importance. I was like a demi-god. A saviour. I had become an instrument of history. The Truly Strong Man.

I was, in fact, nothing but a cheap murderer.

I was vice triumphant.

Soon after, I was wounded – shot in the thigh. We had been patrolling a no-man's-land at night, somewhere near Figueras. We were ambushed. There was confusion. Men running blindly among rocks and trees. At the time, the strike of the bullet felt to me as no more than a slight shock, like an insect bite, or an inconvenience. The pain, unspeakable, came later: the feeling of jagged metal inside you. Indescribable. I was taken in a convoy of the wounded to a hospital, no more than a series of huts that had once been a bicycle workshop, requisitioned from the owners, where men lay on makeshift beds, howling and weeping, calling out in a babel of languages, row upon row of black bicycle frames and silver wheels hanging down above us, like dark mechanical angels tormenting our dreams. I was prescribed morphine and became delirious with nightmares and night sweats. Weeks turned into months. Eventually I was transferred to Barcelona, and then by train to France, and so back home to England, beaten, and limping like a wounded animal.

The adventure had lasted little more than a year.

It seemed like a lifetime.

Ironically, on returning from Spain, I found myself briefly popular, hailed by friends as a hero, and by idling fellow travellers as their representative on the Spanish Front. There were grand luncheons, at Gatti's in the Strand, and speaking engagements in the East End, wild parties at Carlton House Terrace, late night conversations in the back rooms of pubs – a disgusting, feverish gumping from place to place. Unable to comprehend exactly what had happened to me, I spoke to no one of my true experiences: of the vile corruption of the Republicans; the unspeakable coarseness and vulgarity of my fellow volunteers; the thrill of cowardly murder; my privileged glimpse of the future. I spoke instead as others willed me to speak, pretending that the war was a portent and a fulfilment, the opening salvo in some glorious final struggle against the bourgeois. Lonely and confused, attempting to pick up my life again, I ran, briefly, a series of intense love affairs, all of them with unsuitable women, all of them increasingly disagreeable to me. One such relationship was with a married woman, the wife of the headmaster of the Hawthorns, where I had returned to teach. We became deeply involved, and she began to nurture ideas of our fleeing together and starting our lives again. This proposed arrangement I knew to be not merely impossible but preposterous, and I broke off the relationship in the most shaming of fashions – humiliating her and demeaning myself. There was a scandal.

I was, naturally, dismissed from my post.

What few valuable personal belongings and furnishings I possessed – my watch, some paintings, books – I sold in order to fund my inevitable insolvency, and to buy drink. A cabin trunk I had inherited from my father, my most treasured possession – beautifully crafted in leather, and lined in watered silk, with locks and hinges of solid brass, my father's initials emblazoned upon it, and which had accompanied me from school to Cambridge and even on to Spain – I sold, in a drunken stupor, to a man in a pub off the Holloway Road for the princely sum of five shillings.

I had become something utterly unspeakable.

I was not merely an unemployed private school master.

I was a monster of my own making.

I moved into temporary lodgings in Camden Town. My room, a basement below a laundry, was let to me furnished. The furnishings extended only to a bed, a small table and a chair: it felt like a prison cell. Water ran down the walls from the laundry, puddling on the floor and peeling back the worn-out linoleum. Slugs and insects infested the place. At night I tried writing poems again, playing Debussy, and Beethoven's late quartets and Schubert's *Winterreise* – in a wonderful recording by Gerhard Hüsch, which reduced me to tears – again and again and again on my gramophone to drown out the noise of the rats scurrying on the floor above.

I failed to write the poems.

I sold the Debussys, and the Beethovens and Gerhard Hüsch singing Schubert.

And then I sold the gramophone.

During my time in Spain a shock of my hair had turned a pure white, giving me the appearance of a badger, or a skunk: with my limp, this marking seemed to make me all the more damaged, like a shattered rock, or a sliver of quartz; the mark of Cain. I had my hair cropped like a convict's and wore thin wire-rimmed spectacles, living my days as a hero-impostor, and my nights in self-lacerating mournfulness. Sleep fled from me. I found it impossible to communicate with friends who had not been to Spain, and with those who had I felt unable to broach the truth, fearing that my experiences would not correspond to their own. Milton it was – was it not? – who was of the opinion that after the Restoration the very trees and vegetation had lost heart, as he had, and had begun to grow more tardily. I came to believe, after my return from Spain, that this was indeed the case: my food and drink tasted bitter; the sky was filled with clouds; London itself seemed like a wilderness. Everything seemed thin, dead and grey.

I covered up my anxieties and fears with an exaggerated heartiness, drinking to excess until late at night and early into the morning, when I would seek out the company of women, or take myself to the Turkish Baths near Exmouth Market, where the masseur would pummel and slap me, and I could then plunge into ice-cold waters, attempting to revive myself. A drinking companion who had returned from America provided me with a supply of Seconal, which I took at night in order to help me sleep. I had become increasingly sensitive to and tormented by noise: the clanging and the banging of the city, and the groaning and chattering of people. I could nowhere find peace and quiet. During the day I would walk or cycle far out of London into the country, wishing to escape what I had become. I would picnic on bread and cheese, and lie down to nap in green fields, where memories of Spain would come flooding back to haunt me. I bound my head with my jacket, the sound of insects disturbed me so – like fireworks, or gunfire. I was often dizzy and disoriented: I felt as though I were on board ship, unable to disembark, heading for nowhere. I took aspirin every day, which unsettled my stomach. Some nights I would sleep out under the stars, in the shelter of the hedges, lighting a fire to keep me warm, begging milk from farmers and eating nuts and berries from the hedgerow. The world seemed like nothing more than a vast menacing ocean, or a desert, and I had become a nomad. Sometimes I would not return to my lodgings for days. No one noted my absences.

Near Tunbridge Wells one day, in Kent, I retreated to the safety of a public library to read *The Times* – something to distract me from my inner thoughts. Which was where I saw the advertisement, among 'Appointments & Situations Vacant':

Assistant (Male) to Writer. Interesting work; good salary and expenses; no formal qualifications necessary; applicants must be prepared to travel; intelligence essential. Write, giving full particulars, BOX E1862, The Times, E.C.4.

I had, at that moment, exactly two pounds ten shillings to my name – enough for a few weeks' food and rent, maybe a month, a little more, and then . . .

I believed I had already engineered my own doom. There was no landfall, only endless horizon. I foresaw no future.

I applied for the job.

# CHAPTER TWO

THE INTERVIEW for the post took place in a private room at the Reform Club. If I were writing a novel I should probably at this point reveal to the reader the name of my prospective employer, and the reasons for his seeking an assistant. But since I intend to make this as true an account as I can make it of what occurred during our time together, I shall content myself with gradually revealing the facts as they revealed themselves to me. I had, I should stress, absolutely no knowledge during the course of my interview of the nature of the employment to follow. If I had, I would doubtless have scorned it and thus played no part in the strange episodes and adventures that were once world-renowned but which are now in danger of being forgotten.

I arrived at the Reform Club in good time and was shown to the room where the interview was to be conducted. The last time I'd attended an interview was at the party offices on King Street, when I'd had to convince them I wanted to join the British Battalion and go to Spain. That experience had been merely chastening. This was much worse.

Several young men were already seated outside the room,

like passengers at a railway station, or patients awaiting their turn – all of them solid, dense sort of chaps, one of them in an ill-fitting pinstripe suit consulting notes; another, his hair over-slick with brilliantine, staring unblinkingly before him, as though trying to overcome the threat of terrible pain. In my tin spectacles and blue serge suit I appeared a degenerate in comparison, like a beggar, or a music-hall turn. One by one we were called into the interview room. Waiting, I found myself quietly dozing, as had become my habit due to my sleeplessness at night, and dreaming uncomfortably of Spain, of sandy roads lined with trucks carrying displaced persons, of the bodies and the blazing sun.

I was jerked awake, shaken by the man in the pinstriped suit.

'Good luck,' he said as he hurried away, still clutching his notes. He looked shell-shocked.

I was the last to be interviewed. I knocked and entered.

The room was a panelled study reminiscent of my supervisor's rooms at college, a place where I had known only deep lassitude, and the smell of pipe tobacco. Heavy damask curtains were drawn across the windows, even though it was not yet midday, and gas lamps burned, illuminating the room, which seemed to have been established as some kind of operational headquarters, a sort of den, or a dark factory of writing. There were reams of notepaper and envelopes of various types stacked in neat piles on occasional tables by the main desk, and stacks of visiting cards, a row of shining, nickel-sheathed pencils laid out neatly, and a selection of pens, and a staple press, and paper piercers, a stamp and envelope damper, an ink stand, loose-leaf manuscript books, table book-rests crammed with books, and various scribbling and memo tablets. The whole place gave off a whiff of ink, beeswax, hard work, tweed and . . . carbolic soap.

A man was seated at the main desk, typing at a vast, solid Underwood, several lamps lit around him like beacons, with dictionaries and encyclopedias stacked high, as a child might build a fortress from wooden blocks. He glanced up at me briefly over the typewriter and the books, long enough to recognise my presence and to register, I thought, his disapproval, and then his eyes returned to his work. He was, I guessed, in his late fifties, with white, neatly trimmed hair, and a luxuriant moustache in the Empire manner. He wore a light grey suit and a polka-dot bow tie, which gave him the appearance rather of a medical doctor or, I thought – the tapping of the keys of the typewriter perhaps – of a bird. A woodpecker.

'Sit,' he said. His voice was pleasant, like an old yellow vellum – the voice of a long-accomplished public speaker. It was a voice thick with the authority of books. I sat in the leather armchair facing the desk.

From this position I could see him cross and uncross his legs as he sat at the table. He had improvised for himself, I noted, as a footrest a copy of *Debrett's Peerage, Baronetage, Knightage and Companionage, illustrated with armorial bearings* – half-calf, well rubbed – his restless feet jogging constantly upon it. He wore a pair of highly polished brown brogue boots of the kind gentlemen sometimes wear for country pursuits; it was almost as if he were striding through his typing, the sound of which filled the room like gunfire. He continued to type and did not speak to me for what seemed like a long time, yet I did not find this curious silence at all unsettling, for what somehow emanated from him was a sense of complete calm and control, of light, even, a quality of personality of the kind I had occasionally encountered at Cambridge, and in Spain, among both men and women of all classes and types, a personality of the sort I believe Mr Jung calls the 'extravert', a character somehow unshadowed as many of us are shadowed, someone fully realised and confident, completely present, *blazing*. Another word for this kind of determining character, I suppose, is 'charisma', and my interviewer, whether knowing it or not, seemed to epitomise this elusive and much prized quality. He had 'it', whatever 'it' is – something more than a twinkle in the eye. He also seemed, I have to admit, deeply familiar, but I could not at this stage have identified him precisely.

'You are?' he asked, in a momentary pause from his labours.

'Stephen Sefton.'

He glanced at what I assumed were my employment particulars set out on the top of a pile of papers by his right elbow.

'Sefton. Apologies. Must finish an article,' he said. He had a large egg-timer beside the Underwood, whose sands were fast running out. 'Two minutes till the post.'

'I see,' I said.

'You can type?' he asked, continuing himself to beat out a rhythm on the keys.

'Yes.'

Rattle.

'Shorthand?'

Ping.

'I'm afraid not, sir, no.'

'I see. Too much of a' – carriage return – 'hoity-toity?'

'No, sir, I don't think so.'

Rattle. 'You'd be prepared to learn, then?'

'Yes, sir.'

'Good.' Back space.

'Photography. You can handle a camera?'

'I'm sure I could try, sir.'

'Hmm. And Cambridge, wasn't it? Christ's College.'

'Yes, sir.'

Ping.

'Which makes you rather over-qualified for this position.'

'Sorry, sir.'

Rattle.

'No need to apologise. It's just that none of the other candidates has been blessed with anything like your educational advantages, Sefton.' Carriage return.

'I have been very . . . lucky, sir.'

'Not a varsity type among them.'

'I see, sir.'

Ping.

'Curious. Perhaps you can tell me about it.'

'About what, sir?'

'What went wrong.'

'What went wrong? I . . . I don't know what went wrong.'

'Clearly. Well, tell me about the college then, Sefton.'

'The college?'

'Yes. Christ's College. I am intrigued.'

'Well, it was very . . . nice.'

'Nice?'

He paused in his typing and peered dimly at me in a

manner I later came to recognise as a characteristic sign of his disbelief and despair at another's complete ignorance and lack of effort. 'Come on, man. Buck up. You can do better than that, can't you?'

I was uncertain as to how to respond.

'I certainly enjoyed my time there, sir.'

'I believe you did enjoy your time at college, Sefton. Indeed, I see by your abysmal degree classification that you may have enjoyed your time there rather more than was advisable.'

'Perhaps, sir, yes.'

'Too rich to work, are we?'

'No, sir,' I replied. I was not, in fact, rich at all. My parents were dead. The family fortune, such as it was, had been squandered. I had inherited only cutlery, crockery, debts, regrets and memories.

He looked at me sceptically. And then tap, tap, tap, tap, tap, tap, tap, and then a final and resounding tap as the sands of the timer ran out. A knock came at the door.

'Eleven o'clock post,' said my interviewer. 'Enter!'

A porter entered the dark room as my interviewer peeled the page he had been typing from the Underwood, shook it decisively, folded it twice, placed it in an envelope, sealed it and handed it over. The porter left the room in silence.

My interviewer then checked his watch, promptly up-ended his egg-timer – 'Fifteen minutes,' he said – sat back in his chair, stroked his moustache, and returned to the subject we had been discussing as if nothing had occurred.

'I was asking about the history of the college, Sefton.'

'I'm afraid I don't know much about the history, sir.'

'It was founded by?'

'I don't know, sir.'

'I see. You are interested in history, though?'

'I have taught history, sir, as a schoolmaster.'

'That's not the question I asked, though, Sefton, is it?'

'No, sir.'

'Schooled at Merchant Taylors', I see.' He brandished my curriculum vitae before him, as though it were a piece of dubious evidence and I were a felon on trial.

'Yes, sir.'

'Never mind. Keen on sports?'

'Yes, sir.'

'No time for them myself. Except perhaps croquet. And boxing. Greyhound racing. Motor racing. Speedway. Athletics . . . They've ruined cricket. And you fancy yourself as a writer, I see?'

'I wouldn't say that, sir.'

'It says here, publications in the *Public Schools' Book of Verse*, 1930, 1931 and 1932.'

'Yes, sir.'

'So, you're a poet?'

'I write poetry, sir.'

'I see. The modern stuff, is it?'

'I suppose it is, sir. Yes.'

'Hm. You know Wordsworth, though?'

'Yes, sir, I do.'

'Go ahead, then.'

'Sorry, sir, I don't understand. Go ahead with what?'

'A recitation, please, Sefton. Wordsworth. Whatever you choose.'

And he leaned back in his chair, closed his eyes, and waited.

It was fortunate – both fortunate, in fact, and unfortunate – that while at Merchant Taylors' I had been tutored by the late Dr C.T. Davis, a Welshman and famously strict disciplinarian, who beat us boys regularly and relentlessly, but who also drummed into us passages of poetry, his appalling cruelty matched only by his undeniable intellectual ferocity. If a boy failed to recite a line correctly, Davis – who, it seemed, knew the whole of the corpus of English poetry by heart – would literally throw the book at him. There were rumours that more than one boy had been blinded by Quiller-Couch's *Oxford Book of English Verse*. I myself was several times beaten about the ears with Tennyson and struck hard with *A Shropshire Lad*. By age sixteen, however, we victim-beneficiaries of Dr Davis's methods were able to recite large parts of the great works of the English poets, as well as Homer and Dante. We had also, as a side effect, become enemies of authority, our souls spoiled and our minds tainted for ever with bitterness towards serious learning. But no matter. At my interviewer's prompting I began gladly to recall the beginning of the *Prelude*, as familiar to me as a popular song:

Oh there is blessing in this gentle breeze,
A visitant that while it fans my cheek
Doth seem half-conscious of the joy it brings
From the green fields, and from yon azure sky.

These words seemed to please my interviewer – as much, if not more so than they would have done Dr Davis himself – for he leaned forward across the Underwood and joined me in the following lines:

Whate'er its mission, the soft breeze can come
To none more grateful than to me; escaped
From the vast city, where I long had pined
A discontented sojourner: now free,
Free as a bird to settle where I will.

He then fell silent as I continued.

What dwelling shall receive me? in what vale
Shall be my harbour? underneath what grove
Shall I take up my home? and what clear stream
Shall with its murmur lull me into rest?
The earth is all before me. With a heart
Joyous, nor scared at its own liberty,
I look about; and should the chosen guide
Be nothing better than a wandering cloud,
I cannot miss my way. I breathe again!

'Very good, very good,' pronounced my interlocutor, waving his hand dismissively. 'Now. Canada's main imports and exports?'

This sudden change of tack, I must admit, threw me entirely. I rather thought I had hit my stride with the Wordsworth. But it seemed my interviewer was in fact no aesthete, like our beloved Dr Davis, nor indeed a scrupuland like the loathed Dr Leavis, the man who had quietly dominated the English School at Cambridge while I was there, with his thumbscrewing *Scrutiny*, and his dogmatic belief in literature as the vital force of culture. Poetry, I had been taught, is the highest form of literature, if not indeed of human endeavour: it yields the highest form of pleasure and teaches the highest form of wisdom. Yet poetry for my interviewer seemed to be no more than a handy set of rhythmical facts, and about as significant or useful as a times table, or a knowledge of the workings of the internal combustion engine. I had of course absolutely no idea what Canada's main imports and exports might be and took a wild guess at wood, fish and tobacco. These were not, as it turned out, the correct answers – 'Precious metals?' prompted my interviewer, as though a man without knowledge of such simple facts were no better than a savage – and the interview took a turn for the worse.

'Could you give ten three-letter nouns naming food and drink?'

'Rum, sir?'

'Rum?' My interviewer's face went white, to match his moustache.

'Yes.'

'Anything else, Sefton – anything apart from distilled and fermented drink?'

'Cod?'

'Yes.'

'Eel?'

'Satisfactory, if curious choices,' my interviewer concluded. 'You might more obviously have had egg or pea.'

'Or pig, sir?'

'A pig, I think you'll agree, is an animal, Sefton. It is not a foodstuff until it has been butchered and made into joints. A pig is *potential* food, is it not?'

'Yes, sir.'

'Tell me, Sefton, are you able to adapt yourself quickly and easily to new sets of circumstances?'

'I believe I am sir, yes.'

'And could you give me an example?'

I suggested that in my work as a schoolmaster I had encountered numerous occasions when I had been required to adapt to circumstances. I did not explain that one such occasion was when I had been found in a compromising situation with the headmaster's wife. Fortunately, my interviewer did not ask for further elaboration and we returned promptly to questions of more import: the lives of the saints; folk customs; Latin tags; the classification of plants and animals. During the conversation he would glance concernedly at the egg-timer on his desk and thrum his fingers on the table, as though batting against time itself.

'You seem to have a reasonably well-stocked mind, Sefton.'

'Thank you, sir.'

'As one would expect. Languages?'

'French, sir. Latin. Greek. German. Some Spanish.'

'Yes. I see you were in Spain.'

'I was, sir.'

'A Byron on the barricades?'

'I never considered myself as such, no, sir.'

'*No pasaran.*'

'That's correct, sir.'

'Unable to fight in Spain, I learned Spanish instead.'

We spoke for a few minutes in Spanish, my interviewer remarking in a rudimentary way upon the weather and enquiring about the prices of rooms in hotels.

'Your Spanish is certainly satisfactory, Sefton,' he said. 'Good. Do you have any questions about the position?'

'Yes, sir.'

My main question, naturally, was what the position was

and what it might entail – I still had no clear idea. I cleared my throat and tried to formulate the question in as inoffensive a manner as possible. 'I wondered, sir, exactly what it might . . . entail, working as your assistant?'

My interviewer looked at me directly and unguardedly at this point, in a way that made me feel exceedingly uncomfortable. He had a way of looking at you that seemed violently frank, as though willing you to reveal yourself. And when he spoke he lowered his voice, as though confiding a secret.

'Well, Sefton. I hope I can be honest with you?'

'By all means, sir.'

'Good.' He carefully fingered his moustache before going on. The light of the lamps was reflected in his eyes. 'I believe, Sefton, that there is a terrible darkness deepening all around us. We face not *un mauvais quart d'heure*, Sefton, but something more serious. Do you understand what I am saying?'

'I think so, sir.'

I was not at all sure in fact if the serious darkness he was referring to was the darkness I had encountered in Spain, and which haunted me in my dreams, or if it were some other, ineffable darkness of a kind with which I was not familiar.

'I think perhaps you do see, Sefton.' He stared hard at me, as though attempting to penetrate my thoughts, his voice gradually rising in volume and pitch. 'Anyway. It is my intention to shed some light while I may.'

'I see, sir.'

'I hope that you do, Sefton. It has been my life's work. What I see around me, Sefton, is the world as we know it rapidly disappearing: the food we eat; the work we do; the way we talk; the way we consort ourselves. Everything changing. All of it about to go, or gone already: the miller, the blacksmith, the wheelwright. Destroyed by the rhythms of our machine age.' He paused again to stroke his moustache. 'It has been my great privilege, Sefton, in my career to visit the great countries and cities of the world: Paris, Vienna, Rome. I intend my last great project to be about our own enchanted land.'

'England, sir.'

'Precisely. The British Isles, Sefton. These islands. The archipelago. Before they disappear completely.'

'Very good, sir.'

He fell silent, staring into the middle distance.

I felt that my question about the job had not been answered entirely or clearly, and realised I might need to prompt him for a more direct answer. 'And what exactly would the person appointed by you be required to do, sir, on your . . . project?'

'Ah. Yes. What I need, Sefton, is someone to write up basic copy that I shall then jolly up and make good. The person appointed would also be required to make arrangements for travel and accommodation, and to assist me in all aspects of my researches on the project as I see fit.'

'I see, sir.'

'I shan't give you a false impression of my daily rounds, Sefton. There is no glamour. It is tiresome work requiring long hours, endurance and determination.'

'I understand, sir.'

'And do you think you're up to such a task?'

'I believe so, sir.'

'Are you married, Sefton?'

[ 23 ]

'No, sir.'

'Engaged to be married?'

'No, sir.'

'A homosexual?'

'No, sir.'

'Pets?'

'No, sir.'

'Good. We've plenty of those already. You don't mind dogs?'

'No, sir.'

'Terriers?'

'No, sir.'

'Cats?'

'No, sir.'

'Birds?'

'No, sir.'

'Aversions or allergies to any kind of animals?'

'Not that I know of, sir.'

'And you are not in current employ?'

'No, sir.'

'Good. So you'd be able to start immediately?'

'Yes, sir.'

'Very well.'

My curiosity had certainly been piqued by my interviewer's description of his enterprise, but after several rounds of questioning I was still keen to know more about the details. I made one more bid for clarity. 'Can I ask, sir, exactly what the project is to be?'

'The project?' He sounded surprised, as though the nature of his work was widely known. 'A series of books, Sefton, called *The County Guides*. A complete series of guides to the counties of England.'

'All of them, sir?'

'Indeed.'

'How many counties are there?'

'Schoolmaster, aren't we, Sefton?'

'Yes, sir.'

'Well, then? Let me ask you the question: how many counties are there?'

'Forty? thirty-nine?'

'Thirty-nine. Exactly.'

'So, thirty-nine books?'

'We may also include the bailiwicks of Guernsey and Jersey, Sefton. In which case there shall be forty-one.'

'An ... ambitious project then, sir.' It struck me, in fact, not so much as ambitious as the very definition of folly.

'In a life, Mr Sefton, of finite duration I can't imagine why anyone would wish to embark on any other kind of project. Can you?'

'No, sir.'

'I intend the *County Guides* as nothing less than the new Domesday Book. I shall be going out into England with my assistant to find all the good things and to put them down.'

'Only the good, sir?'

'The books are intended as a celebration, yes, Sefton.'

'Works of ... selective amnesia, then, sir?'

My interviewer frowned deeply at this untoward remark. 'Among those I would call the "not-so-intelligentsia", Sefton, I know there to be an inclination to talk down our great nation. Are you one such down-talker?'

'I like to think I'm a realist, sir.'

'As am I, Sefton, as am I. Which is why I am undertaking this project. You may wish to reflect, sir, that you are of a generation that may live to see the year 2000, from which distant perspective you will be viewing a nation doubtless very different from that which you see around you now. It is my desire merely to set down a record of this place before its roots are cut and its sap drained, and the ancient oaks are felled once and for all. I do not wish England – our England – to be unknown by future generations. Do you understand, Sefton?'

'I think so, sir.'

'Good.' He shifted in his seat and he glanced around the room, as though someone were among us. 'Because I believe I can feel the chilly hand of fate coming upon us, Sefton. *The County Guides* I hope shall be clarion calls: they may be memorials.' He paused momentarily for reflection upon this profundity.

'And how long do you imagine this great enterprise will take, sir?'

'I intend to have completed the series by the end of the decade, Sefton.'

'By 1940?'

'1939 I think you'll find marks the end of the decade, Sefton. 1940 forms a part of the next, surely?'

'Yes, of course.'

'So, 1939's our deadline.'

'A book on every county? By 1939?'

'On every county, yes, Sefton. And by 1939. A celebration of England and the Englishman. From the wheelwrights of Devon to the potters of the north, from the shoe-makers of Northampton to the chair-makers of High Wycombe, the books will be—'

'The chair-makers of High Wycombe?'

'Renowned for its chair-making, Sefton. Do you know nothing of the English counties? Anyway, as I was explaining. I envisage this not merely as my *magnum opus*, but as a *magnum bonum. De omnibus rebus, et quibusdam aliis*—'

'But that's . . . dozens of books a year, sir.'

'Precisely. Which is why I need an assistant, Sefton.'

'I see, sir.' The sheer scale of the task seemed ludicrous, lunatic. Which is, I think, what appealed: my own life had already reached the brink.

'I was ably assisted for a number of years, Sefton, by my daughter and by my late wife. But my daughter is . . . maturing. And so I find myself . . . seeking to employ another. Anyway,' he announced, as the final grains of sand gathered to announce the passing of fifteen minutes, '*tempus fugit.*'

'*Irreparable tempus,*' I said.

He glanced at me approvingly. 'The hour is coming, Sefton, when no man may work.'

'Indeed, sir.'

And at this he rose from his seat and walked towards the door. I followed. 'I do hope that you don't imagine that because of our surroundings today' – he gestured into the gloom around him – 'that we shall be going in for ritzy social gatherings, Sefton.'

'No, sir. Not at all.'

'Or chatterbangs. No swirl of the cocktail eddies here.'

'I understand, sir.'

'Good. Well. That'll be all, I think, Sefton. I'll send a telegram.' He went to shake my hand.

'Actually, sir. I have one more question, if I may.'

'Yes?'

There was one question that remained unanswered, and which I was keen to have resolved before leaving the room.

'Might I ask your name, sir?'

'My name? My apologies. I thought you knew, Sefton. My name is Morley. Swanton Morley.'

# CHAPTER THREE

Swanton Morley.

Anyone who grew up in England after the Great War will naturally be familiar with the name, a name synonymous with popular learning – the learning, that is, of the kind scorned by my bloodless professors at Cambridge, and adored by the throbbing masses. Swanton Morley was, depending on which newspaper you read, a poor man's Huxley, a poor man's Bertrand Russell, or a poor man's Trevelyan. According to the title of his popular column in the *Daily Herald* he was, simply, 'The People's Professor'.

Morley's story is, of course, well known: a shilling life will give you all the facts. (I rely here, for my own background information, on Burchfield's popular *The People's Professor*, and R.F. Bolton's *Mind's Work: The Life of Swanton Morley*.) Born in poverty in rural Norfolk, and having left school at fourteen, Morley began his career in local newspapers as a copy-holder. Coming of age at the turn of the century, he had 'stepped boldly forward', according to Bolton, 'to become one of the heroes of England's emancipated classes'. By the time he was twenty-five years old he was the editor of the

*Westminster Gazette.* 'Unyielding in his mental habits', in Burchfield's phrase, Morley had grown up the only child of elderly, Methodist parents. He was a man of strict principles, known for his temperance campaigns, his fulminations against free trade, and his passionate denunciations of the evils of tobacco. He was also an amateur entomologist, a beekeeper, a keen cyclist, a gentleman farmer, a member of the Linnean Society and the Royal Society, the founder of the Society for the Prevention of Litter – and the chairman of so many committees and charitable organisations that Bolton provides an appendix in order to list them and all his other extraordinarily various and energetic outpourings of the self.

On the day of my interview, however, I knew absolutely none of this.

Like most of the British public, I knew not of Morley the man, but of Morley's books. Everyone knew the books. Morley produced books like most men produce their pocket handkerchiefs, his rate of production being such that one might almost have suspected him of being under the influence of some drug or narcotic, if it weren't for his reputation as a man of exemplary habits and discipline. Morley had published, on average, since the early 1900s, half a dozen books a year. And I had read not one of them.

I had *heard* of his books: everyone had heard of his books, just as everyone has heard of Oxo cubes, or Bird's Custard Powder. I had certainly seen his books for sale at railway stations, and at W.H. Smith's. I can even vividly recall a bookcase on the top landing of my parents' home – beneath the sloping roof and the stained-glass window – containing a set of Morley's leather-bound *Children's Cyclopaedia*, which I may perhaps, as a young child, have thumbed through. But they left no lasting impression. Swanton Morley was not an author who produced what I, as a young child, would have regarded as 'literature' – he was no Edgar Rice Burroughs, no Jack London, no Guy Boothby or Talbot Baines Reed, no Conan Doyle – and by the time I had reached my adolescence I had already begun to fancy myself a highbrow, and so Morley's sticky-sweet concoctions of facts and tales of moral uplift would have been terribly infra dig. Finally, Dr Leavis at Cambridge had effectively purged any lingering taste I may have had for the middle- and the lowbrow. Morley and I, one might say, were characters out of sympathy, of different kinds, and destined never to meet.

But I was also, at that moment in time, out of work, out of luck and out of options.

On leaving the Reform Club after my interview, I therefore found myself walking up Haymarket, and then along Shaftesbury Avenue and onto the Charing Cross Road. I thought I might visit Foyle's Bookshop, in order to catch up with a lifetime's reading on Mr Swanton Morley.

Crowds thronged outside Foyle's, the usual overcoated men rifling through the sale books, the publishers' announcements filling the vast windows, one of which was given over to the current 'Book of the Week', a volume optimistically titled *Future Possibilities*. Two dismal young boys in blue berets prodded a shuffling monkey in a red cap to keep moving in circles on the pavement to the sick-making tune of their hurdy-gurdies. The customary beggar stood outside the main door, scraping on a violin, a piece of card hung around his neck. 'Four Years' Active Service, No Pension, Unable to Work'. Pity and loathing made me give him a penny.

To enter into a bookseller's is of course to feel an instant elevation in one's mental station – or it should be. My father had once held an account with Ellis of 29 Bond Street, a bookseller that raised the tone not merely of those entering the shop, but even of those merely passing it by, and I had visited small bookshops in Barcelona, and others in the Palais Royale in Paris, whose elegance seemed to rub off on the browser, like fine print from the daily papers. But Foyle's is not, and never has been, a place of elegance and enlightenment: it is a shop, merely, a very large shop, but most definitely a shop, a place of sales, a department store for books, with its vast stock and signs jumbled everywhere, shelf rising inexplicably above shelf, book upon book, complex corridor upon complex corridor. I squeezed into the main lobby past a young lady in an apron dusting the top row of a long shelf displaying Sir Isaac Pitman's apparently endless Industrial Administration Series, and asked the first shopwalker I could find, a young man, where I might discover the works of Swanton Morley. He turned from casually rearranging an inevitable shelf of those dreadful, faddish books – including *How Not to be Fat, Why Not Grow Young?* and *Eating Without Fear* – and escorted me daintily to a long wooden counter, bearing vivid colour posters advertising a new edition of *Kettner's Book of the Table*, where a young lady – who might easily have been a barmaid were it not for the fact of her wearing spectacles – seemed more than prepared to assist.

'Swanton Morley? One moment, please,' she said efficiently, turning to reach behind her for a large red volume whose embossed spine announced it as *The Reference Catalogue for Current Literature 1936*. 'I'll just check in Whitaker's.' She opened up the book, began rifling through the pages. 'Would you like me to note down the titles for you, sir?'

'No thank you.' I thought I should be able to remember a few titles.

'Very well,' she said, her finger sliding slowly down the page and finally coming to rest. 'Here we are now. *Morley's Animal Husbandry*. That would be in Animal Lore, sir, second floor.'

'Good.' I made a mental note of Animal Lore, second floor.

'*Morley's Art for All*. Aesthetics, sir, second floor.'

I nodded. She continued.

'*Morley's Astronomy for Amateurs*. Astronomy, third floor . . . *Morley's Carpentering*. Carpentering, second floor. *Morley's Children's Songs and Games*, ground floor . . . Cookery, first floor . . . Education, fourth floor . . .'

'Wait, wait, wait,' I said. 'Third floor, second floor, first floor, ground floor.'

'Fourth floor,' she added.

'And how many floors have you?'

'Four. Unless you have a specific book in mind, sir, you might be better simply browsing among our stock. Mr Morley seems to have published many . . .' She slid the big red book around so I could see the entries. 'Gosh. Possibly hundreds of books, sir.'

'I see.' The list of Morley's books ran to two pages of two-columned tiny type: my eyes glazed over at the mere thought of them.

Nonetheless, I wandered contentedly alone for the rest of the afternoon through Foyle's great avenues of books. As readers will doubtless be aware, books in Foyle's are not much arranged; within their categories books seem to be classified variously, and possibly randomly, by name, or by title, or by publisher. Some books seemed to have been undisturbed for many years, and many of the rooms were entirely deserted. But Swanton Morley was everywhere: he seemed successfully to have colonised the entire shop. During the course of a long afternoon I discovered not only books about poetry, and philosophy, and economics, which I had expected, but also campaigning works – *The Cigarette Peril*, *Testaments Against the Bottle*, *War: The Living Reality* – and volumes on gardening, marriage, medicine and mineralogy. In Religion I found *Morley's Children's Bible*. In Music, *Learn to Listen with Morley*. Elsewhere, in and out of their appropriate places I came across *Morley's Happy Traveller*, *Morley's Nature Story Book*, *Morley's Animal Adventures*, *Morley's Adventure Story Book*, *Morley's Book for Girls*, *Morley's Book for Boys*, *Morley's Everyday Science*, *Morley's Book of the Sea*, *Morley's Tales of the Travellers*, *Morley's Lives of the Famous*, *Morley's British Mammals*, *Morley's Old Wild West* . . . The sheer plenitude was astonishing, dumbing. It was as if the man were writing in constant fear of running out of ink. *Morley's Want to Know About . . . ?* series were everywhere. *Want to Know About Iceland? Want to Know About Shakespeare? Want to Know About Trees?* Just the thought of them made me want to give up knowing about anything. *Morley's Book of the World*, a four-volume set I came across misplaced among books on Veterinary Science, made the boast on its dust jacket that a book by Swanton Morley could be found in every household in Britain. They were certainly to be found on almost every shelf in Foyle's.

The books, qua books, varied in their quality from edition to edition: some were lavishly illustrated with pictures, plain and coloured, and mezzotint portraits; others were dense with type; some with fine bindings; others in cheap, flexible cardboard covers. And yet for all their apparent variety, the books were all written in the same tone – a kind of joyous, enthusiastic, maddening tone. The pose was of the jaunty professor – or, dare one say, the eccentric sixth-form master – and yet I thought, leafing through various volumes, that I occasionally caught sight of a desperate man fleeing from the abyss. This, for example, from *Morley's History of Civilisation*: 'Some may say that man is but a speck of mud suspended in space. I say to them, some mud, that can know what suffering is, that can love and weep, and know longing!' Or this, from *Morley's English Usage*: 'The world may be troubled and difficult: our words need not be so.'

But perhaps I was reading my own experiences into the work.

I returned to my room in the early evening, depressed, dizzied and depleted.

As I made my way wearily down the stone steps towards my dank basement, a Chinaman hurried out of the laundry at street level above. He wore his little black skull cap and his long thin black coat turned green with age. We had occasionally exchanged greetings, though he could speak no English and I no Chinese – I was anyway far beyond the desire to be neighbourly. He smiled at me toothlessly, thrust a telegram into my hand, and hurried back to his work.

I tore open the telegram, which read simply:

'CONGRATULATIONS. STOP. HOLT. STOP.

5.30 TOMORROW.'

# CHAPTER FOUR

As it happened, I had no other pressing engagements.

And so, the next day, I packed my few belongings – a spare suit, some thin volumes of poetry, my old Aquascutum raincoat, my supply of Seconal and aspirin – into a cardboard suitcase which I had managed to salvage from the wrack and wreckage of my life, and left my lodgings for Liverpool Street Station. There I found the connections for Holt, spent all my remaining money on the ticket and a supply of tobacco, and set off to meet my new employer, Mr Swanton Morley. The People's Professor.

As the train pulled away I felt a great relief, a burden lifting from my shoulders, and I found myself grinning at myself in the window of the carriage. Little more than eighteen months previously I had left London – Victoria Station, the boat train for France, then Paris – for Spain, a young man full of dreams, about to embark on my great moral crusade, with justice on my side and my fellow man alongside me. Now, gaunt, limping, and my hair streaked with white, I saw myself for what I was: a man entirely alone, scared even of the roar of the steam train and motor traffic, impoverished and rootless. I had of course no idea at that moment, but in giving up on my absurd fantasies of performing on the stage of world history I had in fact unwittingly become a small and insignificant part of the terrible drama of our time. I had imagined that I was to determine the course of history, but history had taken possession of me. And if, as they say, nature is a rough school of men and women, then history is rougher ... But already I am beginning to sound like Morley.

I should continue with the tale.

It had always been my ambition to travel. My father's job as a royal messenger had meant that he had been all over Europe and further afield, scurrying from Balmoral to Windsor and to Whitehall, carrying with him letters of royalty and of state, emblazoned with the proud stamp OHMS. When I was a boy he would recount to me his stirring adventures among the Czechs, and the Serbians, and the Slovaks and Slovenes, dodging spies and brigands who tried to steal his dispatch case – tales in which he would triumph by courteous manners – and although we lived in relatively modest circumstances in a small house in Kensington, I had been introduced at an early age to ambassadors and diplomats from France, and China and Japan, and had imagined for myself a future abroad in khaki, and in starched collars, striped trousers and sun-helmet, upholding the Empire by good manners and breeding alone. In my own country I took little interest: I cared nothing for the Boat Race, or Epsom, or cricket at Lord's. My dreams were of Balkan beauties, of Paris, Hungary and Berlin, of steamers on the Black Sea, and of adventures in Asia Minor. I imagined camels, and consuls and tussles with petty local officials. I harboured absolutely no desires to travel up and down on the branch lines of England.

Nonetheless, as we passed the houses and churches and slums of east London I felt the familiar ecstasy of departure. I took two Seconal, a handful of aspirin, and felt myself released again from the vast jaws of my ambitions, and fell into a troubled sleep – dreams of Spain confused with visions of a ruined London, flying demons dropping explosives overhead, fires raging in the streets, men slithering like beasts, every town and every city throbbing with fear and violence.

I woke thick-headed some time before we arrived in Melton Constable, where I changed quickly onto the branch railway, a little three-carriage local train done out proudly in its golden ochre livery, and which heaved its way slowly through the meadows of East Anglia. I took a window seat in the second-class non-smoker, the only seat remaining, and, gasping for air and desperate to smoke, ignoring the protests of my fellow passengers, pulled down a leather strap on the window – and was immediately assaulted by a dusky country smell of muck and manure. I quickly abandoned all thoughts of a cigarette. I hadn't eaten all day, and the country smells, and the pathetic chugging of the train resulted in my feeling distinctly hag-ridden by the time we made Holt Station at precisely five thirty. I was the only passenger to disembark at Holt – porters hauled a couple of milk crates and packages out of the luggage van, a guard walked down the platform, closing each door, and then the bold little vermilion engine went on its way – and it was too late when I realised that I had left my cardboard suitcase on the train, with my spare suit, my poetry, my tobacco and my pills.

I looked around for any signs of help, welcome or assistance.

There was none. The porters had vanished. The guard gone.

And there was absolutely no sign of Morley.

Nor was there anyone in the station office – though a set of dominoes set out upon a table suggested recent occupation and activity. Outside, in the gravelled forecourt, was a car with a woman leaning up against it, languidly smoking, chatting to the young man who, I assumed from his uniform, should have been manning the station. I could see that the young lady might prove more of a distraction than a solitary game of dominoes. She wore her dark hair in a sharp, asymmetric bob – which gave her what one might call an early Picasso kind of a profile – and she was wearing clothes that might have been more appropriate for a cocktail party down in London rather than out here in the wilds of Norfolk: a pale blue-grey close-fitting dress, which she wore with striking red high-heeled shoes, and buttoned red leather gloves. It was a daring ensemble, deliberately hinting, I thought, at desires barely restrained; and her crocodile handbag, the size of a small portmanteau, suggested some imminent, illicit assignation. She struck one immediately as the kind of woman who attended fork luncheons and fancy dress parties with the Guinnesses, and who had 'ideas' about Art and who was passionate in various causes; the sort of woman who cultivated an air of mystery and romance. I had encountered her type on my return from Spain at fashionable gatherings in the homes of wealthy fellow travellers. Such women wearied me.

'Well!' she said, turning first towards and then quickly

away from me, narrowing her eyes in a glimmering fashion. 'You'll do.' There was a tone of studied boredom in her words that attempted to belie her more than apparent perk.

'I'm sorry, miss, I do beg your pardon.'

She threw away her cigarette, ground it out theatrically under her foot, and climbed into the car. 'Bye, Tommy!' she called to the station guard, who began sauntering back to his office.

'Goodbye, miss,' he called, waving, red-faced, placing his cap back upon his head.

'Excuse me,' I said, addressing him. 'I need to ask about my luggage. It's gone missing. I wonder if—'

'Well, come on, then, if you're coming,' the young woman interrupted, impatiently, patting the smooth white leather seat beside her in the car.

'I'm awfully sorry, miss,' I said, 'I'm waiting for someone and—'

'Yes! *Me*, silly!' she said. 'Come on.'

'I'm afraid you're mistaken, miss. I'm waiting for a Mr Swanton Morley.'

She cocked her head slightly as she looked at me, in a way that was familiar. 'Sefton, isn't it?' she said.

'Yes.'

'Well, I'm here to collect you, you silly prawn, come on.'

'Ah!' I said. 'I do apologise. It's just, I was expecting . . . Mr Morley himself.'

'I'm Miriam,' she said. 'Miriam Morley. And wouldn't you rather *I* was collecting you than Father?'

It was an impossible question to answer.

'Well,' I said, extending my hand. 'Pleased to meet you, Miss Morley.'

She raised her fingers lightly to my own.

'Charmed, I'm sure.'

'If you wouldn't mind waiting a moment I need to see if I can arrange for my luggage, which I'm afraid I've left on the—'

'Tommy'll sort all that out, won't you, Tommy?' she said.

'Certainly, ma'am,' said Tommy obediently.

'There,' she said, her eyes flashing at me. 'Now that's sorted, hop in and hold on to your hat!' she cried. I did as instructed, having no alternative, and as soon as I'd shut the door she jerked off the brake, thrust the gearstick forward, and we went sailing at high speed through the deserted streets of Holt.

'Lovely little town,' I said politely, above the roaring noise of the engine.

'Dull!' she cried back. 'Dull as ditchwater!'

We soon came to a junction, at which we barely paused, swung to the right, and headed down through woods, signs pointing to Letheringsett, the Norfolk sky broad above us.

I felt a knotted yearning in my stomach – a yearning for cigarettes and pills.

'Since we're to be travelling together, miss, I wonder if you might be able to spare me a cigarette?'

'In the glove compartment,' she said. 'Go ahead. Take the packet.'

I took a cigarette, lit it, and inhaled hungrily.

'Manners?' said my companion.

'Sorry, miss? You'd rather I didn't smoke?'

'Don't be ridiculous! Do I look like a maiden aunt?' She did not. 'But I would expect a gentleman to offer me one of my own cigarettes. Unless of course you are not a gentleman . . . ?'

I lit another cigarette from my own, and passed it across.

'So,' she yelled at me, as we screeched around a sharp corner at the bottom of the hill, barely controlling the animal-like ferocity of the car. 'You're not one of Father's dreadful acolytes?'

'No. I don't think so,' I said. 'I—'

'Good. He usually attracts terrible types. Teetotallers. Non-smokers. Buddhists, even! Have you ever met a Buddhist, Sefton?'

'No, miss, I don't think—'

'Dreadful people. Breathe through their noses. Disgusting. Being in the public eye, as we are, one does attract the most peculiar people. Hundreds of letters every week – some of them from *actual* lunatics in *actual* lunatic asylums! Can you imagine! Even the so-called normal ones are rather creepy. And we have people turning up at the house sometimes with cameras, wishing to take his photograph. Quite ridiculous! Isn't it, Sefton?' She looked across at me, searching my face for agreement.

'Yes,' I said, wishing that she'd pay more attention to the road. We passed, in quick succession: a large water mill to the left, offering for sale its own flour and oats; signs for a place called, improbably, Glandford, to the right; a large, rambling coaching inn, charabancs parked outside; a brand-new manor house sporting out-of-proportion Greek columns; and then a gypsy caravan by the side of the road, filthy gypsy children riding an Irish wolfhound before it, a pipe-smoking woman tending a fire alongside it, stirring a black pot of what may well have been goulash, but which was probably rabbit stew and, propped up against a nearby tree, a hand-painted sign advertising 'Gypsy Pegs, Knife-

Sharpening, Card Readings, Puppies'. I was suddenly struck by the rich and exotic beauty of the English countryside, as strange in its way as, say, India, or Port Said. Norfolk: North Africa. 'It really is rather splendid here, miss, isn't it?'

'Oh come on, Sefton! It's dull! Dull! Dull! Dull! I can't stand being stuck up here with Father. But then where's one supposed to go these days? Even London's getting to be so boring. It's becoming like a suburb of New York, don't you think?' She spoke as if having rehearsed her lines.

'I'm afraid I've not had the pleasure of visiting New York, Miss Morley.'

'Well, why don't you take me one day, Sefton, and I'll show you round.'

'Well. I'll certainly . . . think about that, Miss Morley.'

'Call me Miriam.'

'I'll stick with Miss Morley, thank you.'

'Oh, don't be such a stick-in-the-mud, Sefton. What's the point of such formalities? I believe in being brutally frank.'

'Very good, miss,' I said.

'Really. Brutally, Sefton. I'll be brutally open and frank with you, and you can be brutally open and frank with me. How does that sound? The best way between grown men and women, isn't it?'

'I'm not sure, miss,' I said.

'Oh, don't be so solemn! It's terribly boring. I'd hoped you might be more fun.'

'I do my best, miss.'

'To be fun?' she said, taking both hands from the wheel and tossing away her half-smoked cigarette. 'Do you now? I'll be the judge of that, shall I? Anyway, I should warn you, seeing as you're going to be staying with us, that despite what everyone thinks, Father is an *absolute* tyrant, and a *complete* dinosaur.'

'I think, miss, it might be more appropriate if—'

'Appropriate! Are you always so proper and correct, Sefton?'

'Not always, miss. No.'

'Good. I'm only telling you the truth. I'm having terrible trouble persuading him to introduce American plumbing at the moment. He believes in early morning starts and cold baths. He's up studying at five, for goodness sake. I mean, reading before breakfast! Ugh! Rather grisly, don't you think? Imagine what it must do to the digestion.'

'Your father, I believe, is a very . . . diligent and profound student of—'

'Oh, do give over, Sefton! He's a madman. Forever writing. Forever reading. Continually being overcome with wonder at the world. It all makes for terribly boring company. Do you believe in early morning starts?'

'It rather depends what one has been engaged in the night before,' I said.

'Quite so, Sefton! Quite so! You know, you might prove to be an ally about the place after all. What about hot baths?'

'I have no strong opinion about hot baths,' I said.

We had long passed Letheringsett, and were heading for Saxlingham.

'"Hot baths are the root of our present languor,"' she said, in a more than passable imitation of her father. '"The hot bath is a medical emergency rather than a diurnal tonic. It destroys the oil of the skin." Ridiculous! Anyway, Sefton, you're prepared?'

'For what?' I said.

'What do you imagine I'd be asking you to be prepared for, Sefton?' She raised a bold eyebrow beneath her bold asymmetric bob. 'For this ludicrous new enterprise of his, silly.'

'*The County Guides*?'

'Yes. Absurd, isn't it? As if anyone's interested in history these days. Ye Olde Merrie Englande? Ye Cheshire Cheese? Ye Local Customs?'

'I'm not sure that's what he has in mind. I think it's more a geographical—'

'What? *Plunges into Unknown Herts*? *Surrey: off the Beaten*? *Behold, Ye Ancient Monuments*? For pity's sake, Sefton. Who cares? All those dreadful places. Wessex and Devon! Never mind the north! Hardly bears thinking about. I'm afraid I just couldn't be bothered.'

She glanced at me, her Picasso-like profile all the more striking in motion.

'Do you drive, Sefton?'

'I do.'

She then seemed to be waiting for me to ask something back; she was that kind of woman. The kind who asked questions in order to have them asked back, using men essentially as pocket-mirrors.

'This is a lovely car,' I said.

'Oh, this? Yes. Father's mad on cars. He's got half a dozen, you know. Loads and loads. The bull-nosed Morris Cowley, with a dickey seat – dodgy fuel pump. And the ancient Austin, *Of Accursed Memory*. The Morris Oxford, with beige curtains at the windows; sometimes he'll take a nap in it in the afternoons. It's terribly sweet really.'

'Yes.'

'He can't drive, though, of course. And he has all these sorts of crazy ideas. He thinks cars run better at night-time – something to do with the evening air. Claims it's scientific. Absolute clap-trap, of course. But this is my favourite,' she continued, stroking the steering wheel. 'It's a Lagonda,' she said, stressing the second syllable, in the Italian fashion. 'Isn't it a lovely word?'

'Quite lovely,' I said.

'Lagonda,' she repeated. She clearly liked the idea of Italian. Or Italians. 'Only twenty-five of them made. Designed by Mr Bentley himself, I believe. Herr Himmler has one in Germany. Harmsworth. King Leopold of the Belgians. I think you'll find that ours is one of the only white Lagonda LG45 Rapides in England.'

'Really?' I said. She seemed to be awaiting congratulations on this fact. I declined to compliment, and instead silently admired the car's upholstery and its fine walnut dashboard.

Saxlingham outdistanced, we were now beyond signposts, in deep English country.

'She handles very well,' she continued. 'The car, I mean, Sefton.' That ridiculous eyebrow again. 'One of Father's concessions to modernity. He won't buy us proper plumbing, but anything that gets him from here to there more quickly he's happy to fork out for! Honestly! It's the production version of the Lagonda race car, you know. She's really the last word.'

'In what?'

'Cars, silly! Top speed of a hundred and five miles per hour. Would you like me to show you?'

'No, thank you, miss,' I said, suspecting that we were already not far from such a speed. 'I'll take your word for it.'

'Oh come on, Sefton,' she said, fiercely revving the car's engine. 'Don't you enjoy a little adventure?'

'I used to,' I said.

'What? Lost your taste for it?'

'Possibly, miss, yes.'

'Oh dear. Well, perhaps I'll be able to revive your flagging interest then, eh?' And with this she leaned forward eagerly in her seat, stamped on the accelerator, and we began tearing up the roads.

'You're not scared are you?' she called, as our speed increased.

But I now found her absurd flirtatious antics too wearisome to respond to at all, and simply gazed at the hedgerows speeding past inches from the car, which was spitting up stones and dirt – we were now driving along a single-track road that had clearly been made for horses' hoofs rather than high-speed Lagondas.

We breasted a small hill and began careering down the other side, approaching a bend at both unsuitable angle and speed.

'Slow down, miss,' I said sharply.

'What?'

'Slow down.'

As we sped unwisely towards the bend she turned and looked at me and there was a look in her eye that I recognised – the same look I had seen in men's eyes in Spain; and the look they must have seen in mine. Desperation. Fear. Joy. A shameless, stiff, direct gaze, challenging life itself. Terrifying.

She was understeering – out of ignorance, I suspected, rather than daring – as we approached the bend, and I found myself reaching across her, grabbing the wheel and tugging it towards me, attempting to correct the angle and bring the car in more tightly.

'Look out!' she screamed, as we swept down upon the bend, the rear of the Lagonda swinging out from behind us, her foot slamming down instinctively on the brakes.

'Don't brake!' I screamed – I knew it would throw the car – and grabbed down at her ankle and pulled it up, reaching down with my other hand to apply a little pressure in order to transfer weight to the front.

It worked. Just.

We skidded to a halt, engine and tyres smoking, my head first in her lap and then juddering into the Lagonda's pretty dashboard. The engine cut out.

'Oh!' she yelled. 'You maddening man! What on earth do you think you're doing?'

'What do you think you're doing?' I yelled back.

At which challenge she threw her head back and laughed, a great throaty, hollow laugh, as though the whole thing were a mere prank she'd rehearsed many times. Which she may have.

'What am I doing? *I'm living*, Sefton! How do you like it, eh?'

I sat up, straightened myself, opened the car door and climbed out.

'What are you doing?' she called.

'I'm getting out here, miss, thank you,' I said.

'But you can't!'

'Yes I can.' I began walking on ahead. 'I'll find my own way now, thank you, miss.'

'How dare you!' I could hear the stamp of her pretty little foot. 'Get back in here now! Now!'

*The rich and exotic beauty of the English countryside*

I walked on ahead, feeling calm.

'Sefton!' she called. 'Did you hear me, man? Get back in here, now.'

Then, realising that I had no intention of obeying her orders and that she had indeed lost control of the situation, she promptly started up the still smoking engine, stamped her foot on the accelerator, and sped past, hooting the horn as she went.

'See. You. Later. Sluggard!' she called, snatching triumph with one last toss of her head. The look in her eyes remained with me for some time.

It was a trek to the Morley house. My head was throbbing. My foot was sore. I stopped off at a cottage on the road to a place called Blakeney, asking for directions, and the old cottager came out – a fine country figure, rigged out in greasy waistcoat and side whiskers of the variety people used to call 'weepers' – and pointed back the way I'd come. 'But I'm terrible blind,' he warned, as I departed. I wasn't sure if he meant literally, or if it was some amusement of his. Whichever, he sent me the wrong way, and it was long past supper time when I eventually arrived, sans suitcase, sans pills, sans everything.

A thin new moon was set high in the sky.

I felt wretched. Outcast. Like an apparition. Or a newborn child.

# CHAPTER FIVE

THE FAMOUS MORLEY HOUSE, St George's – described by Burchfield as 'a true Englishman's castle' and by Bolton as 'his legacy in bricks and mortar' – was at that time only twenty years old, Morley himself having overseen its construction. Some, I know, have written off the house as a work of Edwardian folly, others have celebrated it as a testament to a great Englishman's passions. But it was far too dark for me to make a judgement that first evening. Country dark is a darkness far beyond what city-dwellers imagine and at St George's, at night, one could almost swim in the thick black swirling around one. I passed up the driveway, between imposing entrance gates – atop which, in glinting moonlight, sat St George on the one hand, dragon dutifully slain, and the *Golden Hind* on the other – and up past what I assumed to be a small lake, and walked, exhausted, between an avenue of old trees and finally up stone steps to the house, with statues of Britannia and lions rampant guarding the entrance. The door, an anachronistic mass of carved oak – like something by Ghiberti for a cathedral – stood open.

*A true Englishman's castle*

'Good evening!' I called, peering into the house's gloom. 'Mr Morley? It's Sefton, sir. I'm sorry I—'

For half a moment there came no reply and then suddenly in the entrance hall there was cacophony, the whole house, it seemed, screaming out in agony in response to my call. The noise was that of cold-blooded murder. Startled, I drew back, almost tripping down the steps, my heart racing. I shut my eyes and actually thought I might be sick – the maddening Miriam, no food, no pills, only a little tobacco. I had slipped back into a dream of Spain. But then, after several minutes, when the incredible noise continued and no one came, and with no intention of retracing my weary footsteps back down the driveway and all the way back to misery and London, I peered cautiously into the hall.

There were, thank God, no demons. It was no dream. The grand entrance hall to St George's – as readers of Burchfield will recall – had been set up as a kind of a zoo and a natural history museum. The walls all around were hung with glass cases and shelves holding displays of skulls and bones, and turtle shells, and sets of teeth and taxidermised beasts: one case seemed to comprise a collection merely of *snouts*. And then below these displays of their ancestors and relatives were the living animals themselves, a literal *tableau vivant*. Rather poor taste, I thought – keeping animals in a kind of animal catacomb. Drawing my eye, directly opposite the great doorway, was the celebrated aquarium, set up on a simple wooden plinth, the whole thing not less than the height of a man and perhaps more than twenty feet across – nothing like it outside the major aquariums of Europe – and designed as a kind of Alpine garden, thick with pebbles and vegetation, and with brightly coloured fish weaving their way through crystal-clear water and decorative stonework. I was drawn towards this extraordinary, oddly luminescent sight and moved mesmerised towards it, noticing a clipboard attached to the plinth, which seemed to record feeding times and observations. 'Dytiscus,' read the notes. 'Dragon-fly larvae?' But I was distracted by all this for only a moment before there came a sudden whoosh and swooping above my head, as a couple of – could they have been? Neither Burchfield nor Bolton make mention of them – jackdaws made their presence known. As my eyes became accustomed to the gloom I glanced all around me and made out among the extraordinary menagerie a goose, a cockatoo, dogs, shrews – and, set apart from the other animals, where one might otherwise expect what-nots or a display of family silver, a large, roomy cage containing what I thought was probably a capuchin monkey. At the sight and sound of me, the monkey raised herself, looked lazily around, and then lay back down to sleep.

As I reeled and tottered slightly, disorientated from these incredible sights and the incessant noise – 'a place of wonder', according to Burchfield, though he evidently had never come upon it unprepared, and at night – I thought I heard the faint tapping of a typewriter coming from elsewhere in the house, and knowing that Morley himself could not be far away I rushed down a long corridor lined with thousands of books and bound piles of newspapers, pursued by various loping and persistently swooping creatures, until I burst in upon a kitchen. Which, like the entrance hall, both was and was not what one might usually hope and expect.

St George's was not so much a home as a small, privately funded research institute. The kitchen resembled a laboratory. Indeed, I realised on that first night, judging merely by the ingredients, chemicals and equipment lining the shelves, that it was both kitchen *and* laboratory, home for both amateur bacteriologist and amateur chef. Up above the fine Delft tiles and the up-to-the-minute range and the sink, up on the walls, were pretty collections of porcelain and china, flanked by row upon row of frosted and dark brown bottles of chemicals. And recipe books. And below, at a vast oak refectory table scarred with much evidence either of meals or experiments, sat Morley, my very own Dr Frankenstein, in colourful bow tie, slippers and tartan dressing gown.

I breathed a sigh of relief.

The cockatoo came and settled on his shoulder, two terriers at his feet. The jackdaws circled once, then fled away. Cats, geese – and a peacock! – warmed and disported themselves by the range.

'Ah, good, Sefton,' he said, glancing up from what I now regarded as his customary position behind a typewriter, surrounded by books, and egg-timer at his elbow. 'You found us then?'

'Yes, sir,' I said, panting slightly, regaining my composure.

'Glass of barley water?' He indicated a jug of misty-looking liquid by his elbow. It was his customary evening treat.

'No, thank you.' I was rather hoping for strong drink.

'And you met my daughter, I hear.'

'Yes, sir.'

'She's rather eccentric and strong-willed, I'm afraid.'

'That's . . . perhaps one way of describing it, sir, yes.'

'Yes. Women are essentially wild animals, Sefton. That's what you have to remember.'

'Well . . .'

'Untameable,' he said. 'Not like these.' He stroked a terrier at his side, gestured at the bird, the cats. The peacock. 'And what with the bobbed hair, I have to say, about as unlovely as a docked horse. After her mother died – my wife – we tried her at a convent school in Belgium. No good. No good at all. Wild animals,' he repeated. 'Scientifically proven, Sefton. I've made quite a study of animal behaviour, you know.'

'Yes, I was . . . admiring your . . .'

'Menagerie?'

'Yes. And the aquarium. On the way in.'

'Good. Yes. We've an aviary as well. And a terrarium, of course. And then there's the farm. Model farm only. But. You're familiar with ethology, Sefton?'

'I don't think I am, actually, sir, no.'

'Sit down, sit down. No need to stand on ceremony now.' I perched precariously on a round-backed chair by the table, its wicker seat half caved in and piled with books. 'Ethology,' continued Morley. 'Study of gestures, Sefton. Or rather, interpretation of character through the study of gesture. Applies in particular to animal behaviour.'

As usual, I wasn't sure if I was expected to answer, or to listen. But then Morley went on, kindly resolving my dilemma for me.

'Can also be applied to humans, of course. So you'd have to ask, what was she signalling to you?'

'Who, sir?'

'My daughter, Sefton. She's told me all about it. The journey.'

'I see, sir.'

'This is where our friend Herr Freud goes wrong, I believe. Confusing mental qualities with behaviour. Most of our fraying is a kind of animal suffering, you see. I do wish psychoanalysts would spend more time studying animal communication.'

'I'm afraid I don't quite—'

'I'll be honest with you, Sefton. You'll need to watch her carefully. Attend to her gestures. And the eyes – everything is in the eyes. The face, as you know, speaks for us. We must learn to read it. Which is becoming more difficult all the time. With women's faces, I mean. Foreheads tightened. Creases erased. Extraordinary. You've read about this? Young women having their bosoms unloaded and ... uploaded? American, of course. Jewesses do it with their noses, I believe. Dreadful. Nothing to be ashamed of, surely? And many women now of course supporting their entire families, you know. Businesswomen. *Mater*familias. *Noblesse industrielle*. Waitresses in dinner jackets in London – it's a fashion from France.'

'Is it, sir?'

'The feminine question, it seems, no longer requires a masculine answer, Sefton.'

As usual, Morley's mind seemed to be spinning up and around and away from the conversation into realms where it was difficult to follow. Fortunately, he brought himself back down to earth – I was far too tired to have tried dragging him down myself.

'Anyway, we're setting off tomorrow, Sefton.'

'Tomorrow, sir?'

'Yes. Research for the first book. *The County Guides*. Remember? Book one. *Numero uno. Un. Eins*. In Polish, do you know?'

'No, I'm afraid . . .'

'Numbers one to ten, in the major Indo-European languages? Essential knowledge, I would have thought, for every man, woman and child in this day and age.'

'No, I'm afraid I . . . *Jeden*?' I hazarded a guess.

'Excellent!' said Morley. 'I knew I'd made the right choice with you, Sefton.'

I silently thanked my father for all the ambassadors who'd trooped through our drawing room all those years ago, jabbering in their languages and teaching us children cards, much to my mother's dismay.

'Anyway, all the arrangements have been made. You'll have the cottage on your return, but for tonight you have a room upstairs. The upper room. I hope it's sufficient.'

'I'm sure it'll be more than sufficient, sir.'

'Good. And there's no need to call me sir.'

'Very well, sir.'

'You may call me Mr Morley.'

'Very good, Mr Morley.'

'We'll be leaving by 7 a.m. I like to get an early start. Now. You'll be wanting some supper?'

'Well . . .'

'The maid has set something out in your room, I think. You're not a vegetarian?'

'No.'

'Marvellous. All very well for Hindus, for whom I have the very greatest respect, I should say. But, the boiled beef of England, isn't it? Cold meats for you, mostly, I think. Seed

[ 58 ]

cake. You know the sort of thing. And you're travelling light, I see. Good good. Russian tea?' he asked, indicating a tall glass of brackish-looking liquid by the typewriter, which one might have mistaken for typewriter fuel. 'I developed a passion for it after my time in Russia.'

'No. I'm fine, thank you.'

'Well, good. That's us then. You go on ahead. Make yourself at home. I've an article to finish here. *Chronicle.* On the history of the folk harp. Fascinating subject. One can see in its history the spread of certain common craft skills across civilisations. I'll see you first thing.'

'Certainly.' I made back towards the door, avoiding animals, in the hope of finding my room without further adventure. 'Just one question, Mr Morley, if I may.'

'Yes. Of course, Sefton.'

'Which county will we be beginning with tomorrow, sir?'

'I thought we'd start close to home, Sefton. With God's own county.'

'Yorkshire?'

'Norfolk. "I am a Norfolk man and glory in being so." Who said that, Sefton?'

'I don't know, Mr Morley.'

'Nelson, of course! Horatio Nelson! Adopted son of the county, whose native sons include . . . ?'

'Hmm. I—'

'The aboriginally Norfolk, Sefton? The autochthones? The Sparti, as it were? The old Swadeshi, as our friend Mr Gandhi might have it? Come, come.'

'I'm sorry, I—'

'People from round here?'

'I don't know, Mr Morley, I'm afraid.'

'Boadicea? Elizabeth Fry? Thomas Paine? Dame Margery Kempe? Sir Robert Walpole! You'll need to be reading up on your Norfolk folk, Sefton. The character and the *characters* of Norfolk, Sefton, that's what we're after! Plenty of flavour. Plenty of seasoning. I've left some of the relevant maps and guides in your room, so you can get started tonight.'

'Very good, Mr Morley.'

'Seven, no later,' he called, as I left the kitchen and he returned to his work, almost as in meditation, animals happily around him, tap-tap-tapping at the typewriter.

# CHAPTER SIX

'Was it Edward IV who breakfasted on a buttock of beef and a tankard of old ale every morning?' asked Morley.

'It may have been, sir.'

'Well, we don't.'

'No,' I agreed.

'Cup of hot water with a slice of lemon. Bowl of oatmeal,' said Morley, tapping his spoon decisively on the side of his bowl. 'Sets a man up for the day. Full of goodness, oatmeal. Steel-cut. Pure as driven snow.'

'Pass the sugar, would you?' said Miriam. 'Indispensable, wouldn't you say, Sefton? Utterly tasteless without, isn't it? Like eating gruel.'

'Gruel? Gruel?' said Morley, before embarking on a short excursion on the history of the word, punctuated by Miriam's protests and my own occasional weary agreements.

It was the morning after the night before, and I was enjoying my first taste of breakfast in the dining room at St George's, which was not a household, I came to realise, that liked to ease its way into the day. There was neither a halt nor indeed even a pause in the relentless clamour of argument and quarrelling that echoed around the place like trains at a continental railway station. The conversation – to quote Sir Francis Bacon, or possibly Dr Johnson, or Hazlitt, certainly one of the great English essayists, who Morley liked to quote at every opportunity, and who I now, in turn, like to misquote – was like a fire lit early to warm the day and once lit was inextinguishable. Even when engaged in apparently casual conversation, Morley and his daughter exchanged verbal thrusts and parries that could be shocking to the outsider. For his part, Morley was not a man who brooked much disagreement, and his daughter was not a woman who liked to be bested in argument: and so the sparks would fly. All houses, of course, have an atmosphere – some pleasant, some not so pleasant, and some merely strange, no matter how humble nor how grand. The atmosphere of St George's was one of a noisy Academy, presided over by Socrates and his rebellious daughter.

'Sleep well?'

'He's not a child, Father. "A dry bed deserves a boiled sweet."'

'Sorry, I—'

'Ignore her, Sefton. She only does it to provoke.'

'Are you feeling provoked, Sefton?' asked Miriam.

'Erm. No. I don't think so.'

'Good,' said Morley. '*Dies faustus*, eh? *Dies faustus*! All set?'

'I think so, Mr Morley.'

'Good, good. First day. *Gradus ad Parnassum*. Miriam will be driving us, in the Lagonda.'

'Very well.'

'Until you get the hang of it.'

'Get the hang of it!' snorted Miriam.

'Anyway, I thought it would be nice for you to accompany us on the first outing. And I'll need to brief Mr Sefton properly.'

'Brief him? It's hardly a military operation, Father.'

'Have you exercised, Sefton?'

'Not this morning, sir, no.'

'Pity. Never mind. No time now. But in future I'll expect you to be in fine fettle for our little trips. You're welcome to use the swimming pool, you know. Down by the orchard.'

'Thank you.'

'Not at all. You have a bathing gown?'

'No, I'm afraid my clothes ... I left my luggage on the train.'

'I see.' He eyed my blue serge suit with a tailor's precision, his eyes like tiny chalks.

'Oh. We'll have to see what we can do. I think we might have some clothes that fit you. Miriam, do you think?' They both looked me up and down.

'About the same height,' said Miriam.

'Same build,' agreed Morley. 'You know where the clothes are?'

'Yes, Father.' Miriam sighed. There was an awkward – and unusual – silence. Miriam poured more coffee, the remains of the coffee from a flask.

'Anyway,' said Morley. 'Bathing suit. I'll lend you one of mine. Fifty lengths, I'd say? Controlled Interval Method of training I prefer. We need you in tip-top shape. This is not going to be a holiday, you know.'

'Of course.'

'So,' continued Morley, 'let us set out, shall we, since all our party are assembled, our aims, principles and methods.'

'Father!'

'What?'

'Do give the poor man a break, will you? He's not had a cup of coffee, and you're offering him this muck—' She gestured towards the bowl of oatmeal.

'Oatmeal.'

'Muck for breakfast, and he looks like he's half asleep.'

'I'm fine, thank you, Miss Morley,' I spoke up.

'Oh, good grief, Sefton, come on. Be honest. Tell him. He's as ... as tedious as a tired horse, a railing wife, and worse than a smoky house!'

'Shakespeare?' said Morley.

'Correct!' said Miriam. 'Play? Sefton?'

'*Much Ado About Nothing*?' I offered lamely.

'*Henry IV*,' said Miriam, simultaneously sighing and raising her eyebrows – in a manner not unlike her father's, I would say – as though I had proved the end of civilisation.

'Part?' said Morley.

'What?' said Miriam.

'*Henry IV* part . . . ?'

'One,' said Miriam. 'Obviously.'

'Correct,' said Morley. 'Now, where were we?'

'Aims, principles—'

'And methods,' I said.

'Exactly. Basic principles first, Sefton. If we're going to meet our targets we can't loaf.'

'No loafing,' I said.

'Jolly good. And no funking.'

'No. Funking,' said Miriam. 'Did you hear that, Sefton?'

I ignored her provocation.

'Do you take a drink?'

'Well, occasionally—' I began.

'And absolutely no drinking while out researching. Have I made myself clear?'

'Abundantly, Mr Morley,' I said, scraping the rest of my oatmeal.

'Good, good. And let's just remember that procrastination—'

'Is the thief of time,' said Miriam wearily, rolling her eyes. 'I'm going to go and get ready, Father.'

'Are you not ready already?'

'In this old thing?' Miriam smoothed down the sides of her dress, flashing her eyes at me. 'Now, no man of any consequence would allow me to accompany him on any adventure in this old thing, would they, Mr Sefton?'

'Erm.'

'Miriam, please. We need to leave . . .' Morley glanced up at a clock on the wall. 'In forty-seven minutes.'

'I'll be ready, Father.'

'And bring those clothes for Sefton, won't you?'

'I shall.' She sighed again. 'Now do let Sefton enjoy his breakfast. If enjoy is the right word. Which it is not.'

And with that, she flounced out.

'I do apologise, Sefton. As I was saying to you last night: animal. Wild animal. Untamed.'

'Quite, sir.'

'You don't drink coffee, do you? Didn't have you down as a coffee man.'

'Well, I . . .'

'I'll get cook to make some more.'

'No, it's fine. I'll manage.'

'Good. Now, where were we?'

'Aims?'

'Aims. Precisely. So, aim is, book about once every five weeks. That gives us a chance to get there, gen up on the place, get writing, get back here for the editing. What do you think?'

'It's certainly an ambitious—'

'Though Norfolk I think we can do rather more quickly. Because a lot of it's already up here.' He tapped his head. 'As far as research is concerned we'll be relying mostly on the archive, Sefton.'

'The archive?'

'Yes. Here.' He tapped his head. 'Mostly. *Archive*. From the Greek and Latin for town hall, I think, isn't it? Is that right?'

'Probably.' My Greek and my Latin were not always immediately to hand.

'Yes. Denoting order, efficiency, completeness. The principles by which we work. We'll have books with us, of course. But the books are the reserve fund, if you like.' He smiled and stroked his moustache. 'Up here, you see, that's where we do the real work. It's all about connections, our project, Sefton. Making connections. And you can only make them here.' He tapped his head again. 'And context, of course. Context. Very important. Topicality. The *topos*. Where we find it. You see. If you are digging, you don't simply make an inventory of the things you discover. You mark the exact location where the treasures are found. Think Howard

[ 66 ]

Carter, Sefton. Another of Norfolk's sons – make a note. Like Carter we are engaged in a struggle to preserve, Sefton. To find and preserve.' He checked his watch. 'Forty-three minutes to departure, Sefton. I have a few things to attend to. You'll need an overnight bag.'

'I'm not sure I—'

'Cook'll sort you out with something.' He checked his watch again. 'Forty-two minutes. See you anon.'

Forty-two minutes later – or near enough – I made my way outside, where Morley was supervising Miriam packing the car.

'Forty-*five* minutes, Sefton,' he said, without glancing at a watch. 'Forty-*five*. *Tempus anima rei*, eh? *Tempus anima rei*. You're putting us behind schedule. Don't do it again. Now, you'll be wondering, of course, about method,' he continued, picking up on the threads of the conversation we'd had forty-five minutes earlier, as though nothing else had intervened between. 'No, not there, Miriam!'

'Why, what's wrong with there?'

'There,' he said. 'Clearly, it fits *there*.'

Miriam slightly readjusted some bags packed around the large brass-bound travelling trunk that was strapped on the back, numbered 'No.1'.

'Do you need a hand at all?' I said.

'*Forty-five minutes!*' said Miriam mockingly, tightening straps. 'You have us all behind, Sefton.'

'You know the word *verzetteln*, Sefton?' continued Morley.

'No, I'm afraid I don't, sir.'

'From library science. "To excerpt". To arrange things into individual slips or the form of a card index.'

'I see.'

'Place for everything.'

'And everything in its place,' said Miriam, handing me an old Gladstone bag. 'You'll be needing these, Sefton.' The bag was stuffed to overflowing with clothes and dozens of notebooks.

'Ah. The notebooks,' said Morley. 'Jolly good. Notebooks are the fundamental equipment for those who devise things,' said Morley. 'Are they not, Miriam?'

'Yes, Father.'

'One should always avoid haphazard writing materials, Sefton. Remember that.'

He then gestured towards the car, and daintily climbed into the back seat, whereupon, to my astonishment, Miriam began fitting a wooden desk around him, transforming the rear of the vehicle instantly into a kind of portable office. Safely wedged into his seat, Miriam then hoisted, seemingly from out of nowhere, a small, lightweight typewriter onto a couple of stays on the desk, and stood back to admire her handiwork.

'Home from home,' said Morley.

'Do you like my dress, Sefton?' said Miriam.

'Very nice,' I said, bewildered, as so often in their company. 'Brown.'

'It's "donkey", actually,' she said.

'Donkey? Is that a colour?'

'Of course it's a colour. Have you ever seen a donkey?'

'Yes.'

[ 68 ]

'And what colour is it?'

'It's—'

'*Donkey* is the colour of donkeys, Sefton.'

'Well—'

'Enough tittle-tattle, children,' said Morley. 'Do we have everything, Miriam?'

'Yes. Of course. Now, you've remembered I'm going to London later, Father?'

'But—'

'I told you yesterday. Margaret Whitwell is having a party and she absolutely insists that I'm there. So Sefton will be in charge of things once I've dropped you off. Get in, then, Sefton.'

'Where?'

'There.'

I clambered into the back with Morley.

'You know I don't hold with these London parties, Miriam.'

'I know that, Father.'

'I'm just reminding you, that's all.'

'Repetition is a form of self-plagiarism, I think you'll find, Father.'

'Anyway. We have everything? Pens?'

'Yes.'

'Pencils?'

'Yes.'

'Koh-i-noor pencils?'

'Yes, of course.'

'You use Koh-i-noor, Sefton?'

'I can't say that I—'

'They're terribly good. Hardtmuth's. Sounds German.

But they're American. Seventeen degrees. Smooth. Durable. Unsnappable. Four shillings per dozen from my wholesaler. Which isn't bad for pencil perfection, eh? Notebooks, Miriam?'

'Yes.'

'Typewriters?'

'Yes, of course, Father.'

'Camera for Sefton?'

'Yes. Yes. The new Leica.'

'Good. Portable desk?'

'Yes. Of course.'

'Blotting paper?'

'Yes!'

'Writing paper.'

'Yes! Father!'

'Airmail paper?'

'Yes, yes, yes. And the elephant rifle, the muskets, the swords, the daggers and the boar spears!'

'Good.'

'We don't really have——' I began.

'Of course not!' said Miriam. 'But we have everything we need, and now we are going.'

At which, without further ado, Miriam started up the car and set off down the driveway in much the manner she had been driving the day before, which is to say, suicidally. Thrilling at the speed, Morley sat bolt upright, gazing all around like a child, his fingers playing across the keys of his typewriter so much like a pianist about to perform that I almost expected him to play a scale.

'It's a Hermes Featherweight,' he said loudly, leaning across.

'Very nice,' I agreed.

'Nobody else cares about your typewriters, Father!' called Miriam from the front.

'Tools of the trade,' said Morley. 'Sefton needs to get to know them.'

'They're just typewriters!' said Miriam. 'Lesson over.'

'They're not just typewriters!' said Morley. 'Sefton. Look. They've only just started manufacturing them. Had it imported from Switzerland. Tremendous craftsmanship.' He stroked the casing of the machine. 'I use Good Companions as back-ups,' he said, 'but the Swiss do seem to have the upper hand when it comes to precision engineering, don't you think? Watches and what have you.' He held up both wrists to me—a watch on each wrist. 'Luminous dial,' he said, pointing with his right hand to his left wrist, and then pointing to the right wrist, 'And non-luminous dial.'

'Super,' I said.

'Beautiful, isn't she?' continued Morley, addressing the typewriter.

'She's certainly a very nice typewriter,' I said.

'And incredibly light. Here.' He pulled the typewriter towards him, removed it from its wooden stays and handed it across to me.

'Extraordinary, isn't she?'

'It's certainly very light.'

'Eight pounds.'

'Very light.'

'You could sit her on your lap almost, couldn't you? Never mind portables, Sefton. Lapwriters, that'll be the next thing, mark my word. Five, ten years, we'll have typewriters you can fit into your pocket!' He was always coming up with absurd predictions about machines of the future – he corresponded, of course, for many years with H.G. Wells about the nature and practicalities of time travel – and there was also his famous shed, more like a barn, at St George's, mentioned by all the biographers, and which contained the carcasses of many engines, clocks and bicycles, the mechanisms of which he was continually seeking to improve, or, more likely, confuse: there were clocks made from bicycle parts, and bicycles made from clock parts. The story of Morley's ill-fated steam-paraffin-driven bicycle I shan't repeat here, for we were sweeping out onto the open road, and I was having trouble keeping up with the briefing . . .

'So, that's me,' he said, wedging the typewriter back into position. 'You, meanwhile, will mostly be using the notebooks. Have them imported specially from Germany. The very best. Waterproof.'

I picked up one of the notebooks from the bag Miriam had handed me. And it was indeed a fine notebook: octavo, morocco-bound, lined, with a red ribbon marker dangling from it, like a fuse.

'Feel the heft of it,' said Morley.

I weighed the notebook in my hand.

'Beautiful, isn't it?' he said.

'Yes, again, it's quite . . . beautiful,' I said. I had never before met a man who cared so much about his writing equipment. I had always managed to get by with pencils and the backs of envelopes and cigarette packets.

'Leave the poor man alone!' cried Miriam from the front. 'Nobody wants to hear about your stationery fetish.'

'My what?' said Morley.

Miriam groaned. 'Never mind.'

'My advice to novice writers when they write to me, Sefton, is very simple. "Avoid haphazard writing habits. And haphazard writing materials." And that's it.'

'That's it?' I said.

'That's it,' agreed Miriam, from the seat in front.

'That's it,' said Morley. '*That* is the secret of my success.'

In fact, as his own notebooks clearly show, Morley's work was forever verging on the haphazard, with sketches, diagrams, coordinates and figures of all sorts crowding the pages, not to mention the words themselves. He wrote – as anyone familiar with the biographies will know – not only continuously and prodigiously, and in the same note-books for almost forty years, but also in a tiny, lunatic hand. Indeed, over the years of our relationship, his hand-writing became progressively smaller and smaller, almost to the point of being unreadable except by the use of a magnifying glass. His stated ambition was to squeeze in a hundred lines per page. Sometimes, pausing in between his labours, I would notice him counting the lines, again and again.

'Blast it!' he would say.

'A problem, Mr Morley?'

'Ninety. Blast it.'

'Ninety?'

'Lines.'

'Ah.'

There was, I came to realise, a relationship between the size and density of his writing and his lavishness of aim and ambition in wishing to capture reality as he felt it existed: it was as if by making things small he also some-how emphasised their magnitude and significance. I, on the other hand, averaged at best twenty lines a page. Which he believed to be a sign of moral turpitude.

'Now. Norfolk. Norfolk. What do you think of, Sefton, when you think of Norfolk?'

'"Very flat, Norfolk"?' I said, regretting it immediately.

Morley groaned as though I had prodded him in the side with a spear. 'Spare us the Noël Coward, Sefton, please. Terribly overrated. Not a fan. Poor man's Oscar Wilde. Who was himself, of course, the poor man's Dr Johnson. Who one might say was the poor man's Aubrey. Who was the poor man's Burton … Who was … Anyway … A quip is not an insight, Sefton. And besides, it's not, actually, Norfolk.'

'What?' I did my best to keep up.

'Flat. Ever been to Gas Hill, in Norwich?'

'No, I—'

'Precisely. West Runton? Beacon Hill?'

'Again, no, I—'

'There you are, then. It's actually made up of three very distinct geological areas, Norfolk.' He made cupping movements with his hands, as though the entire county was within his grasp. 'Flatlands in the west. Chalklands and heathlands of the north and the centre. And the rich valleys of the south and east.'

'I see.'

'From which we might learn much about the history of the place. "Very flat, Norfolk!" Worthless. Ignorant. Stupid. We can learn everything about a place from its landscape, Sefton, if we bother to pay attention to it. You're going to have to clear your mind of cant, if you wouldn't mind, when we're discussing these things. I want to know what *you* think when you think of Norfolk, Sefton, not Mr Know-All

Coward. Independent thought, Sefton. That's the thing. The mind unshackled. So. Let's try again, shall we? When I think of Norfolk I think of . . .'

'When I think of Norfolk I think of—'

'Churches. Exactly. Very important. Beguiling county of great religious art and culture.'

'I see.'

'Write it down, Sefton.'

And so I took up a pen and began to write; my first notes of our grand project.

'Saxons, Normans, came, built their churches. Churches. That's the way in to Norfolk. Not a lot you can't learn from churches. Norfolk has some six hundred medieval churches, I think. Check that. Most of them of the Perpendicular.' He pulled a piece of paper from a pocket. 'Here. I have a little list.' He brandished a scribbled list. I read it. It was a list of churches: three columns per side, one hundred lines apiece.

'There's certainly a lot there,' I said.

'Six hundred,' he said.

'Yes, that's a lot.'

'Don't worry, Sefton. We're not going to visit them all.'

'Right. Good.'

'Four or five hundred should do us. I thought we'd start with the churches. Get them out of the way. And then we've got all of Norwich to do. Carrow Road. "Come on, the Canaries!" Though I'm not a great fan of association football. And I thought we might do something on the speedway at Hellesdon – terribly popular, you know, speedway. Are you a fan, Sefton?'

'I can't say—'

'And then something on the flora and fauna – lavender

*Norfolk, county of mills*

and what have you. And Thetford Forest, I suppose. Largest lowland pine forest in Britain, I think I'm right in saying, though we'll have to check, of course.'

'Of course.'

'And all the little curiosities: Whalebone House in Cley. And the windmills and the water mills. Brick mills. Drainage mills. County of mills, Norfolk. And some of the modern industries, of course – we mustn't forget Colman's. But the churches first. Need to get our priorities right, eh?'

'Yes.'

'Definitely Trunch.'

'Trunch?'

'You know the font canopy at Trunch?'

'I can't say I do—'

He sniffed the air, as though he could actually smell the font canopy at Trunch, like the lure of wild game beckoning to him across the East Anglian tundra.

'And Ranworth,' he said. 'Wonderful. And the crypt at Brisley – used for prisoners on their way to the Norwich jail, did you know?'

'No, I can't say I—'

'The Labours of the Month at Burnham Deepdale. Early Gothic leaf carving at West Walton, curvilinear windows at Cley and at Walsingham. Oh, yes. It's going to be a wonderful few days, Sefton. All on the list there, if you look.'

I stared at the list as Morley continued to recite the wonders of many of Norfolk's six hundred churches, and Miriam kept gunning the engine.

'. . . the hammerbeam roof at Cawston, the giant St Nicholas in Yarmouth, the Seven Sacraments font at Dereham, the four great churches of Wiggenhall . . .'

We paused briefly, and thankfully, at a crossroads, Morley and engine idling.

'All sounds fas-cin-ating,' yelled Miriam from the front, yawning loudly.

'Yes, I think it will be.'

'I was being ironical, Father.'

'Oh? Were you? I do wish you wouldn't, Miriam. It's terribly bad manners.'

'It's the height of sophistication, actually.'

'Really? Sefton?'

'Sorry, Mr Morley?'

'Irony?'

'What about it, Mr Morley?'

'An adjudication, if you please?'

'On?'

'Irony. Good thing, or a bad thing? What do you think?'

'It certainly shows a certain . . . detachment,' I said. 'And an energy of response.'

'Energy of response,' he said. 'I like that. Very nice, Sefton. That's why we've hired you. He admires your energy of response,' he called out loudly to Miriam.

'Really?' said Miriam. 'I'm flattered, Sefton. I shan't return the compliment, though, thank you. Now, which way?'

'Left,' said Morley.

Miriam swung the vehicle left, and we began to pick up speed.

'Anyway,' said Morley, tapping at the keys, with one eye on the surroundings. 'Ah!' he cried. 'Notable roof!'

'Sorry, Mr Morley?'

'A notable roof. There. See?'

He pointed towards what looked like an entirely average Norfolk roof of blackish-red pantiles.

'See?'

'Yes,' I said.

'Make a note,' said Morley.

I wrote down the words 'Notable roof'.

'Sorry, Mr Morley, notable in what sense?'

'Blackish tinge around the chimney?' he said.

I turned and looked behind me as the house and its chimney vanished into the distance.

'Yes.' The chimney was indeed blackened.

'And what make you of that?'

'I don't know.'

'And he doesn't care!' cried Miriam.

'Don't care was made to care,' said Morley. 'And don't know isn't an answer.'

'Yes it is!' said Miriam.

'A chimney fire, perhaps?' I said.

'Oh, come on. Go for the obvious answer first, Sefton, shouldn't you? Before indulging in fantasies? A blackened chimney? Logical explanation? Primary cause?'

'A hot fire?'

'Aha! Exactly. And why would this particular house, among all the other houses in the village, have such a hot fire, do you think?'

'Because the inhabitants are colder than the others?'

'Possible, I suppose. Except that we know nothing of the inhabitants. Context?'

'A house in a village?'

'Correct. And moreover?'

'Erm . . .'

'A house in *the middle* of a village. Significant, surely? Small village, house centrally located, with blackened chimney, suggesting hot fire, suggesting . . .'

'I'm afraid I don't know, Mr Morley.' I was rather exhausted from his mental exertions.

'What about a little one-man bakery, Sefton? No market here for bakers' vans from the town, or your Woolworth's.'

'Ah.'

'The baker's house, I'd warrant.'

'I see.'

'And there's the peep of history, you see, Sefton! By studying the small things we might be able to understand the larger things. As a leaf will tell us about a tree, and a rivulet about the river, and the minute reveals the day, and—'

'Yes, all right, Father, we get the picture.'

'People have come far too much to rely on the far-off voices of Savoy Hill, Sefton, in my opinion. We need to use our own eyes, Sefton. And own ears. This is our England that's disappearing, Sefton, right around us. The granary of England, Sefton. Destroyed by our mania for shop-bought bread.' He stared across at me. 'You look like a man who eats shop-bought bread.'

'I suppose I am, Mr Morley, yes. Or, I mean, I have eaten—'

'That'll be a section in the book, Sefton. The Granary of England. Against Shop-Bought Bread. Make a note.'

I made a note.

The journey continued in like manner, with Morley variously interpreting the landscape and growing overcome with a sense of wonder at the world, while I made notes: lime trees; ash woods; sea-lavender; seals; squirrels; snakes;

| | | | | | |
|---|---|---|---|---|---|
| Gt Northern Diver | Brent Goose | Woodcock | Razorbill | Great Tit | Chiffchaff |
| Red-throated Diver | Barnacle Goose | Curlew | Guillemot | Blue Tit | Wood Warbler |
| Great Crested Grebe | Canada Goose | Whimbrel | Puffin | Coal Tit | Goldcrest |
| Little Grebe | Mute Swan | Black-tailed Godwit | Stock Dove | Marsh Tit | Spotted Flycatcher |
| Manx Shearwater | Whooper Swan | Bar-tailed Godwit | Woodpigeon | Willow Tit | Pied Flycatcher |
| Fulmar | Bewick's Swan | Green Sandpiper | Turtle Dove | Long-tailed Tit | Hedge Sparrow |
| Gannet | Sparrow Hawk | Wood Sandpiper | Collared Dove | Nuthatch | Meadow Pipit |
| Cormorant | Buzzard | Common Sandpiper | Cuckoo | Treecreeper | Tree Pipit |
| Shag | Marsh Harrier | Redshank | Barn Owl | Wren | Rock Pipit |
| Heron | Hen Harrier | Spotted Redshank | Little Owl | Dipper | Pied Wagtail |
| Bittern | Peregrine | Greenshank | Tawny Owl | Mistle Thrush | Grey Wagtail |
| Mallard | Merlin | Knot | Long-eared Owl | Fieldfare | Yellow Wagtail |
| Teal | Kestrel | Purple Sandpiper | Short-eared Owl | Song Thrush | Red-backed Shrike |
| Garganey | Red Grouse | Little Stint | Nightjar | Redwing | Starling |
| Gadwall | Red-legged Partridge | Dunlin | Swift | Ring Ouzel | Hawfinch |
| Wigeon | Partridge | Curlew Sandpiper | Kingfisher | Blackbird | Greenfinch |
| Pintail | Pheasant | Sanderling | Green Woodpecker | Wheatear | Goldfinch |
| Shoveler | Water Rail | Ruff | G. S. Woodpecker | Stonechat | Siskin |
| Scaup | Corncrake | Arctic Skua | L. S. Woodpecker | Whinchat | Linnet |
| Tufted Duck | Moorhen | G. Black-backed Gull | Woodlark | Redstart | Twite |
| Pochard | Coot | Lesser B-b. Gull | Skylark | Nightingale | Redpoll |
| Goldeneye | Oystercatcher | Herring Gull | Swallow | Robin | Bullfinch |
| Common Scoter | Lapwing | Common Gull | House Martin | Grasshopper Warbler | Crossbill |
| Eider | Ringed Plover | Black-headed Gull | Sand Martin | Reed Warbler | Chaffinch |
| R-b Merganser | Little Ringed Plover | Kittiwake | Raven | Sedge Warbler | Brambling |
| Goosander | Grey Plover | Black Tern | Carrion Crow | Blackcap | Yellowhammer |
| Shelduck | Golden Plover | Common Tern | Rook | Garden Warbler | Corn Bunting |
| Grey Lag Goose | Turnstone | Arctic Tern | Jackdaw | Whitethroat | Reed Bunting |
| White-fronted Goose | Snipe | Little Tern | Magpie | Lesser Whitethroat | House Sparrow |
| Pink-footed Goose | Jack Snipe | Sandwich Tern | Jay | Willow Warbler | Tree Sparrow |

*From Morley's Field List of British Birds (Simplified)*

the history of flint-knapping. Idling at another junction, over the roar of the engine, we could just about hear the sound of birdsong.

'Birds, Sefton.'

'Yes,' I agreed, feeling on reasonably solid ground.

'Recognise them?'

'Ah.' I had never learned birdsong.

Morley repeated the noises himself. 'Now, what's that, Sefton?'

'I'm afraid I don't know, Mr Morley.'

'Have you no idea at all, man?'

'I'm afraid not.'

'Well, hie ye and buy a bird book. Hie ye and buy a bird book. Snipe, sandpiper. And the wonderful song of the thrush,' cried Morley. 'Or the mavis, of course, as he is called hereabouts. Ah! The local names of birds – make a note, Sefton. Worth a little list in our book, isn't it? Hedgeman for the sparrow, ulf for the greenfinch. Are you familiar with them?'

I confessed that I was not.

'We'll include a little checklist, shall we, in the *County Guides*? For bird-spotters? What do you think?'

'I think it's—'

'Spink, I think, is the local term for a chaffinch, isn't it? Miriam?' he shouted.

'What?' she yelled back from the front.

'Spink?'

'What?'

'Spink!' yelled Morley.

Miriam glanced around at me. 'Sorry, Father, I misheard you.'

'Which reminds me,' continued Morley, on another of his detours, 'there's a man in Great Yarmouth who claims to be able to speak seagull language. Make a note, Sefton. We must remember to call in on him.' I made a note, and Morley began to sing: '"He sings each song twice o'er, / Lest you should think he never could recapture / The first fine careless rapture." Good omen, isn't it? The song of the thrush. Let's on in careless rapture, shall we? To Blakeney!'

I glanced at my watch. It wasn't yet nine o'clock in the morning. It had already been a long day.

# CHAPTER SEVEN

OUR ADVENTURE PROPER BEGAN, as all adventures begin – as Morley himself might say – *in media res*.

We arrived at the old seaport of Blakeney, the song of the thrush preceding us, by nine o'clock, exactly according to schedule. Unscheduled, however, were the vast cloud shadows and the creeping fog that came upon us as we arrived. I had never before travelled in Norfolk and was struck immediately by the remarkable combination of vast golden fields, green trees, wide never-ending skies, the flatlands and the fog, creating the illusion of a vast oasis in a desert. I mentioned it to Morley.

'Very good,' he said. 'Make a note. Just the thing we're after. Norfolk: an oasis.' He was given always to such phrases – summings-up, gists and piths. His goal was always 'the telling fact'. 'The telling fact,' he would sometimes murmur to himself, searching for it among the lumber of his mind. 'All we need here, Sefton, is the telling fact.' It was the legacy, I suppose, of so many years spent as a journalist and editor: he thought in captions and headlines. 'Minimum words. Maximum information,' was one of his many mottoes.

'*Cacoethes loquendi, cacoethes scribendi,*' was another. He was a man of contradictions.

We had travelled – at accelerating speed, which seemed to thrill Morley almost as much as his daughter – on the winding road from Cley, over the bridge across the River Glaven.

'Note,' cried Morley, in full flow, 'there are three great rivers in Norfolk: the Great Ouse, the Yare and Stiffkey. Among the smaller rivers and tributaries the most beautiful is perhaps the Glaven, which rises in Bodham and flows down to Blakeney Point, through the majestic mills and quiet ponds of the lower Glaven valley.' He paused for breath, as I hurried to note it down. 'Too touristy?' he said.

'Well, it is perhaps –' I began, but he had already passed on to his next observation.

'Wiveton Hall, majestic, halfway 'twixt the church and shore. And then the quaint charm of Blakeney, the name possibly derived from the Scandinavian, Blekinge in Sweden. Others say the name derives from the Black Island, the finger of land we know as …'

It felt like being dragged into the wheels of some kind of endless writing machine.

'Am I speaking too fast for you, Sefton?' he would sometimes ask.

'Perhaps a little fast, Mr Morley,' I would say.

'I'll slow down then, shall I?'

'Please,' I would say. And he'd slow down – for about a minute. And then he'd be off again: the crow-stepped gables on the houses; the cry of the bittern; the history of flint-tipped arrows. The entire duration of our trip – as on every trip – he perched high in the back of the car, the typewriter

*Blakeney: the Florence of East Anglia*

across his lap, tap, tap, tapping away, dictating to me, and glancing around continually at the scenery for all the world like a bird seeking where it might find to make its nest.

The soft, grey morning fog was borne in from the sea, muffling Blakeney in silence as we drove down to the quay, swaddling and concealing the village from us as though a mother were wrapping it tight in a blanket of muted grey-blues and grey-gold. The place seemed not yet to have come awake – or to have come awake many hours ago, and left to go to work – and we drove through narrow, deserted streets. Out across the mudflats there were only wading birds, and a few walkers.

'Holidaymakers,' pronounced Morley decisively as we parked at the quay.

'Oh, Father, how can you tell from this distance?'

'Distance is hardly the problem, I think, Miriam.' Morley consulted his watch. 'Time, not space, my dear.'

'Meaning?'

He consulted his watch. 'Nine ten a.m. Two people out walking. What does that suggest?'

'They could be going to work.'

'With a walking stick?'

'They might have a bad leg?'

'Clearly not,' said Morley, peering after the disappearing shapes.

'Fishermen?'

'In grey mackintoshes and gum boots?'

'Oh, whatever,' said Miriam, yanking on the handbrake.

Morley carefully levered himself from his seat, and then climbed down from the car, and sniffed the air.

'Great day!' he announced.

'No. It is not a great day. It is a *grey* day, Father,' said Miriam. 'Grey, foggy, and—'

'If there's enough blue to make—'

'A pair of sailor's trousers—'

'Is what I always say.'

'We know,' said Miriam.

'Gamey, isn't it?' continued Morley, sniffing again, while I scrambled after him as he began to stroll purposefully past the deserted pleasure boats along the quay. 'Muttony, almost. Reasty. Wouldn't you say? Make a note, Sefton. Blakeney. Reasty. Do you know the word?'

'No.'

'Hmm. Sometimes said of bacon. But it'll do us here, don't you think?'

I took a sniff.

'Smell of the tidal estuary,' continued Morley. 'Yeasty. Rank. Gamey. Yes?'

'Something rotten in the state of Denmark,' I ventured.

'Strictly speaking, I think the Bard is referring to something rotten in the body politic at that point, Sefton. The smell here is simply a smell. We shouldn't get carried away with ourselves, should we? Now, camera. Miriam?'

Miriam duly produced the camera from one of the trunks and proceeded to give me a basic lesson while Morley offered a brief history on the development of photography.

'It's the innovations in shutter speed and focal planes that makes them now so light, of course; and as for our Leica D.R.P. Ernst Leitz Wetzlar IIIa here … Best that money can buy, Sefton. Always worth getting the right kit, isn't it, Miriam?'

'True, O King!'

'I do wish you wouldn't say that, Miriam.'

'Why? That's the response he's looking for, Sefton. You might as well get used to it. Book of Daniel,' she said.

'Chapter three, verse twenty-four,' added Morley. 'Do you remember your first 35mm, Miriam?'

'I do, Father, indeed.' She glanced at me again.

'The Coronet?'

'Yes. Nice camera.'

'And before that, what was it?'

'A Contax, Father. And a Rolleiflex roll-film, that was rather fun.'

'Yes, of course. Anyway, all set? Got the gist of it, Sefton?'

'Say "Yes, O King,"' said Miriam.

'Yes, Mr Morley.' I seemed as prepared as I was ever going to be.

'You know the work of Gisèle Freund?' he asked, striding ahead.

'I'm not sure—'

'*Life* magazine.'

'No, I don't think I—'

'Anyway, that's not what we want. I'm thinking more Cartier Bresson, Brassai, Sefton. You know the sort of thing.'

I did not know the sort of thing, but agreed, and began making notes and taking photographs as instructed. It took me a while to get the hang of the thing, but eventually I seemed to work it out and started snapping away: the old Guildhall; detail of some of the fine Flemish brickwork; the little red-roofed cobble cottages jammed together among the boat sheds and alleyways. Instantly I liked the feel of the camera in my hands. It felt like a form of protection. Morley, meanwhile, continued composing aloud, on the hoof, as it were, adding captions to the photographs as quick – and often quicker – as I was taking them.

'The town, with its little red-roofed cobble cottages. Marvellous, aren't they, Sefton? The pantiled dormers, with their gentle slopes like the curves ... like the curves of a woman's body, eh? Actually, strike that, Sefton. Do you know the domes of Burma and India?'

'Not personally, Mr Morley, no.'

'Things of incomparable beauty. I'm a great fan of Indian architecture. All that copper and gold on the temples and the mosques. Sort of oriental versions of the roof of Westminster Hall, I always think. Don't you?' I did not answer: it did not matter. 'Which of course – I think – is the biggest oak roof of its kind in England. We'll need to check that. Timbers fashioned from oak which were saplings when the Romans ruled the land.' He glanced at the roofs around him. 'But these? They are like an Italianate city. Italianate, wouldn't you say, Sefton? The alleyways and what have you?'

'Yes.'

'Florentine,' he mused. 'Yes. There we are. "Blakeney: The Florence of East Anglia." That'll do. Make a note.' And on. And on.

～ ～

Miriam soon made her excuses and took herself off to the Blakeney Hotel down on the quayside, where, she informed us, she hoped to procure coffee, smoke cigarettes and, if at all possible, scandalise the natives – an objective, I fancied, that might not take more than a quarter of an hour. Morley and I meanwhile walked up through the streets, bidding good morning to the occasional passer-by, Morley noting both out loud and in his notebook some of the more notable roofs, gables and architectural features that took his fancy. Eventually we made it to the top of the village, a slight breeze coming up behind us, splitting the fog, and a church rising before us like a . . .

'Galleon on the high seas,' said Morley, who as usual was several steps ahead.

As we approached the church I noticed a pair of owls were busy around an old alder.

'Owls,' said Morley. 'Note.' Which I already had. 'And the arched roofs of the alder, gabled like porches,' he added. Which I had not. He was always able to find and describe the unexpected, even among the unexpected. 'And so, Sefton,' he continued, striding through the graveyard, spreading his hands before him as if introducing a fairground attraction, or a troupe of music-hall performers, 'as if coming to announce itself to us: the mystery of the church at Blakeney.'

'The mystery?'

'Indeed.' He stopped in his tracks and turned to face me, the church looming behind him. 'There is mystery all about us, Sefton, if only we would open our eyes and perceive it. Is this not the lesson taught to us by all the great mystics?'

'Perhaps,' I agreed.

'Look at these headstones, for example. Hundreds and hundreds. And each one with a story to tell if only we would let them tell it, eh?' He knelt down by a gravestone. 'The *joie de vivre* of the English stonemason, Sefton. Quite extraordinary. Humbling.' He traced the words on the stone with his fingers. 'Traditional English letter forms, Sefton. Quite unlike their continental counterparts: bolder strokes, thinner strokes; the abrupt transition from thick to thin. See? Inspiring, isn't it?'

'Yes,' I said, trying to sound inspired.

He stood up. 'Now, what is it that strikes you about the church, Sefton?'

I gazed up at what appeared to me to be simply . . . a church. A faded board outside announced that it was St Nicholas, Blakeney, with service times at 8 a.m., 10 a.m., 4 p.m. and 6 p.m. on Sundays and matins during the week.

'A typical example,' Morley continued. 'I would say – wouldn't you say, Sefton? – of fifteenth-century Perpendicular architecture. Though of course with one very peculiar and distinguishing feature.' He paused. 'Which is?'

I gazed along from the west tower to the—

'Two towers,' he exclaimed.

'Ah.'

'Indeed. Like an aft-mast and a main mast, aren't they?'

I agreed that indeed they were.

'Now, note, Sefton.' I took out my notebook and began to write. 'The chancel tower, the east tower, is believed by many to have been a lighthouse.'

'Really?'

'Yes. But does it look like a lighthouse to you, Sefton?'

I looked up again. 'It could be a lighthouse, I suppose.'

'Hmm. But what is it lacking, would you say, in its potential capacity as a lighthouse?'

'Lights?' I suggested.

'Of course. But it is not night. And even now without, lights it once might have had. Lights there may have been.' He pointed up to the top of the tower. 'So, the lack of lights, we are agreed, is hardly a sufficient reason for what we

*The mystery of the church at Blakeney*

suspect to have once been a lighthouse indeed to have been such. Is that correct?'

'I suppose.'

'Good. So, to return to the question: what is the *other* essential condition of a lighthouse functioning as a lighthouse, Sefton? Not only light, but . . .'

'I'm sorry, I don't know.'

'Think about it.'

'Sorry, I don't— '

'Don't give up! A lighthouse needs . . .' He stood on his tiptoes, and stretched his hands high above his head.

'Height?' I said.

'Height!' said Morley. 'Exactly! Yes! Indeed. There we are. So if you were building a lighthouse, might you not have made the east tower here a taller tower?'

'Yes, I suppose I would,' I agreed.

'Or simply installed your light in the west, the taller tower, which clearly predates the other?' The west, taller tower, I could confirm, looked older.

'So why didn't they make it taller?'

'You see, you see. *That*, Sefton, is the mystery of the church at Blakeney. Make a note now. Come, come. Let's venture in.'

But just as I was about to write down this latest insight, a woman came rushing out of the church and out of the fog towards us, like a wraith or a demon.

'Oh! Oh!' she cried when she saw us, grabbing hold of Morley's arm. 'Oh, oh!' she continued to wail.

'What seems to be the problem?' said Morley. 'Madam. Are you all right?'

The woman had the look about her of someone who

was not at all all right, and who was indeed so not all right that she was about to collapse and become very un-all right indeed. Sensing that this might be the case, Morley promptly produced a bottle of smelling salts from his waistcoat pocket; he never travelled without it, regarding it as an essential pick-me-up. (If I ever saw him begin to fade – and it happened, perhaps, no more than half a dozen times during the course of our long association – he would instantly produce the smelling salts, take a sniff, and straight away be off again to a fresh start.)

. 'The reverend . . . is . . .' the woman began, momentarily revived by the first whiff of the smelling salts. But she was unable to finish the sentence, as if caught by the throat by an invisible hand.

'Yes?' said Morley, waving the bottle now more vigorously beneath her nose.

The woman took in deep breaths, and again the smelling salts seemed to have a momentary effect.

'The reverend . . . He's . . .' But again she seemed about to go under.

'Goodness,' said Morley, taking the woman gently by the arm. 'A three-sniff problem, Sefton,' he said to me. 'Come and sit down here,' he instructed the woman, brushing some moss from a gravestone – Arthur Cooke, Surgeon of Addenbrooke's Hospital, Cambridge, 1868–1933, R.I.P. He set her gently down. 'There. I'm sure Mr Cooke won't mind.'

The woman looked dazed.

'Now. Are you sick?' asked Morley. 'Unwell?'

'No. No. The reverend.'

'He's sick?'

'He's not sick, no!' the woman said, before losing the

power of words again. 'He's . . .' She pointed towards the door of the church.

'Yes, you said. Now what's your name, my dear?' asked Morley.

'Snatchfold,' she said. 'Snatchfold.'

'Right, well. If you can tell us what's wrong, Mrs Snatchfold, we might be able to help.'

'He's . . .'

Mrs Snatchfold was clearly going to be unable to tell us anything further.

'Well, how about we go and see the reverend, shall we?' said Morley, taking charge of the situation. 'Is he here in the church?'

'Yes, yes. In the church.'

'Very well. Come on, Sefton. Something's up. Let's not dilly-dally. Would you rather stay here, my dear?'

'No!' she said. 'Don't leave me!' At which she sprang up from her sitting position and held on tight to Morley's arm.

'Very well, then,' said Morley, glancing at me, perturbed. 'Clearly a serious business. Lead on.'

As she led us into the church I was surprised to see another woman, standing by the font, her hands folded, almost in the pose of Mary at the foot of the Cross. She had her back to us.

'Hannah,' said Mrs Snatchfold. 'This is Mr . . .'

'Morley,' said Morley. 'Swanton Morley.'

'And I'm Sefton,' I said. 'Stephen Sefton.'

'Hello,' said Hannah, who did not turn fully towards us, but merely looked over her shoulder, as if in fear or contempt. She seemed about to speak further, but then thought better of it and bit her lip. She nodded towards the altar.

Mrs Snatchfold led us through the nave. The church was much larger than I had expected, almost a small cathedral, and Morley, even in the midst of this unexpected adventure, could not help himself from remarking as he went. 'Ah yes,' he said, rubbing his hands together, speaking only to himself, 'font, octagonal; nave – one, two, three, four, five, six bays; chancel with a rib vault; seven-lancet east window; grand Victorian pulpit; extraordinary rood screen; angels up in the hammerbeam, I think; and Nativity figures, altar ... Oh.'

We had duly proceeded into the chancel at the east end of the church, and then through a curtain by the altar, up a steep, tight spiral staircase, and into a room where we discovered the cause of Mrs Snatchfold's distress.

The reverend was hanging by the neck from a bell-rope, his features horribly distorted, his face staring up at nothingness, his lips pulled back in a grimace – an expression that Morley later remarked reminded him of a Barbary ape that he had once seen on his travels in the Atlas Mountains. A trail of phlegm-like liquid stained the front of his dog collar. Mrs Snatchfold stood by the door, shaking, but Morley strode towards the dangling body, peered at it, removed his spectacles, glanced around the room, and peered again.

'Is he ... dead?' asked Mrs Snatchfold fearfully.

'I think we can safely assume so, madam, from the evidence,' said Morley. 'What do you think, Sefton?'

I had stayed unwittingly by the door myself, not so much from fear but from surprise. I had seen so much of death in Spain, but this was in some way much worse: it was the incongruity. Morley waved me forward.

'Come, come, second opinion please. Sefton. Quickly.'

I stepped forward.

'Dead?' said Morley.

I nodded.

Nonetheless, Morley reached up and tried to find a pulse on the reverend's wrist. There was nothing.

'Skin still warm,' Morley said, stepping back and standing up straight. 'What do you think? Suicide?'

Mrs Snatchfold gave out another wail, and then promptly fainted. I rushed over towards her.

'Leave her,' commanded Morley, not turning round.

'But, what about the smelling salts?'

'What about them?'

'Shouldn't we—'

'You've never seen a woman faint before?'

'Yes, but . . .'

'Yes but nothing, Sefton. We've got work to do. Come on, we need to move fast and take notes while the scene is fresh. Priorities, Sefton. We have a dead body here. We can deal with our fainting lady in due course.'

Morley had already produced one of his German notebooks from his jacket pocket and was surveying the scene. He leaned forward and sniffed at the chalice on the table, touched the back of his fingers to the side of it. He consulted the time on his pocket-watch. Consulted the time on his wristwatch. And his other wristwatch. Scribbled something in his notebook. Then he turned his eyes from the body, looking carefully around the rest of the room, his eyes roaming over every detail, taking careful note of what he saw.

'Note?' he said.

'Sorry?' I assumed he wanted me to make a note.

'Any sign of a suicide note?'

'Not that I can see,' I said.

'No,' said Morley. 'There rarely is. Never mind.'

There was the sound of Mrs Snatchfold stirring.

I began to go over to assist her up.

'Leave her,' said Morley. 'You're fine, Mrs Snatchfold,' he called across to her, continuing to make notes. 'You've simply fainted, that's all.'

'Oh, I'm sorry,' said a tearful Mrs Snatchfold weakly from the floor, 'it's just . . .'

'No need to apologise,' said Morley. 'Tell me, have you called the police?'

'Yes. I sent a boy over to the rectory, sir. There's a telephone there.'

'Good. You did the right thing.'

Mrs Snatchfold lay, staring at the reverend's body. 'What's that smell?' she said.

'He's evacuated his bowels, I'm afraid, Mrs Snatchfold. Very common, I believe, in such cases. This stain here . . .' He moved over towards the table and began pointing to the various stains.

Mrs Snatchfold gave another small cry, and fainted again.

'Leave her, Sefton,' he said once more as I went to assist. 'Leica.'

'What?'

'The camera, man. You've got it?'

'Yes.' I brandished the camera.

'Good. Well. Go on. Some photographs.'

'Of the church?' I was shocked. This hardly seemed the time to be working on the book.

'No, not the church, man. Here. This.' He gestured at the body, and the room.

'Here?'

'Yes.'

'Isn't that a bit macabre?'

'This could be a scene of crime, Sefton. *Corpus delicti.*'

'I hardly think—'

'Come in useful, anyway,' said Morley. 'Before the police arrive and make a mess of things. Come on. Snap, snap. Just for our own records.'

I took a series of photographs while Morley strode around the room, stepping carefully over Mrs Snatchfold's prone form, making copious notes and talking the whole time.

'Many as you like, Sefton. Come on. Chop, chop. This, please. Photo.' He pointed to a small coat of arms mounted on the wall. *'Zelo Zelatus sum pro Domino Dio exercitum.* Translation, Sefton?' I couldn't come up with a convincing reading. 'Look,' said Morley, pointing beneath the words. 'Tells us the verse, for those of us without the Latin: 1 Kings 19:14. Any idea?'

'No.' But then, as Morley turned away to study some of the books on the shelves, and thinking I was doing the right thing, I put down the camera, picked up the Bible that lay on the table at the reverend's feet, and was about to flick through to 1 Kings 19:14 when Morley turned.

'No!' he said.

I stopped, about to turn the page.

'Don't move!' said Morley.

'What?' I said. 'Why?'

He removed the Bible carefully from my hands, looked at the page where it was open, and made a note in his notebook. 'Photograph,' he said, waving at the page. 'Please.'

'Of the Bible?'

'Of course.'

'Why?'

'What's the passage it's at?'

I looked down at the Bible. 'Judges chapter 16.'

'And do we know if that is the lesson for today?'

'I don't know. Does it matter?'

'It might, Sefton. Or of course it might not.'

'Right,' I said.

'Carry on,' said Morley. 'Chop, chop. Snap, snap, snap.'

When I had taken sufficient photographs to satisfy Morley's needs – which were many – and Mrs Snatchfold had sufficiently revived, Morley ushered us both back towards the stairs.

'No point upsetting ourselves further here. Clearly a matter for the police. I'm sure they'll be here soon. Why don't you wait outside, Mrs Snatchfold. You wouldn't want to distress yourself further.' At the top of the stairs he whispered to me, 'You first, Sefton. In case we need to break a fall.'

We made it safely without incident back through the church. The woman who Mrs Snatchfold had introduced to us as Hannah stood inside the porch, and as we approached I saw her reach into her pocket for a cigarette and light it. She pulled in a deep breath of smoke.

'Would you mind?' I asked.

'Of course,' she said, and offered me a cigarette, surveying me carefully as she did so. There was something shockingly direct and frank about her gaze. It was chilling. I could think of nothing to say.

'So?' she said.

'He's dead.'

'Of course,' she said, and gave a little laugh.

# CHAPTER EIGHT

MORLEY WAS CHECKING his wristwatch every few minutes, and then his other wristwatch, and then his pocket-watch, and then his wristwatch again, in the hope, presumably, of time speeding up for us so we could move on and get back to our schedule. But time passed in its usual way, Morley notwithstanding, and it was clearly impossible for us to leave until the police arrived, and so we retired to the rectory with a rather shaky Mrs Snatchfold, who kindly offered to provide us with tea and cake while we waited. The sun had pierced the morning's fog, and it began to look as though it might turn into a fine day – though of course this made no difference to Morley. If anything, it made things worse.

'*Tempori parendum*,' he was intoning to himself, mantra-like. '*Tempori parendum*.'

'Everything OK, Mr Morley, sir?'

'Fine,' he said. 'Fine. Absolutely fine.'

He was getting fidgety.

We were served in a melancholy silence by Mrs Snatchfold in the drawing room, but Morley immediately suggested that we take the tea outside and look over the garden: he

*Mrs Snatchfold, thoroughly recomposed*

needed the stimulus, needed to take his mind off things; and he was, of course, a keen horticulturalist, ranking the role of gardener as only slightly lower than his own profession of letters. (He often spoke of his friend E.A. Bowles, in fact, the popular author of gardening books, as though he were Homer himself – 'The greatest bulbsman of our time!' he would declare – and certainly of the same rank as his other literary hero, E.V. Lucas, whose green-buckram-bound *The Open Road: A Little Book for Wayfarers* accompanied us on all our trips, Morley often reading choice passages aloud.)

'Ah! Ah! Ah!' said Morley, in a crescendo of delight, forgetting himself in the moment, as he so often did, when we made our way out onto the terrace. 'A Snake's Head Iris. Snapdragons. Forsythia. Roses. And a magnolia! Look at this, Sefton! Wonderful. Beautifully conceived!' He took a long sniff and breathed out. 'And the fragrance, Mrs Snatchfold! An assault on the senses, is it not, as we step outside. Like a door opening into paradise.' He sniffed again. 'What do you think? Hot spiced lemon, mixed with ...' – he took another deep breath, and held out his hand and wafted the scent towards him, as though grasping not only the smell but also the colour and the very taste of the garden – 'mixed with dry earth and plum, and something perhaps vaguely liliaceous ...'

'If you say so,' said Mrs Snatchfold, clearly alarmed at Morley's sudden enthusiasm, setting the tea tray down on a sturdy wooden table, and proceeding to pour a saucer of milk and place it on the ground. 'I can't say as I'm an expert myself.'

'Pussy!' cried Morley suddenly.

'I beg your pardon?' said Mrs Snatchfold.

'Pussy, pussy, pussy!' he continued.

'Stop!' said Mrs Snatchfold, a look of grief on her face. 'Oh no, Mr Morley, please! Stop!'

'I'm terribly sorry,' said Morley. 'I was just calling your cat. I saw the—'

'He's dead,' said Mrs Snatchfold. 'I forgot for a moment. But he's dead!'

'Yes, I know,' said Morley. 'And it is a terrible shock. But I'm sure the police will do everything they can to investigate the reverend's—'

'Not the reverend,' said Mrs Snatchfold, plainly on the verge of tears. 'The cat.'

'Oh dear,' said Morley. 'That is awful. When was this?'

'Last month,' sniffed Mrs Snatchfold. 'He came in from the garden one day and started vomiting, and then he had this little . . . seizure, and then he went to sleep and . . . Oh!' She began howling again, and rushed back into the house.

I looked at Morley.

He looked at me.

And then he looked at his watch, again.

'*Tempus edax rerum,*' he said woefully. 'Eh, Sefton? *Tempus edax rerum.*'

∽ ∾

'Sorry, gentlemen. More tea?' said Mrs Snatchfold, re-emerging from the house some time later, thoroughly recomposed.

'Alas and alack, I think not, my dear Mrs Snatchfold. We do appreciate your hospitality, under these most unfortunate circumstances, but I'm not sure we can stay much longer.' He ostentatiously consulted his watches again. 'We have our book to write, you see, and an appointment with a flint-knapper over in Dereham this afternoon, so—'

'You'd surely not be leaving me here alone, Mr Morley, until the police arrive?'

'Well . . .'

'It could be hours, and there's no one here except me and—'

There were signs of an upswelling of emotion, which Morley might have been happy to ignore, but which I sought to quell.

'Of course we won't leave you, Mrs Snatchfold,' I said.

'Thank you, Mr Sefton, sir. *You* are a gentleman.' She eyed Morley suspiciously, as though my being a gentleman precluded him from being the same. 'You'll have more tea then?'

'Well . . .' said Morley, clearly agitated at the thought of his timetable being further rearranged.

Mrs Snatchfold poured more tea regardless. 'There you are, Mr Sefton. And you too, Mr Morley.'

Morley sighed and muttered something – something that sounded very much like 'Stupid woman' – and went reluctantly back to the plants and was soon once again in the grip of a botanical fervour. I, meanwhile, lazily and in-expertly gazed around the garden, which stretched far distant.

'He had quite an eye, the reverend?' I said.

'Quite an eye?' said Mrs Snatchfold.

'For the garden, I mean?'

'I'm not sure I can say, sir.' She caught her breath. 'And

actually I'm not at all sure we should be talking like this with him only . . .' She took a deep sigh, and looked as though she might again be overcome with tears.

'Now, now,' said Morley, rising up from his place half concealed within a border, sensing danger. 'I'm sure the good reverend would have wanted us to enjoy the garden he's created, wouldn't he?' He leaned over and took another deep sniff of something. 'Ah. The enchanting scents of Araby. And these anemones, Mrs Snatchfold. Quite magnificent. I've never seen anything quite like them outside Italy.'

'Those things?' said Mrs Snatchfold, sniffing, and pouring herself another consoling cup of tea. 'That's all her doing.'

'Look at this, Sefton.' Morley stood by what appeared to me to be simply a purple bush; I could never share Morley's enthusiasm for the plant world. 'Wild purple anemones.' He stepped back and squinted, as though surveying an Old Master hanging in a gallery. 'Has a tremendous freedom to it, doesn't it, the anemone? Tremendous self-assertion. A sort of carelessness and innocence. You have a veritable Garden of Eden here, Mrs Snatchfold, if I may say so.'

'And her the Eve,' said Mrs Snatchfold, mumbling rather. 'Cake?' She offered Morley a slice of what was a rather dry seed cake.

'I beg your pardon?' said Morley.

'Cake?' she repeated. 'Made yesterday, but still good today.'

'No, before that, what did you say?'

'Nothing, sir,' she said.

'No, there was something,' said Morley.

'Her the Eve?' I said.

'Did you mean the maid, Mrs Snatchfold?' said Morley.

'Hannah?' I said.

'She's responsible for the garden?'

'Yes,' said Mrs Snatchfold.

'She's an expert in the botanical? The striking young woman at the church?' said Morley.

'She knows about plants, sir, but I'm afraid I can't comment on her strikingness. I've heard it said such. I can't say I see it myself.' She reached for a slice of her own dry cake.

'Beauty being in the proverbial eye of the proverbial beholder,' said Morley.

'Exactly,' said Mrs Snatchfold, taking a bite.

'I don't know if you know much of the science of physiognomy, Mrs Snatchfold?' asked Morley.

'I don't, sir, no.'

'It is what one might call a sub-subject in the sciences. Lamarck and etcetera. Popularised by the phrenologists and the criminologists. Eyes too close together, forehead too high – these things taken as signs of criminal intent – or indeed behaviour. External signs of some internal malady. You know the theory?'

'It's the nose on her,' said Mrs Snatchfold with some distaste, wiping dry seed cake crumbs from her lower lip.

'Entirely discredited, of course,' added Morley. 'As a subject. Tells us next to nothing. If we were to attempt to read your face aright, Mrs Snatchfold' – Morley squinted towards Mrs Snatchfold inquisitively – 'what would it tell us?'

'Why, nothing at all, sir!'

'Perhaps not. But the maid has a nose, you say. She's a Jewess, do you mean?'

'Yes,' said Mrs Snatchfold defiantly. 'She is.'

'And yet she was with you in the church?'

'We'd gone to arrange flowers,' said Mrs Snatchfold. 'And then ...' Her voice cracked and her eyes started to well with tears.

'Now, now, now!' said Morley, always uncomfortable at any show of emotion, his own included. 'Let's not start any of that again, Mrs Snatchfold. Look! Look! Fine wisteria,' he said, panicking rather, as Mrs Snatchfold began to crumble. 'Perhaps you'd like another cup of tea yourself, or another slice of your delicious cake?' He nodded towards me, indicating that I might wish quickly to pour tea and dispense cake, in an attempt to quell another damburst of emotion. But it was too late. No tea or cake, however dry, was going to calm this new outpouring. Mrs Snatchfold's tears fell against her heaving bosom, like waves lapping up against the shore.

Morley took immediate action: he excused himself.

'I think I'll take a little botanising tour around the garden, Sefton, if you don't mind.' He set off purposefully in the direction of the trees in the distance. 'See what other treasures are hidden away here. You're all right there, of course, with ...?'

'Fine,' I said, leading Mrs Snatchfold back into the house.

It wasn't until the bells of the church had rung out a melancholy twelve – and Mrs Snatchfold's wave of emotion had subsided, with the assistance of several cups of strong, sweet tea, and several slices of cake – that the police finally arrived. I say 'police', though this implies that their arrival was in some considerable force, or in phalanx. In fact, the police in north Norfolk on a summer's day in August consisted entirely of a young constable named Ridley, no older than twenty-two or twenty-three, who sported a thin moustache, whose fingers were stained yellow from smoking, and whose uniform looked decidedly greasy. I thought him rather a disappointment, but Mrs Snatchfold seemed calmed and reassured by the presence of some official authority, and so I quickly rounded up Morley from the garden – who was in ecstasies over some geraniums – and we agreed to accompany the unsuspecting young constable back up to the church.

'Well,' said Ridley, when he saw the reverend dangling from the bell-rope.

'Indeed,' said Morley. 'What do you think?'

'He's dead,' said Ridley decisively, as though saying it was the thing that confirmed it was the case.

'Dead,' agreed Morley, who drew closer, on the same principle – he adored the naming of parts. 'Deceased. Departed. I don't think there's much doubt about that, Constable. I meant rather what do you think? Circumstances? Cause of death? Time of death? Details? Hypotheses? The latter derived from the former?'

'I couldn't say,' said Ridley, staring at Morley with some concern; a common reaction, I found. 'He looks like he's been dead a while.'

'Oh,' said Morley, clearly disappointed. His faith in humans was such that he often expected people to be able to solve problems and puzzles in the same way he solved crosswords: which is to say quickly, and with little fuss. 'Psmith is baffled, eh?'

'Sorry?'

'Psmith is baffled?'

'My name's Ridley, sir.'

'Yes,' said Morley briskly. 'And you've really no idea? Can't work it out?'

'This is my first dead body, actually, sir,' said Ridley. 'On duty, I mean.'

'Really?' said Morley. 'Well, congratulations. You, Sefton?'

'Sorry, Mr Morley?'

'Dead body, seen one before?'

'Yes,' I said.

'Good. And I, during the course of my long – and some might say undistinguished – career, have come across a few. Which means, Constable, that you have the great advantage of coming at things from first principles.'

'Do I?'

'You do. Opportunity for you to exercise your skills and judgement, I'd say. Young man like yourself. I smell promotion, Ridley, if you were to get to the bottom of this, show a little initiative.'

'I don't really think I'm in a position to show initiative, sir.'

'Of course you are. Skills. Judgement. Initiative. You are a policeman, aren't you?'

'Yes, but—'

'And it's your job to sort all this out, isn't it? Untangle the skein, as it were? Proceed by due process to a logical conclusion.'

'Yes,' said Ridley, whose skein-untangling skills were

*Self-portrait in the garden*

clearly already at their limit. 'I suppose. Police work does
. . . proceed via certain . . . due process, Mr Morley, which I'm
sure you'll understand I have to—'

'Follow. Of course, yes, though I'm surprised you're not
prepared to hazard some educated guess as to what tragedy's
occurred, based on the evidence.'

'We've not gathered any evidence so far, Mr Morley.'

'What? What about all this?' said Morley, sweeping his arm
round with a vigour and intensity that seemed to penetrate
the very walls, indicating not just the room, but the whole
church, its surroundings, and indeed the whole county of
Norfolk as a potential field of evidence. 'No evidence? It's all
evidence, isn't it? *Ex pede Herculem*. You know the expression, Constable?'

'No, I'm not sure that I do, sir.'

'Really?'

'Is it Latin?' asked Ridley, whose moustache was beginning to look weaker and more downcast by the minute.

'It is.'

'I'm afraid I did not have the benefit of a classical education, sir.' The moustache bristled rather with this, I
thought. Weakly bristled, but bristled nonetheless: I began
to warm to Ridley.

'Neither did I, Constable,' retorted Morley. 'Neither did I.
But the disadvantages of one's youth, however great, should
hardly restrain the ambitions of one's adult self, should
they?'

'Well, sir . . .' Defeated, Ridley looked to me for moral
support.

'Otherwise all achievements – intellectual, moral, scientific – would depend entirely upon the hereditary principle,

would they not? Do you believe only in the hereditary principle, Constable? The pharaonic line? The rule of primogeniture?'

'I—'

'*Ex pede Herculem*,' continued Morley, who was now pacing round and round the body, as calmly as a man might pace before his own fireplace. 'Any guesses?'

'No.'

'Come, come. Herculem? Ring any bells? Classical gods?'

'Hercules?' I said, hoping to help Ridley out of the undignified hole Morley had unceremoniously thrown him into.

'Very good, Sefton. But let's allow the young constable here to work things out for himself, shall we? *Pede*?'

'I'm afraid I don't know, sir.'

'But you do know what a podiatrist is?'

'I don't think I do, sir, no.'

'Podiatrist.' Morley spelled out the letters.

'No, sir.'

'Of the foot, Ridley. *Pede*.' He stuck out a leg, shook a foot in demonstration, and pointed at himself. 'So?'

'From the foot, a Hercules,' I said.

'Correct, Sefton. We'll make a classical scholar of him yet, won't we? But, back to the matter in hand.' Morley pointed at the reverend's body, which remained as mute witness to our discussion, like a non-speaking character on stage. 'From a single pertinent fact, Ridley, we might begin to piece together the whole, might we not? You know Pythagoras?'

'Sorry, I don't, no, I . . .' He looked to me again for moral support, but Morley continued, pacing round.

'The sixth-century Greek mathematician and philosopher who calculated the height of Hercules by measuring and comparing the length of his stadium in Athens?'

'His stadium?'

'His stadium, being much longer than that of other men. And thus—'

'This is perhaps not the time for history, Mr Morley, is it?' I interrupted. Restraining Morley from taking a detour, both literal and metaphorical, even in the smallest of rooms, was a hopeless task at the best of times, and one often doomed to failure, but one I nonetheless felt often obliged to perform.

'Indeed,' said Morley, both acknowledging while simultaneously ignoring my attempt to reroute him, 'indeed' being one of his favourite rhetorical devices, allowing him to pretend to account for the opinions and arguments of others while maintaining the force and direction of his own. 'Indeed. It's the principle, though, Sefton. I think the constable here would be willing to spend a minute of his time trying to grasp an important principle, don't you?'

'I think we might be better spending our time—' I began.

'*Ex pede Herculem. Ex ungue leonem.* Constable?'

'Yes, sir?' said Ridley, who by now was flushed bright red with frustration and embarrassment as Morley – insensitive to the finer feelings, and seizing the moment, as ever, as an opportunity for teaching and learning – ploughed on with his questioning.

'*Ex ungue leonem.* A little effort here, please. *Leonem?*'

'Lion?' said Ridley pathetically.

'Correct. So? *Ex ungue leonem?*'

'From something we get the lion?'

'Correct! *Ungue*? Think.'

Ridley had the look of a man whose reserves of thinking had long since been exhausted.

'Come on.'

'The mane?' said Ridley. 'Seeing as it's a—'

'No.'

'The roar?'

'No.' Morley held up his arms as if he were a roaring lion.

'The legs?'

'Closer.' Morley shook his hands.

'The foot?'

'Lions do not have feet, Constable. I think you'll find the word "foot" can be applied, strictly speaking, only to bipeds.'

'Paw?'

'Closer!'

'Claw?' said Ridley.

'Excellent!' exclaimed Morley. 'Lion. Claw. From the claw, a lion. *Ex uno disce omnes*.'

'From the one the many,' I said quickly, saving either Ridley or myself from another round of guess-the-Latin word games.

'So, any ideas?' said Morley. 'Based on the evidence? On the principles? On the details? Lion's claw? Hercules' foot?'

Ridley looked forlornly round the room, as did I, rather hoping for an actual lion's claw – or a Herculean foot – to make itself apparent.

It did not. The body of the reverend seemed to be all we had to go on.

'I'm afraid it's not for me to say what's caused ... this,' said Ridley, nodding towards the body. 'We'll need to get someone from Norwich to look at it.'

'From Norwich indeed!' said Morley.

'That's right, sir.'

'Very well. And when might we expect these wise men from Norwich to arrive, following yonder star?'

'This evening, at the latest. I called ahead for them when I received the phone call earlier.'

'Jolly good,' said Morley, patting Ridley on the back. 'Quick thinking, man.' It was his way. One moment he would be tearing you apart, as though in some impromptu university viva; the next, he'd be slapping you on the back and congratulating you on your perspicacity. With Morley, it was only ever about the truth. The little niceties often seemed not to matter. It made him seem somehow both highly civilised, and an unfeeling brute.

'So there's really nothing for us to do here except wait,' said Ridley.

'You're not going to amaze us with some deductive *tour de force*?' asked Morley, rather teasingly, I thought.

'No, sir.'

'Well, in that case, while we wait, would you mind, if I ...?' Morley took a pen from his top pocket.

'You want to make some notes?' said Ridley.

'No,' said Morley. He pointed with the pen towards the body.

'You want to what?'

Morley then stepped closer to the body, brandishing the pen as though he were going to use it to cut the body down, or scratch some weird graffito upon it.

'You mustn't touch the body, sir!'

'I have no intention of doing so, Constable. But, if I might just explore a little? Prompt poor Mercer here to answer some questions? With the aid of the pen?'

Ridley looked at me, uncomprehending, as I looked at him.

'*Timon of Athens*, gentlemen? Mercer: one of Shakespeare's ghost or mute characters?'

'I see,' I said, not really seeing at all.

'What do you have in mind?' asked Ridley.

'Only this, gentlemen,' said Morley, standing by the body and then, with some considerable degree of dexterity, lifting up the reverend's cassock, using the pen, and then proceeding to expose the poor man's trousers, pulling open a trouser pocket, from wherein he extruded a handkerchief, which, holding it carefully by a corner, he then tugged and tugged, like a music-hall magician, until out it came, tumbling out of the pocket, bringing with it a clatter of coins, a penknife and a flutter of some small pieces of paper. The reverend's body swung ever so slightly.

'Worked almost like a slot machine, didn't it?' said Morley, delighted.

'What do you think you're doing?' said Ridley.

'Now, now! I haven't touched the body.'

'No, but you've . . . tampered with the evidence.'

'I thought you said there was no evidence?'

'Well, not evidence. But . . . things.'

'You don't mind if I examine some things, then?' He indicated the pile on the floor.

'I suppose it would be all right,' said Ridley, whose resistance to Morley, once weak, was now non-existent.

Morley scooped up the items and set them on the table, the reverend's body still swinging slightly above him. He placed a single finger on one of the reverend's brogues.

'Still now, Captain Swing.' The body stilled. 'So, gentlemen, what do we have here?' He picked up a small salmon-pink ticket. 'A ticket stub for the cinema. I see. In Norwich.'

'Rather a long way to travel to a cinema, isn't it?' I said.

'Yes, indeed,' agreed Morley. 'And why would a man travel all that way to see the latest film, do you think?'

'It was a film he wanted to see?'

'Possibly so. Or perhaps a film he didn't want to be seen seeing.'

'Something . . .' I began.

'What?' said Ridley, looking at the cinema ticket.

'Something . . . unsavoury?' I said.

'I don't know exactly what you mean by unsavoury, Sefton, but, yes, I suppose that is what I mean.'

'I hardly think so,' said Ridley. 'He was a vicar.'

'So was the vicar of Stiffkey,' said Morley.

Morley stood examining the rest of the contents of the reverend's pockets: some coins, a pocket penknife. He arranged them on the table.

'What do you think, Constable? Anything significant?'

Ridley stared at the contents of the reverend's pockets, as though he were a haruspex examining chicken entrails. He was unwilling to hazard a guess.

'I can't see anything significant there, but—'

'Quite right,' said Morley. Ridley looked relieved. 'But if you come close to the body, Constable, there's a smell.'

'A smell of what?' Ridley backed away again.

'I don't know,' said Morley. 'Something apart from the obvious . . . Come here, Sefton. Can you smell anything?'

I came closer to the reverend's body and sniffed. Nothing.

'No? Ridley. Come here, man. Don't be squeamish, come on.'

Ridley came closer and sniffed also. Nothing.

'Well, perhaps I'm imagining it.' He sniffed. 'Lily of the valley? Daphne? Chrysanthemums? Can't quite put my finger on it. Something . . . We really need a botanist. Or someone in medicine.'

'There's the professor,' said Ridley.

'Professor?'

'Professor Thistle-Smith. Lives in Blakeney House. Retired.'

'Well!' cried Morley. 'I wonder you didn't mention him before, a real live professor on hand to assist us.'

'I didn't know we'd be needing a professor,' said Ridley.

'One always needs a professor, Ridley, doesn't one? Always. Can't have enough of them professing, eh? Proffing. Proffering. Profiteering. What did you say his name was?'

'Thistle-Smith.'

'A double-barrelled professor, Sefton!'

'I could go and fetch him,' said Ridley. 'He's only five minutes away.'

'Perfect,' said Morley. 'Professor Double-Barrelled will have this all cleared up in no time and we'll be on our way! Marvellous! Should we perhaps stay here by the body?'

'Yes,' agreed Ridley, who then realised that this might be a problem. 'I suppose . . . Someone better had. But you won't touch anything?'

Morley held up his hands, and his pen.

'*Dictum meum pactum*, sir.'

'Is that a yes or a no?' said Ridley.

'He won't touch anything,' I said.

Ridley left, Morley continued to examine seemingly every mote and speck of dust in the room, and I, exhausted again from Morley's strenuous mental exertions, and with a pounding headache induced by a lack of pills and tobacco, excused myself to go outside to smoke.

# CHAPTER NINE

THE WOMAN, HANNAH, was outside in the graveyard. She looked up as I approached. She'd clearly been crying – you could see tears clinging to her eyelashes – but her gaze was somehow dry and flat, entirely unemotional. Her eyes were dark, like proverbial pools: Morley would later describe them as 'private' and 'turbulent'. Her hair was tied back tight off her face, which made her face shine, without shadow. She wore no make-up. Her hands seemed dirty, stained bluish, yellow, as if she had scraped her face clean. She was perhaps twenty-five, twenty-six years old. You could see her breathe as she spoke.

'Are you all right?' I said. 'You've been here the whole time?'

'Yes, sir. Thank you. I'm fine, thank you.'

I handed her my handkerchief. She wiped her hands first, and then her face.

'Would you like me to escort you somewhere, perhaps?'

'No. I can't leave if . . . his body is still in there. Someone should be with him.' There was in her voice some slight hint of something foreign; I couldn't help but stare at her mouth as she spoke.

'Mr Morley's in there with him, madam. He'll look after him.'

'Cigarette?'

I patted my pockets. I didn't like to scrounge, but, 'Thank you,' I said.

I lit her cigarette, and then my own, and since there seemed nothing else to do, we fell into step together, and slowly paced our way around the churchyard.

'How long had you known him?'

'About five years.'

'That's a long time.'

'I came when ... It was my job to help around the house.'

'Ah, yes, we were just there, with Mrs Snatchfold.'

She didn't respond.

'You don't get on?' I asked.

She turned as we walked and stared at me – that frank look again. 'We get on very well. Who did you say you are?'

'Sefton. Stephen Sefton. I work with Mr Morley. I'm his assistant.'

'I see. Like me.'

'Perhaps ... A little. And Mrs Snatchfold said your name was Hannah?'

'Hannah Tuchosky, yes.'

'It's a lovely name.'

'Thank you.'

'Not a Norfolk name?'

She threw her head back. 'No.'

'A foreign name?'

'Yes, Mr Sefton. If you must know about me, my family came here in 1932. From Germany.'

'I'm sorry, I didn't mean to pry.'

She laughed her dry, pitiless laugh.

'"*Pry*." Pry. Nobody around here means to "pry".' And then she suddenly stopped walking, turned her body fully towards me, and stood in my way. 'Do you know Rilke?' she asked. '*The Duino Elegies*?'

'Yes,' I said. 'A little . . . I think.'

'"*Wer, wenn ich schriee, hörte mich denn aus den Engel Ordnungen?*"' Her eyes suddenly filled with tears. '"Who, if I cried out, would hear me among the angelic orders?" Do you understand?'

'I think so.' I wasn't sure.

'He's committed suicide, I suppose?'

'I'm afraid it looks like it.'

'Do you know how?'

'It looks like hanging. But we're waiting to find out now.'

She took both my hands in her own – her hands were warm, and so soft – and stared at me for what seemed like a long time, waiting to tell me something else. But she did not speak, and indeed refused to say anything more before Ridley arrived back at the church with Professor Thistle-Smith, a vast, lumbering man in his sixties, dark-suited, cheeks florid, panama hat in hand, with rich, exaggerated, almost fruity features that might have been painted by the great Arcimboldo himself. The professor ignored Hannah, looking past her, and round her and over her, I noticed, but introduced himself courteously enough to me, and I accompanied him with Ridley back inside the church, the professor wheezing his way up the stairs, growing ever more crimson as we approached the vestry, where he did not for a moment balk or hesitate or flinch at the sight of the hanging body, but instead strode over, wheezing all the while, staring at and sniffing around the corpse.

'Oh dear,' he said, breathing in deeply, like a seething wind, 'oh dear . . . oh dear . . . oh dear.'

Morley stood close by, watching him; Typhon, he referred to him as later, in private, another of his references.

'I wondered, Professor, if you could smell anything . . . different?'

'No, can't smell anything unusual,' he said.

'Are you sure?' asked Morley.

'Quite sure. Apart from the fouling, of course – perfectly normal in these cases.'

'So you're familiar with such incidents?'

'I am, indeed, sir. Thirty years as a Professor of Medicine – one becomes accustomed to all sorts of cadavers in all sorts of unpleasant states and forms. Nothing odd or unusual here that I can see. Seen it all before.'

'Except of course in this instance you knew this particular cadaver before its death?' said Morley.

The professor stepped back from the body then and peered at Morley, as if seeing him clearly for the first time. 'I'm sorry, sir. You seem not to have introduced yourself. You are?'

'*Civis Romanus sum.* Swanton Morley, at your service.'

'Morley, eh? And can I ask exactly what are you doing here, Mr Morley?'

'I'm here writing a book, actually, Professor, and we happened to be passing—'

'Happened to be passing?' The professor exchanged suspicious glances with Ridley. 'I see. A book?'

'That's right.'

'Novelist, are we?'

'No.'

'No. You don't look like a novelist.'

'I'll take that as a compliment, sir.'

'Not intended as one,' said the professor. 'And you're the chap who found the reverend's body?'

'Not exactly, Professor, no. Mrs Snatchfold found the body, and we then found Mrs Snatchfold. So we are one – if you like – step removed from the discovery.'

'One step removed?'

'Quite so. But you knew the reverend well, yourself?'

The professor was busying himself, wandering around the body, fascinated.

'I'm a congregant here, Mr Morley, if that's what you mean.'

'Ah, I'm Methodist myself,' said Morley.

'Hmm,' said the professor disapprovingly. 'You may not know then, Mr Morley, that in the Church of England – unlike the Methodists – we tend not to befriend our reverends.'

'Dead or alive,' said Morley.

'Indeed.'

Ridley, meanwhile, seemed to have overcome his initial distaste for the body, and was also looking closely at the reverend.

'So you think he definitely killed himself, Professor?' he said.

'That would be my opinion, yes,' said Thistle-Smith. 'Is that all?'

'We've someone coming from Norwich who'll perhaps want to speak to you. I hope that's all right.'

'Of course. Ugly business,' said the professor. 'You know where to find me, Ridley?'

'Yes,' said Ridley.

'And I'm sure your colleagues will be keen to speak to Mr Morley as well,' said Thistle-Smith as he made for the door. 'First at the scene of the crime and what have you.'

'Second, actually,' said Morley.

'So you said. I'm sure your colleagues will be very keen to talk to him, won't they, Ridley?'

'Actually,' said Morley, 'we were hoping to move on. We have a tight schedule to keep, with the writing of the book.'

'I'm sure you have, Mr Morley. But I assume there are strict police procedures to be followed, are there not, Ridley?'

'Oh yes, Professor,' said Ridley, who was clearly beginning to sense where Thistle-Smith's suggestions might be leading. 'I'll have to ask you, Mr Morley, and your companion, to remain here until my colleagues arrive.'

'You'll be needing a death certificate, isn't that right, Constable?' said Thistle-Smith.

'I think so,' said Ridley.

'Have you sent for Dr Sharp?'

'No, I haven't. Would it help if I were to go for him?'

'I think it would, young man. I think that would be most helpful. Perhaps I should stay with our ... witnesses here, and make sure nothing happens to the body ...'

There followed a stand-off between Morley and Professor Thistle-Smith, as we waited for Dr Sharp. The few words they exchanged were challenges and retorts rather than conversation proper, the reverend's body hanging between them as referee and witness.

'Who *are* you, exactly, Morley?' drawled the professor,

who had drawn up a chair by the table, while Morley and I remained standing; it felt as though we had been summoned before a court.

'Who am I?' asked Morley.

'Yes.'

'I'm terribly sorry, I'm not sure I understand your question, Professor.'

'Don't understand my question?' Professor Thistle-Smith's large face drooped in an expression of deep contempt, his features changing from the merely unpleasant to the unmistakably menacing. 'Really?' He straightened up in the chair and took a deep, gargling breath. 'Don't know who you are? Hmm. Interesting. I, *for example*, am a farmer, landowner, retired professor, of solid yeoman stock, a magistrate, a Liveryman of the Worshipful Company of Scriveners, a Knight Grand Cross of the Supreme Military Order of the Temple of Jerusalem, and a Knight Grand Cross of the Military Order of the Collar of St Agatha of Paterno. And I am simply asking … in similar kind, sir, Who. Are. You?'

'I see. My apologies. *Davus sum, non Oedipus*. My name is Swanton Morley, sir. I am a journalist and author.'

'Journalist as well, are we, eh, as well as an "author"? Which newspaper?'

'The *Daily Herald*, sir.'

The professor snorted. 'Muck-raking rag,' he said.

'I think of it rather as a working man's paper,' said Morley. 'And—'

'I'll make up my own mind about the quality of the *Daily Herald*, if you don't mind, Morley. Self-made man, are we?'

'We?' said Morley.

'You,' said Thistle-Smith. 'Obviously. Not me.'

'What little I have achieved I have achieved by my own efforts, yes.'

'Well, *well done you*, but some of us do not want to live in a self-made man's communist republic, thank you very much, where everyone has to read the *Daily Herald*.'

'That seems unlikely,' said Morley.

'Not if you and your lot get your way.' The professor spoke with singular force. 'And what about this book you claim you're writing?'

'It is a major literary project—' began Morley.

'Ha!'

'Called *The County Guides*, in which my assistant and I travel the country and produce a guidebook to each of England's counties.'

'Ha!' The professor snorted again and stared at the two of us as if we were obvious impostors. 'Ridiculous. You're going to live till one hundred and twenty, are you?'

'*Dum spiro spero*,' said Morley.

'What?'

'It's Latin.'

'Some of us left Latin behind with other childish things when we left medical school, Morley. So in English, man, in England. What did you say?'

'While I breathe I hope,' said Morley. 'Though at the moment, obviously, we are being prevented from working on the project while we wait here with you for the police.'

'Oh, what a pity,' said Professor Thistle-Smith, who had clearly perfected his vile sneer over many years.

'Might I perhaps ask about your relationship with the reverend, Professor? Seeing as we're here?'

'You might, sir. But you might not get an answer.'

'I see.'

'Do you now? All I will say is, if he'd taken the church any lower, it would have been crawling.'

'Too low for your tastes then?' said Morley.

'Too. Low. Indeed. Sir.'

'And personally?'

'Personally? Though I can't see that it's any of your business, I'll admit I didn't much like him,' said the professor.

'I see,' said Morley. 'And was it mutual?'

'Mutual?'

'Did he not like you?'

'I know what mutual means, sir. I'm not a bloody idiot. And nor am I a mind-reader. Are you?'

'No, I'm not.'

'Clearly. So I have no idea about the reverend's feelings towards me, Mr Morley. And, frankly, could not care less. A gentleman does not speak of such things.'

'Quite so. But . . .'

∽ ∾

After about fifteen minutes of this rough jousting, Dr Sharp arrived. 'The superlative little doctor,' Morley later called him: he was brisk; efficient; sober in manner and in suit. He greeted Professor Thistle-Smith warmly and Morley and I watched as they examined the body.

'Oh dear, oh dear, oh dear,' said the doctor, echoing the professor's words.

'The professor here thinks he died by hanging,' said Morley.

'Yes, I think we can safely assume so, gentlemen,' said the doctor, 'although of course we'd have to perform an autopsy to be absolutely sure. There's not a lot we can do here.'

'Will you perform the autopsy?' asked the professor.

'If Ridley here approves.'

'I see no reason why not,' said Ridley

'Can I ask when?' said the professor.

'It would probably be this evening,' said Dr Sharp. 'By the time I've seen my other patients. Perhaps eight o'clock. Would that suit, Constable?'

'Of course, if it suits you, sir.'

'And would you mind if I attended?' said Morley. 'Purely for the purposes of research, you understand. I write a number of books and columns.'

The doctor looked dubious. The professor was scowling. Ridley picked up the hint.

'I don't think that would be appropriate, Mr Morley,' he said. 'Under the circumstances.'

'Which circumstances?'

'My colleagues will be wanting to speak with you this evening, sir, so you'll have to make yourself available for them, if you wouldn't mind. And then if everything is in order you'll be able to be on your way.'

'And we wouldn't want this getting out to the papers, would we, eh?' said the professor.

'I wouldn't dream of writing about it,' said Morley.

'Anyway,' said the doctor. 'I'm sure we could let you know about the results of the autopsy, if you're interested, Mr Morley. Couldn't we, Constable?'

'Yes,' said Ridley.

'Thank you,' said Morley.

'Now, shall we find you somewhere to stay?' said the doctor. 'In case you're going to be with us for a while?'

Morley took one last forlorn look at a wristwatch. We were outnumbered.

'*In manus commendo me*,' he said.

'It's probably Latin,' said Ridley.

'Thank you, Constable,' said the professor.

As we made our way out of the church, a woman came marching towards us. She was in her fifties, fashionably dressed, red lipstick, a vast silk scarf flung about her shoulders, like a pelt. We had just reached the doors of the church – Morley and me, the professor, the doctor and Ridley – and I could see Hannah still hovering outside by the graves. This other woman now confronting us seemed as vivid and as bold as Hannah seemed modest and reduced.

'Is it true?' she said, addressing us all.

'I'm sorry, madam,' began Ridley, but she cut him short with a wave of her hand.

'Is he dead?' she said, speaking directly to the professor.

'I'm afraid—' began the doctor.

'I want to see him,' she said.

'I really think it would be better if you didn't,' said the doctor. 'Don't you . . . Mr Morley?'

'I think if Mrs . . .'

'Thistle-Smith,' the woman said, not looking at Morley, her eyes directed, it seemed, only at the professor.

'Well, I think if Mrs Thistle-Smith – your wife, Professor?' – the professor gave a curt nod of assent – 'if she wishes to see the reverend I think we should accede to her wishes, don't you?'

'Out of the question,' said the professor.

'What happened?' she said, addressing herself now to Morley. 'Was it poison?'

'Hanging,' said Ridley.

'Hanging,' she repeated. 'Well, well.'

'Are you all right, Mrs Thistle-Smith?' asked Morley.

'Yes, thank you,' she said.

'I'm sure it has come as a shock.'

'A shock, yes,' she agreed.

'When was the last time you saw him?' asked Morley.

'Alive?'

'Yes, of course . . . alive.'

'The last time I saw him alive was . . .' She studied Morley's face before she answered, as though calculating. 'I think the last time I saw him was on Sunday. At service, of course.'

'That'll be all, thank you, Morley,' said the professor, who took his wife firmly by the arm, and proceeded to walk with her through the graveyard back towards the village, the rest of us following behind.

# CHAPTER TEN

WE PUT UP IN THE BLAKENEY HOTEL. Miriam had long since departed for London. After a light supper we adjourned to the hotel's public bar. Morley always insisted on the public bar, believing saloon bars to be places of ill-repute. 'Strictly for duchesses, cads and travelling salesmen,' he would say. 'And hoity-toits like you, of course, Sefton.'

The bar was busy: locals. The ritualistic sound of pint glasses, and of low, muddy, murmuring Norfolk voices. And then there was the sound of Morley, cutting through.

'"Set 'em up, Joe,"' he said, unfortunately, to the barman.

'I beg your pardon, sir?'

'I said, "Set 'em up, Joe."'

You could hear men squint, and the sound of calloused hands being rubbed.

Morley, as everyone knows, had a predilection for reciting nursery rhymes, and tongue-twisters, and indulging in verbal games of all sorts – it was the flipside, I suppose one might say, of his fluency, an aspect of his character much remarked upon and cherished; another sign of his droll English eccentricity. His habit of imitating phrases from

# Tariff

| Inclusive Terms : | £ | s. | d. |
| --- | --- | --- | --- |
| Per Week .. .. .. .. .. .. | 3 | 3 | 0 |
| Per Day .. .. .. .. .. | | 12 | 6 |
| Bedroom and Breakfast .. .. | | 7 | 6 |

*The Entrance*

## Miscellaneous Charges :

| | |
| --- | --- |
| Early Morning Tea or Coffee .. .. | 6d. |
| Baths .. .. .. .. .. .. .. | |
| Garage .. .. .. .. .. .. | No charge |
| Dogs .. .. .. .. .. .. | per week 2/6 |

*Tariff from the Blakeney Hotel*

American films and novels, however, and often at the most inopportune moments, was one of his lesser known and less endearing characteristics.

'What can I get you, sir?' said the barman stoically.

'"Set 'em up, Joe!"' Morley said again, rolling the phrase around in his mouth. 'Extraordinary phrase, isn't it? I don't know if you're a fan of the Western?'

'No.'

In the public bar of the Blakeney Hotel that evening, it suddenly felt like a Western, and we were the unwelcome strangers just ridden into town.

'No? *The Texas Rangers*? *Custer's Last Stand*? Gene Autry, the Singing Cowboy? "Mexicali Rose"? "Mexicali Rose, stop crying—"'

I stepped in quickly before Morley got into the swing of his cowboy singing.

'A pint of beer for me, please.' Morley looked at me disapprovingly. 'Under the circumstances,' I said.

'Very well,' said Morley.

'And what would you like to drink, Mr Morley?'

'A pint of Adam's ale for me, please.'

The barman looked at Morley – as barmen often looked at him – with a sort of weariness bordering on contempt.

'You serve Adam's ale?' said Morley.

'Adam's ale?' said the barman.

'Aqua vitae. The—'

'Water,' I said. 'Please. If you don't mind.'

'Water?' said the barman to me, having given up on a sensible conversation with Morley. 'He's wanting to drink water?'

'That's it,' said Morley. And this of course was *another* of his exotic habits: the ordering of water in pubs and bars. Indeed, among all his habits – the punctiliousness, the hastiness, the continual quoting of Latin tags and English verse, his archaic Edwardian manners, the inopportune quoting of phrases from American movies – it was the drinking of water in public bars that was perhaps the one habit that over the years got us into more trouble than anything else.

'I'm not sure I'd drink the water,' said the barman.

'It'll be fine,' said Morley, raising his considerable eyebrows in friendly reassurance. 'Fine. Nothing finer than a glass of English water.' He turned around to address the now silent men of the bar. 'Isn't that right, gentlemen?' Reply came there none, and if in Norfolk there were tumbleweed, tumbling it would come. 'The true and proper drink of Englishmen, barman, if I might paraphrase George Borrow.'

'George Who?'

'Borrow?' said Morley. 'Late of this parish? Local hero, surely?'

'Who?'

'Borrow. George Borrow?'

'Anybody know George Borrow?' the barman asked of the silent drinkers.

'No.'

'Really?' said Morley.

'And you say he's from Blakeney?'

'Norfolk, certainly. Dereham, I think. You're not acquainted? Linguist. Novelist. Friend of the Romanichals?'

'No,' said the barman decisively, and he stared at Morley for a moment, attempting to get the measure of him, and then – having got the measure of him – sniffed, wiped his hands slowly on his apron and retreated to the back kitchen, where there could be heard the sound of muttering; and wherefrom an ample-bosomed and rosy-cheeked woman – who might have stepped straight from Maugham's *Cakes and Ale* such was her perfectly formed barmaidliness, her body and manner expressing, if one might say so, boundless tolerance, or 'A woman of robust and welcoming construction', as Morley later put it – appeared.

'Everything all right here, gentlemen?'

'All fine, thank you, madam,' said Morley, and then turning to me added, *sotto voce*, 'Would I were in an alehouse in London, eh?'

'Indeed, Mr Morley,' I said, taking the comment merely as a remark.

'Quotation, Sefton,' he said.

'Oh.' I had come already, within days, rather to dread his love of quotations.

'Guess?'

'Shakespeare?'

'Of course.'

'Of course.'

'And which play?'

'I don't know. Sorry. I'm tired, Mr Morley.'

'Tired, Sefton?' Morley turned his steely blue gaze upon me.

I don't think in all our years of acquaintance that I ever knew Morley to admit to feeling tired. He would, on occasion, recite out loud, 'Let us not be weary in well doing; for in due season we shall reap, if we faint not' – something from the

Bible – which seemed to work for him as a kind of charm, or a pick-me-up, like his smelling salts, the proverbial hair of the dog, as it were. 'What we need is a biblical bracer,' he would sometimes say, in search of a quote to support some argument or other, as though Scripture were the equivalent of a raw egg with a dash of Worcester sauce. These biblical bracers tended to have the opposite effect on me, making me despair of ever making it through the day.

'*Titus Andronicus*?' I said, when it was obvious – his peering at me enquiringly over his moustache – that he was still waiting for an answer to the question.

'"Would I were in an alehouse in *London*?"' he said.

'Not *Titus Andronicus*?'

'Henry V at battle!' he cried, as the barman returned and placed a glass of rather cloudy-looking water before us on the bar. 'Cry havoc, and let slip the dogs of war!'

'Water,' said the barman, spilling the contents of the glass slightly.

'Adam's ale!' said Morley, raising the – rather grimy-looking – glass to his lips and then drinking a long draught. The barman watched him keenly, grinning, arms folded, from behind the bar. 'Ah. Delicious,' continued Morley. 'A drop of the old aqua vitae. You know the word derives ultimately from the Irish and Scottish Gaelic *uisge beatha*?'

'Does it now?' said the barman.

'And what does this phrase mean, you might ask?'

'I might.'

'Indeed.'

'But I won't, thank you, sir. That'll be—'

'Water of life,' said Morley. 'Or more commonly—'

I quickly handed some money to the barman and led

Morley away to a quiet corner by the fire, where he could do no harm and cause no further irritation.

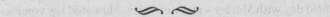

Eventually men returned to their drinking and smoking and playing darts, carefully lobbing, I noted, their cigarette ends into the fire with the same accuracy they were scoring on the dartboard, while Morley sat twisting the ends of his moustache, a sign he was deep in thought, as though he were jiggling the wires on a crystal set, trying to tune in to some obscure Hertzian wave or stream of thought. On a table opposite two men sat silently playing a game of shove-halfpenny, clearly listening to every word we spoke.

'In the church,' said Morley. 'Why in the church? Why would he kill himself in the church?'

'Because that's where he was?' I ventured.

'But he could have been anywhere, could he not?'

'He could, but he wasn't.'

'Exactly. Which brings us back to the question, why in the church? Why not in the rectory? Or out in some woods? Plenty of opportunities for a man to take his own life, aren't there?' He took a long sip of water and twisted his moustache some more. 'Where would you take your own life, Sefton, if you were so inclined?'

The two men opposite listened ever more intently and suspiciously in our direction. This was clearly not everyday pub talk in rural north Norfolk. Though it would hardly have been everyday pub talk in any village, town or city throughout the length and breadth of England: it was simply Morley's habit to ask the simple, direct sort of question that the rest of us usually see fit to avoid; he was a man who had somehow released the mental valve that most of us manage to keep tight shut. Freud, I often thought, would have had a field day with Morley – and vice versa. I lowered my voice as I replied, my own mental valve being turned firmly clockwise a number of times. I had, in fact, as it happened, considered taking my own life on a number of occasions, and only recently: in Spain, and in London, and by various methods: poisoning; shooting; hanging; jumping from some high place; starvation; lying down in front of a train. The options seemed endless, in fact, though ultimately unattractive. If I could simply disappear, that might have been the answer. Though travelling through England with Morley for all those years, I suppose I did in a sense disappear, or was constantly in the state of disappearing.

'I'd probably go somewhere quiet,' I said quietly.

'Precisely!' said Morley, too loudly. 'Any sane man would kill himself somewhere quiet! *Not* in the vestry.'

'Probably not, no,' I agreed, shushing Morley, who could never satisfactorily be shushed.

'Because there'd be a chance, wouldn't there, Sefton, of someone walking in, preventing you from going through with it, popping a proverbial spanner in the suicidal works, etcetera?'

'I suppose so, yes.'

'So, why run the risk?'

'Perhaps he was suddenly overcome with despair?' I suggested, as another cigarette end hit an ember, dead centre. The whole bar seemed to have grown quieter as Morley grew more vivid. I felt the eyes of every man watching us.

'And in his moment of despair,' said Morley, 'he fetched

[ 142 ]

a bell-rope, climbed up on a table, onto a chair, tied the bell-rope into a noose, looped it around the beam, kicked the chair away, and hanged himself? Quite a moment, wouldn't it be? Not so much a moment, in fact, as a short episode, which implies not only premeditation but also—'

'I might get myself another drink, actually,' I said, unable to bear the scrutiny of the other – now once again silent – customers any longer.

'Good idea,' said Morley.

'Good idea,' I agreed, getting up.

'I smoked marijuana once, you know, Sefton,' he continued, 'through a hookah, in Afghanistan. Herat. Wore a turban. It's not all it's cracked up to be. Either the turban or the marijuana.' He would often throw these googlies into conversation. It was best to ignore them, I found, though the darts-players were clearly having trouble doing so, staring at this white-haired, middle-aged, moustached man as though he had escaped from a lunatic asylum.

'Another pint of—'

'The old aqua vitae,' he said. 'Yes. Wouldn't that be lovely?' And he pulled out a notebook and began writing.

'Does anyone commit suicide on impulse, as it were?' he continued, on my return, tapping his notebook, which was now covered with furious little notes and diagrams. Fortunately, the novelty of having a one-time turban-wearing, marijuana-smoking autodidact among them seemed to have worn off, and men had returned to their conversations, their darts and their shove-halfpenny.

'I'm sure they do,' I said.

'Young people, perhaps. Adolescents. Young Werther and what have you. But a grown man, Sefton? And a vicar, at that. With an eternal perspective? Hardly.'

I took a restoring sip of my beer, and chose not to answer, which was always the best course in such circumstances, I found, since after a few moments Morley was always prepared to pick up a ball and run with it alone.

'So, what do you think, Sefton, reasons for suicide?'

'Erm.'

'If we had to draw up a shortlist. Number one reason?'

'Erm . . .'

'Number one. Mental or physical infirmity. Can't say at the moment about the physical infirmity – he seemed a fine specimen, but we'll have to wait for the results of the autopsy to confirm. No one has mentioned the reverend being doolally, have they?'

'No, not to me,' I said.

'Me neither,' said Morley. 'One might have expected Mrs Snatchfold to have mentioned it, if he was crazy?'

'Yes.'

'So that rather rules that out. Which leaves us with our number two reason for anyone committing suicide. Which would be?'

'Sorrow?'

'Precisely! Yes. But sorrow over what exactly?'

'I don't know.'

'Loss? Mourning? Grief, as we know, abides by its own peculiar timetable; but it seems unlikely, I think. What do you think?'

'Erm . . .'

'He may of course have been in some sort of practical discomfort. Financial distress, possibly. Debt? A gambler? In which case someone locally would be able to tell us. Which leaves us a long list of other reasons for sorrow, including perhaps remorse, shame, fear of punishment – God's or otherwise – despair due to unrequited love, thwarted ambition—'

'Quite a lot of possibilities.'

'Exactly, Sefton. Which means it's probably the wrong question to ask. Too many answers: wrong question. So, let's work on the basis of what we do know rather than what we don't, shall we? Let's imagine, just for a moment, Sefton. Let's put ourselves in the role of the poor departed reverend. This man who decides to kill himself in his own church.'

One of the darts-players scored a triple top, to much celebration.

'Bravo!' said Morley, joining in, and then continuing without a break. 'Let's just think about it for a moment, Sefton. The life of a country priest.' He pointed to a diagram in his notebook: a series of circles and letters, and noughts and crosses, like a set of primitive pictograms or strange celestial symbols. 'Here he is. The reverend.' He pointed to a small black cross inside a large black circle. 'Now, what does a reverend do, on a daily basis?'

'Preaches?'

'Yes, of course, he preaches. Though weekly, we might assume, rather than daily. But, you're right of course, he does preach. Hence ...' He pointed to a line that led from the large black circle to a smaller circle containing a capital P. 'Anything else?'

'He visits the sick?'

'Again, yes,' and he traced his pen along another line out towards another circle containing the letter S. 'He does indeed. Chum to the weak, and what have you. But what is most important about the role of the priest, town or country, in the Holy Roman and Apostolic Church?'

'I don't know, Mr Morley.' My mind sometimes wandered when Morley was pursuing a theory, adumbrating a theme, or sketching.

'The sacerdotal role, is it not?' He drew a circle around all the other circles, creating a kind of wheel with spokes. 'The priest is set apart from the community, Sefton. Everything that represents worldliness – the love of pleasure, of art, of ourselves. The priest is supposed to be essentially different from us.' He drew half a dozen small arrows attempting to penetrate the large circle.

'I see.' I had absolutely no idea what was the point of the diagram now.

'He's a symbol, isn't he?'

'I suppose.'

He took a long draught of his water.

'So, the point?'

'It's just an illustration, Sefton, to help us think.'

'Right.'

He tore the page from his notebook and fashioned it into a small dart.

'Now, Sefton. Watch.' He squinted. 'On the oche!' he said and leaned back, and then promptly threw his little dart straight into the heart of the fire, where it burst into flame. 'One hundred and eighty!' he cried. The darts-players responded with a polite round of applause. Morley bowed in his seat and took a couple of celebratory twists of his moustache. 'You're a city person, Sefton, aren't you?'

'Yes. Born and bred in London.'

'Can you imagine for a moment, then, living somewhere like this?' He swept his arm wide, almost knocking our drinks to the floor.

'Well . . .'

'And every day you'd have to meet the same people. The same people in your place of work. The same people in the pub. Our darts-playing friends here . . .' Our darts-playing friends glanced over. 'Day in, Sefton, day out. Week in, week out. Year in, year out. People you might not like. And who might not like you. And yet you can't leave, Sefton. You can't go anywhere. Because your role as parish priest is to serve them. All of them.' He threw his arms wide again, once more narrowly missing our drinks. 'And in return, Sefton, they are expected to respect you, to look up to you, to see you as a representative if not of Christ exactly, then at least of the Church, and for you to express and uphold its values, and yet and yet and yet' – a final arm fling, which fortunately I saw coming, and had snatched away our glasses – 'they see you every day, conducting your duties in the same way we all conduct our duties, which is to say inconsistently and incompletely. They see your failings and your petty grievances and faults. Might not the temptation eventually be . . .'

I placed the drinks safely back down on the table. 'To kill yourself?' I said.

'Wrong!' cried Morley, this time finally throwing his arm wide enough and quickly enough to knock both our glasses successfully to the floor. The unmistakable sound, first, of breaking beer glasses; second, of the absolute silence following the breaking of beer glasses; and third, and finally, of the fulsome barmaid, on uncertain heels, hurrying to resolve the breaking of beer glasses. And then . . . the equally unmistakable sound of Morley, continuing on.

'*Terra es, terram ibis,*' he said.

'Sorry, sir?' said the barmaid.

'Dust thou art, to dust thou shalt return.'

'If you say so, sir.'

'I really am terribly sorry. I have an awful habit of talking with my hands, I'm afraid. A touch too much of the old *Schwärmerei,* eh?'

'I'm sure it is, sir. But not to worry,' said the barmaid of boundless tolerance, who was bending over to pick up the larger shards of glass from the floor, and mopping at the beer and water with a dishcloth. 'We'll have this cleared up in a moment, sir.'

I got down on my hands and knees to help, not least because the barmaid's heels and clothes rather inhibited her free movement. She was dressed primarily for display purposes.

'Don't you be troubling yourself with that, sir.'

'Nonsense,' I said. 'It's the least I could do.'

'Mind your fingers.'

'I will,' I said. And for a moment – something to do with the light, the woman, the smell of beer – I was back in a bar in Barcelona where there was a banner up outside: 'Las Brigades Internacionales, We Welcome You'.

Between us we made a pretty good job of clearing up, and the bar chatter gradually resumed.

'I'll help you get rid of this,' I said, my hands cupping broken glass.

'There's no need,' said the barmaid.

'It's fine,' I said. 'I need to get us both another drink anyway.'

'*Ubi mel ibi apes*, eh, Sefton?' said Morley.

'Is he foreign, your friend?' whispered the barmaid as we walked to the bar with all the sharp little pieces.

'He's just . . . eccentric,' I said.

'All right, Lizzie?' asked the barman, as we dropped the broken glass into a bucket behind the bar.

'We're fine, John.'

'Can't you keep your friend under control?' said the barman.

'Yes,' I said. 'I mean, no. Not really, no, I'm afraid he's . . .'

'He's harmless,' said the barmaid. 'Leave him alone, John.' She straightened up and faced me, cocking her head to one side. 'You're staying in the hotel?'

'Yes, we are. Just for a night or two.'

'Well, we'll see lots of you in here then, I hope. You make a nice change.'

'Indeed,' I said.

～ ～

'The temptation, Sefton,' continued Morley, once I had brought us fresh drinks and settled down again, 'would not be to kill oneself, surely, but to kill them, would it not?'

'What?' By this stage all I wanted was to drink my beer quietly and get to bed.

'Does it seem so strange?'

'I'm sorry, Mr Morley, I can't quite seem to understand what it is you're suggesting.'

'I'm not suggesting anything, Sefton. I'm simply remarking on the obvious fact that anyone and everyone might at some time be tempted to kill themselves. Or indeed others. Your experience in Spain would bear that out, would it not?'

'I don't know.'

'Do you know Durkheim?'

'No, I'm afraid not. Not personally no.' I had no idea who he was talking about.

'German. Cranky. Beard, etcetera. But useful distinctions between types of suicides. We are assuming that the reverend's is an act of egoistic suicide, self-directed, an act of self-harm. But what if it's not? What if it's a suicide aimed specifically at others? An aggressive suicide, if you like? What if the question is not, why would the reverend want to kill himself, but rather why would the reverend want to kill others?'

'No. I'm sorry, I don't follow.'

'Put yourself in the sacerdotal shoes for a moment, Sefton. Try imagining yourself as a vicar in a small Norfolk village, squeezed into the reverend's shoes – four-eyelet tan brogues, were they not? With rubber cleated soles? Cordovan leather, possibly.'

'I didn't notice,' I said.

'Doesn't matter,' said Morley. 'Not literally, metaphorically I mean, of course. So how do they fit? Eh? The good reverend's shoes?'

'A bit uncomfortable,' I admitted.

'Indeed. Tight fit, isn't it? Tell me, do you really hate anyone, Sefton?'

'Well . . .' At that moment, one obvious example came to mind.

'Absolutely hate their guts, I mean? Loathe them, despise them? Regard them as lower than vermin? As worms? Ants? Fit only to be crushed under your heel?'

'Maybe not.'

'Don't be afraid to admit it, Sefton. These are human emotions, after all. Perfectly normal.'

'Well, I suppose . . . yes.'

'Good! And we know you to be a fine young man. So is it not possible therefore that the reverend felt likewise, or that others felt likewise towards him?'

I had to grant this was indeed possible.

'Which is how we might end up with . . . this.' He jerked a hand up behind his neck, as though hanging himself by a rope. The darts-players looked suspiciously in our direction. I looked nervously towards them.

'I think perhaps you should keep your voice down, Mr Morley, actually, to be honest.'

'Really?'

'Yes. I'm not at all sure about your theory, and I think—'

'Well, why don't we ask one of these chaps what they think?' He nodded in a friendly fashion towards the men playing darts.

'I'm not sure they want to be disturbed, actually.'

'Everyone wants to be disturbed, Sefton.'

'I'm not sure about that, Mr Morley.'

'And yet simultaneously everyone wants to be left alone. There's the rub, you see. What about that chap there?' Morley pointed towards a man just about to throw a dart. 'He's the man to ask.'

'Is he?'

'I think you'll find he's the bell-ringer in the church.'

'How do you know?'

'Broad shoulders. Heft. Broken nose – could be a boxer. But one arm, as you'll note, overdeveloped. Hence not a boxer. Most likely from pulling on ropes.'

'Or playing darts.'

'Yes, I suppose, it could be either.'

'Well, I'll wager you, Mr Morley, that I'm as likely to be correct in this as you.'

'I'll not accept the wager, Sefton, thank you. We should abstain from the appearance of evil. But I wonder, would you mind awfully buying him a drink and asking him over?'

'Now?'

'When you're ready.'

I got up to go over.

'And Sefton?' Morley added.

'Yes, Mr Morley?'

'I think you'll find that I am correct.'

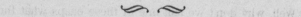

He was correct.

The bell-ringer's name was Hackford. He had bright blue eyes, bristly red hair, a drinker's nose, hands like smoked hams and a stinking black pipe. He also wore, perched atop his head, a regimental beret.

'Royal Warwickshire Fusiliers?' asked Morley.

'That's right,' said Hackford.

'My son was in the 16th Battalion, London Regiment,' said Morley.

'Was he, now?'

'Yes.' Morley gave a slight cough and changed the subject. 'Did you know the reverend well?'

Mr Hackford tugged on his pipe and took a long time to answer, in the traditional Norfolk fashion.

'As well as any man knows his vicar.'

'And what did you think of him?'

'It's not for me to say, sir, is it?'

'No, of course,' said Morley. 'A terrible tragedy, though.'

'He was a good vicar,' agreed Hackford, raising his tankard from the table.

'Really? And what makes a good vicar, do you think?' said Morley.

Hackford took a long draw on his pipe, blew out great rings of smoke, as though he were ringing a peal of bells, and swallowed a vast mouthful of beer.

'He was a good preacher. And he'd listen if you had a problem.'

'I see. And you went to him with problems yourself?'

'I did not, no.'

'But others did?'

'Maybe so.'

'So he was popular with the congregation, I'm sure.'

'I suppose.'

'Not popular, then?'

'You always gets your grumblers,' said Hackford.

'So not universally popular?' said Morley.

Hackford fixed his eyes steadily on Morley. 'Might I ask you a question, sir?'

'Of course,' said Morley.

'Are you universally popular?'

'Perhaps not, Mr Hackford.' Morley laughed. 'Perhaps not. Can I ask, though, did you speak to the reverend during the service on Sunday?'

'I rang the bells, same as usual. Then I made my way home.'

'What did you ring, if you don't mind my asking?'

'On the bells?'

'Of course.'

'You're a bell-ringer, sir?'

'No, not myself, alas, but there's a very good book, by Dorothy L. Sayers. *Nine Tailors*. Novel. Do you know it?'

'I can't say as I do, sir, no.'

'Very good. Lot of campanological stuff in it.'

'I'm afraid I don't know what you're talking about now, sir.'

'Campanology is the study of the subject of bell-ringing, Mr Hackford. Surely you—'

'I don't study 'em, sir, I just ring 'em.'

'Of course. And was there anyone in the vestry, that you were aware of? Anyone who shouldn't have been there?'

'I don't think so. But I was in the other tower, ringing.'

'And did you notice anyone in the congregation you hadn't seen before?'

'No.'

'You're absolutely sure?'

'I know everyone in the congregation of St Nicholas by now, I think, sir. I've been worshipping there for sixty-one years.'

'The family of the church,' said Morley.

'That's what they say, sir, yes.'

'Jolly good!' said Morley. 'Quite right.'

Hackford set his empty tankard down on the table, and looked at me. 'Is that it?'

'Yes, that's it,' said Morley.

'Another drink, Mr Hackford?' I said.

'I'll not, thank you,' said Hackford. 'I have to say, you're a great man for the fine words and phrases, Mr Morley.'

'I shall take that as a compliment, Mr Hackford, thank you.'

'As a compliment it's meant.'

'Well, thank you.'

'But you've no business being here,' said Hackford, getting up and walking off.

'Seem to have upset him,' said Morley. 'Strange.'

I tried to persuade Morley to leave the bar then with me, but he insisted that he wanted to stay. It was his reading hour: he set aside a portion of every evening to read a book on a subject he knew nothing about, and tonight, he said, would be no different. And so I left him, among the hostile bar staff and darts-players of Blakeney, perfectly content, and about to start – and doubtless finish – a book on eighteenth-century French furniture. I, on the other hand, excused myself and said I would retire early.

'Resembles the Hayter portrait of Queen Caroline, doesn't she?' said Morley, as I got up to leave.

'Sorry? Who does?'

'The barmaid. Very striking-looking. Regal of bosom, wouldn't you say?'

'I can't say I've—'

'And her dress – rather daring, isn't it?'

'Is it? I don't know. I didn't notice.'

Morley raised an eyebrow. 'The effect is *inquiétant*, I think is the French, is that right?'

'I don't know.'

'Hmm. Word to the wise, Sefton. *Omne ignotum pro magnifico est.*'

'Everything ... unknown ... is—'

'Distance lends enchantment, Sefton, is all I shall say. Tacitus. *Agricola*. Look but don't touch, eh? Highest standards to be maintained at all times on your journeyings, if you don't mind.'

'Of course.'

'I'm sure she appreciated your assistance, Sefton. Very selfless of you.'

'Yes.'

'Sleep well.'

'Yes, you too, Mr Morley. Goodnight.'

He produced his egg-timer from his jacket pocket, and propped his book before him.

'There we are. All set.' He caught me looking at him. 'The elusive waywardness of time, Sefton,' he said mildly, as if in explanation. 'We must do everything we can to capture it, must we not? Not a moment to waste.'

∽ ∾

As it happened, I slept for no more than an hour or two that night, before finding myself jerked awake, as was often my habit, in a cold sweat, the same persistent nightmares troubling me. I opened the curtains in my room, and saw that

[ 156 ]

a blood-red moon had set outside. It was ten past midnight. I felt unaccountably excited and fearful, as though something was about to happen that I could not prevent, nor wish to avoid. I sat smoking for some time – until almost one o'clock – and then, still unable to sleep, I dressed, and found myself wandering through Blakeney village. I was inexorably drawn to the church.

Constable Ridley was stationed outside, with a candle lantern.

'Evening, Constable,' I said as I approached.

He jumped out of his skin, pulling a truncheon from his pocket, and bringing his shiny whistle to his lips.

'It's only me!' I said.

'Ah. Thank goodness,' said Ridley. 'Good evening, sir. Sorry, I was maybe dozing there for a moment. You won't mention it to anyone.'

'No, of course not.'

'Good. Meant to keep awake, to watch the church, in case anyone tries to tamper with the evidence.'

'Quite right. Your chaps from Norwich are here, then?'

'Yes, sir. Just arrived a couple of hours ago. They'll be wanting to talk to you tomorrow, no doubt.'

'Good.'

'And then you can be on your way.'

'Let's hope so.'

'Yes.'

'Well. Lovely evening, isn't it?'

'It is indeed. A little late for a stroll though, sir?'

'I couldn't sleep.'

'Ah. You're not the only one.'

'Really? Why? Who else is out?'

'Her.' He nodded his head.

'Who?'

'The reverend's maid.'

I looked across the graveyard and saw Hannah. The brightest stars shone through the evening mist. Her cigarette glowed in the distance.

'She's been here the whole time?'

'I'm afraid so. I can't persuade her to leave.'

'Is everything all right?'

'I don't know. She won't say a word to me.'

'Should I . . . ?'

'Be my guest. Can't do any harm.'

I approached her across the graveyard. There was the hooting of an owl.

'Hannah? It's me, Stephen Sefton. Is everything all right?'

She looked at me with those dark, intelligent, sorrowful eyes, and reached out a hand towards me.

I took her hand and she drew me immediately into an embrace. I could feel her breath in the silence. She held on to me for a long time and then, suddenly, I felt her weight shift, as if her body had made some decision, and she tilted her head up and forward, and kissed me on the mouth.

I was shocked, of course, but I kissed her back, and again we stayed that way for a time, calmly, without urgency, as though lovers long familiar, and then something changed again and I felt her breasts press urgently against my chest, and her arms grow tighter around my shoulders, and suddenly we were moving together deeper into the shadow of the church, now out of sight of Ridley.

And then . . . her back was pressed against the wall, and we were kissing, and then we were moving frantically together, her moaning a little as we did so, pressing against me, turning her head as she placed my hand gently over her mouth as she rocked her body against mine.

It was not the right place, or the right time. It was real, and yet had the substance of dreams.

It was just something that happened.

I returned to the hotel around two in the morning, took two sleeping tablets, and fell into a troubled sleep, confusing the softness of Hannah's body and her dark flashing eyes with memories of couplings in Spain, when we were all maddened by war, and under threat, and desperate, our lives glowing white-hot in the heat of the burning sun, the sands of time running out before us.

# CHAPTER ELEVEN

I CAME DOWN to breakfast late the next morning, Morley having long since eaten, and his breakfast table having been cleared and converted into his portable office – typewriter before him, pens and pencils lined up in a row, fresh paper stacked neatly, books on the floor, and the ever-present egg-timer at his elbow. He was dressed, as usual, in bow tie, light tweeds and his stout brogue boots, spruce and ready for adventure.

'Early start?' I said, feeling rather grisly. It was difficult to measure up to Morley at any time of day or night, but particularly first thing in the morning. He didn't mean to make people inadequate: in his presence, one simply felt that one *was* inadequate. It wasn't a matter of shame or guilt, or, at least, it wasn't *always* a matter of shame or guilt; it seemed merely a fact.

'Ah, good morning to you, Ishbosheth,' he said, without looking up.

'Sorry?' I said. It was too early in the morning.

'Good morning to you, Ishbosheth,' he repeated, still without a glance of recognition. I didn't say that I didn't know what on earth he was talking about; it was too often and too obviously the case for me to need to say so, and anyway Morley could sniff out incomprehension at a hundred paces, and so instantly clarified.

'Second Book of Samuel, Sefton. Look it up.'

'I shall, Mr Morley. Thank you.'

'Now,' he said, reaching down beside him and handing me a Bible, which sat conveniently stacked in his portable reference section, which included also a *Pocket Oxford*, which he insisted on calling 'the mini-Murray', a *Roget's*, and Fowler's *The King's English*: 'Roget, Murray and Fowler,' he would say. 'My business partners.' He found the Second Book of Samuel for me. 'There we are. No time like the present, and what have you.'

I took a deep sigh, Morley raised an eyebrow, and I dutifully read the story of Ishbosheth – one of those grisly and apparently pointless biblical stories, in which, in this case, a bunch of chaps come into someone called Ishbosheth's bedroom and cut off his head.

On which merry note, and without further comment from Morley – who clearly felt he had proved his point – I ordered coffee and toast, while he turned back to the task in hand. He had brought with him on our trip the proofs of his latest book, *Morley's Last Words*, another in his seemingly endless works of anthology, which he somehow produced alongside all his other work, without ceasing, sometimes as many as three or four volumes a year. His procedures in compiling the books were essentially the same as his procedures for composing all his books, and is the method he famously describes in *How To Write – A Lot!*, a little pamphlet published in 1935, in which he set out his *modus operandi* as an encouragement to others, though the effect was almost certainly the opposite. (Personally I felt the exclamation mark – another of his tics – was in itself off-putting enough, though he often defended its use stoutly in argument. 'Readers must be herded!' he would say. 'For like sheep we have gone astray.') In *How To Write – A Lot!* Morley ascribes genius merely to method and exertion of effort, conveniently overlooking the fact that there is always genius at work in the application of method, and forgetting also that encouragement by the great and the good can in itself be dispiriting. Nonetheless, for the purposes of explanation, and at the risk of dispiriting yet more readers, the method is perhaps – briefly – worth restating here.

Thus: for newspaper articles, speeches, lectures and the like, Morley's first draft would always be composed straight onto the typewriter, 'The rhythms of the typewriter,' as he remarks in *How To Write – A Lot!*, 'representing and resembling the very rhythms of our minds' (the very rhythms of his own mind, perhaps, with its clicks and clacks and endless returns, but a rhythm quite unlike my own and, I fancy, the rhythms of others). He would then augment this first typescript with notes from his notebooks, and would type it again, making further corrections to the new typescript by hand. He would then type a third and final draft of the article, and send it away. In this fashion he could average a thousand words an hour, or precisely four turns of the egg-timer, enabling him to write three or four articles before lunch. When it came to the books, the process was similar. Once he'd finished a typescript of a book – having worked on each chapter in the fashion as outlined above – he would then send it to his publishers, who would send back the proofs, which Morley would then amend, sometimes as many as three or four times, until he agreed on the final proofs, which were sent for publication. 'By application of this simple method,' he concludes in *How To Write – A Lot!*, 'a man may comfortably write whate'er he might, and indeed whate'er he will.'

And so as he continued at whate'er he might and whate'er he will on that dark morning, I sat and drank my coffee in silence.

'Soap dish?' he said suddenly, and apropos of nothing, as I crunched my way through a piece of hotel-hardened toast.

'Sorry?'

'Soap dish? How was yours?'

'It was . . .'

'And the enamel on the bath?'

'Erm . . .'

'Width of the bed?'

'Was . . .'

'Tooth tumbler? Notice anything strange?'

'No. Should I have done?'

'Unwashed tooth tumbler a major source of bacteria in hotels, I would have thought. Do you take no note of your surroundings at all, Sefton?'

'Yes, I do, Mr Morley, but—'

'I have already made a list of deficiencies, and suggested improvements, and given them to the management.'

'I'm sure they appreciated that,' I said.

'They seemed to, Sefton, yes. Certainly, rather more than the chambermaid, who I had to show how to mitre a corner correctly. Rather ungrateful, I thought.'

'Really?' I took another sip of coffee.

'Balsa cement,' he continued, without pausing.

'I didn't have any balsa cement in my room, I don't think . . .'

'Not in your room, Sefton. Eighth wonder of the world.' In the moments between correcting the proofs on *Morley's Last Words*, it turned out, he was also mulling over an article that he was about to write for a newspaper on how to make a model of Mevagissy Harbour out of balsa wood. And in the moments between annotating the one thing and typing the other, at each turn of the egg-timer, he made a few brief notes for an article on British woodland birds from one of all four volumes of Thorburn's *British Birds* which were set at his left elbow. He was, in other words, behaving exactly as always. Which made his next announcement all the more shocking.

'Time to bear the sacred *plume de littérature* over another ridge, then?' I said, having by now drunk enough coffee to raise my spirits. I knew Miriam had already arranged a number of trips and interviews with locals for us: there was an itinerary.

'Terrible business last night,' said Morley.

'Last night?' I said.

'You haven't heard then?'

'Heard what?'

'She's dead.'

'Who's dead?'

'The German girl.'

Sometime during the night, moments after we had been together, Hannah had committed suicide. She had set light to herself on Blakeney quay, having doused herself in petrol.

The flames were seen by the night porter of the hotel, who had rushed down to try to save her.

Morley narrated the story as though reading a clipping from an old newspaper. I made out only snatches of detail: just before dawn; unable to quench the flames; locals shocked.

I was speechless.

Having recounted the news to me, Morley then got up and started gathering his papers.

'Come on then, Sefton, up, up, please, and doing.'

'I . . .'

'What's the matter? Cat got your tongue?'

'I'm sorry. I . . .'

'What?'

'I can't believe it.'

'Can't believe what?'

'That . . . I'm just . . . astonished.'

'About the girl you mean?'

'Of course.'

'Ah. Yes, well. Terribly sad. But, *abyssus abyssum invocate*, I'm afraid, Sefton. Isn't that right? Hell calls to hell. One tragedy bids forth another. In fact, it has often seemed to me there is nothing astonishing in this world, except our absolute inability to understand our capacity for making ourselves and others miserable. Definitely hanging, by the way, according to the doctor. Autopsy. Would have liked to see it myself. But. We have work to do. With Miriam away in London, you'll be driving the Lagonda and in charge of logistics. I'll meet you in the lobby in, say' – he glanced at both wristwatches – 'twenty-one minutes?'

I stared at him, disgusted. His buoyancy – though there

was never anything forced or exaggerated about it, nothing unnatural – seemed nonetheless at that moment irresponsible, arrogant, childlike and appalling.

'How can you keep on working, with . . .'

'How can I keep on working, Sefton?' He looked shocked. 'Surely, rather, the question is how can one not? Do you know Bruegel's *The Fall of Icarus*?'

'No, I don't think I—'

'Worth looking up, Sefton, I'm afraid. Worth looking up. The Old Masters. Never wrong.' He gazed fixedly into the middle distance for a moment. 'And anyway, ink is our lifeblood and words – think you not? – our only friends. So. Doesn't do to dwell on these things.' With which he turned his back on me and strode sharply from the dining room.

I didn't know what to do. Despite Morley's admonitions, vast miserable spaces seemed to open up in my mind, horrible fantasies and imaginings, abysms of despair, and yet of course the normal business of the hotel continued all around me. I felt a buzzing in my head. It was Spain all over again. I smoked several cigarettes, went to my room, lay down. Got up.

And then drove with Morley to our first appointment in total silence.

# CHAPTER TWELVE

'HIDEOUS STATUARY,' he said, as we pulled up a driveway flanked by three carved female figures. 'What do you think: Pandora, Eve, Aphrodite? Difficult to tell. Could be the Furies. Could be the Graces. Could be the Gorgons. What do you think, Sefton?' My mind was elsewhere; statues were not my concern. 'Hideous anyway. And a house that seems to have been designed for a maharajah by a Chinaman. Make a note, Sefton.' I did not make a note; I was driving; the two tasks were incompatible, though this mattered not to Morley. 'Sefton?' he repeated. 'Sefton?' When answer came there none he simply continued. 'Why do the English love to dress their buildings in other people's clothes?' I was thinking of Hannah's clothes going up in flames. 'The Gothic and Grecian country house, our Romanesque gaols. Our Italianate villas. Or – as here – our eccentric Indian country houses? Is it the imperial impulse, Sefton, do you think? Or simply our love of narrative, of telling stories about ourselves and other cultures?'

'I don't know, Mr Morley.'

'Cool, dark and mysterious,' he said, referring to what it

*Miss Harris's house: the imperial impulse*

was not clear. 'Come on, Sefton, concentrate, please. Eyes open. Mind alert. Mouth shut. We do have work to do.'

We were greeted and ushered into the house by a maid, who showed us into a drawing room – a sick-making combination of pale green walls, swirling red paisley fabrics and assorted knick-knacks – where a middle-aged woman sat on a straight blue wooden chair by a bay window hung with damask, apparently having framed herself deliberately, as though for a photograph. She was in her late fifties, possibly older, and wore a long flowing dress in faded magenta, with a pair of low-heeled black boots that might suit for a fishing or hunting trip, and her hair, which was a dusty grey, she wore cropped close to the head, like a weak-featured man going deliberately for the look of a powerful Roman emperor. Her eyes were a piercing blue, and her lips, though thin, suggested the potential of passion – violent passion even, one might say. She wore a black silk shawl draped around her shoulders, which made her look as though she might at any moment rise up, throw it off, and declaim, which she might have done, had the shawl not been fixed firmly in place with a silver brooch of the most horrible design, in the form of a dog's head, with tiny, pinprick red jewels for eyes. In my troubled and downcast state, the room, and the woman, struck me as bogus, vile and somehow as harbingers of doom.

'Miss Harris,' said Morley, going over.

Miss Harris, in regal fashion, raised her hand to be kissed, nodded, but said nothing.

'It is an honour to meet you, Miss Harris.'

'Indeed,' said Miss Harris, who was – Morley had briefed me – a faded star of the stage, with a sideline in light opera, and who clearly felt that honour should indeed be granted where honour was due.

'This is my assistant, Mr Sefton,' said Morley.

I nodded. Miss Harris forced a smile.

'It's a wonderful place you have here,' said Morley, rather convincingly, I thought, since he later described the house to me, with characteristic frankness, as being more like a stage set than a home. He thoroughly disapproved of interior decoration, believing in simplicity and spartan values in all things except cars, books, stationery, pets and of course his own eccentric home and its furnishings, which he believed to be exemptingly and self-evidently exquisite in every regard. I had described the place, in my notes, as containing fine examples of antique furniture. 'It was not antique furniture,' Morley corrected me. 'It was furniture with antique pretensions. There is a difference, Sefton.' Fortunately, Miss Harris was not privy to this later conversation.

'I know, I know, we are frightfully lucky,' said Miss Harris. 'The house came up a few years ago, just when we were looking to move out of London. I can't tell you, Mr Morley, how much we appreciate it. It was designed by John Norton. Do you know him?'

'I'm afraid I don't, madam, no.'

'He designed the Maharajah Duleep Singh's house at Elveden?'

'Ah. Yes. Our first Sikh settler.'

'Indeed. Norton specialised in houses in the Indian manner, after he had created Elveden.'

'I see.'

'This is on a very modest scale, of course, but it has been a labour of love, restoring it and updating it. But it has been worth it, don't you think?' Miss Harris was the sort of woman who spoke as though she were speaking a citation – to herself – or reciting verse to an audience of the hard of hearing in a large auditorium. She measured each sentence as though she were handing out precious gifts, or fifty-guinea notes, fully aware of the worth and weight of every syllable, and the price in pence and pounds of every slight change in tone and pitch. She also happened to have at her feet a willing audience and accompanist, in the form of a continually snorting Pekinese, whose rhythmic snufflings made it sound as though it was either about to die, or to leap enthusiastically into life, though during the course of our visit it did neither, and acted merely as a small furry metronome, drawing attention to the forced tempo of Miss Harris's pronouncements. 'Times have changed so in London, have they not, Mr Morley?'

'They have indeed, Miss Harris. You prefer Oxford, I think?'

'Yes, I do. How did you know?'

'I was just admiring your mezzo-tints in the hallway, on the way in. Balliol, was it?'

'Yes, my brother attended college there. We shared many happy times together.'

'All of you as a family?'

'That's correct. It seems like another age. Barbarousness everywhere these days. I blame three things, Mr Morley: the war; the Spanish flu; and the Americans. And Emily Davison. But that makes four. Do you agree?'

'It's certainly one argument, Miss Harris.'

'Particularly the Americans. I have no time for Americans, Mr Morley, even though I spent much time there in my youth, touring with the D'Oyly Carte. We might as well be living in America these days, wouldn't you say?'

'I'm not sure, Miss Harris. I think Norfolk is still quite—'

'Clothes. Jazz. Conversation. All fashions follow a very simple and direct route, Mr Morley, in my opinion. They come first from the Negroes, and then on to the brothel, and then to "movie" stars, and then hence to high society, and finally to maids and servants and secretaries in the suburbs, where they meet again with their origins. Do you see?'

'A vicious circle,' said Morley.

'Precisely,' said Miss Harris. 'A positive cyclorama of degradation. The amount of young women one sees these days in high heels, Mr Morley, even in Norwich. It's really quite extraordinary. High heels might be suitable for the salons and arcades of Paris, but they are hardly practical for country living.'

'You haven't met my daughter,' said Morley.

'No,' said Miss Harris. 'Why? Has she fallen for the current fashions?'

'I'm afraid she has,' said Morley.

'"Dainty skirts and delicate blouses aren't much use for pigs and cows-es. The answer is overalls and trousiz,"' sang Miss Harris, rather tunefully, I have to admit. The Pekinese, for a moment, stopping grunting and staring up at her.

'I beg your pardon?' said Morley.

'It's a popular tune, Mr Morley, or was, in my youth.' She pursed her lips in an unfriendly fashion at the mention of her youth. Make-up would not have sat well upon her features, which resembled the kind of contour map of the more mountainous regions of England.

A woman entered the room and came and spoke to Miss

*The drawing room*

Harris. She was considerably younger than Miss Harris –
in her thirties, perhaps – improbably tall, and dressed in a
dark trouser suit. Morley referred to her henceforth, though
in private, as Glumdalclitch, another of his allusions that
passed me by entirely, until, with his usual upbraiding, he
pointed out that it was the name of Gulliver's nurse. 'Dean
Swift, Sefton? Never heard of him? Doesn't feature on the
Tripos these days?'

'Sorry, you must excuse us, Mr Morley,' said Miss Harris.
'This is Miss Spranzi. My secretary.'

'An Italian name?' asked Morley.

'Yes,' said Miss Spranzi, smiling.

'*Lieto di conoscerla*,' he said, staring up at her.

'*Molto lieto*,' replied Miss Spranzi.

'*Di dov'è?*'

'*Di Firenze.*'

'*Una bella città!*'

'We should perhaps speak in English, though, Mr Morley,'
said Miss Spranzi. 'For the sake of the others?'

'Of course. Sefton, you don't have Italian?'

I shook my head.

'The language of Dante?'

'Nor I, Mr Morley,' said Miss Harris. 'I have never felt
the need to acquire it.' She spoke as though 'it' were an unnecessary purchase in the food hall at Selfridge's.

'And I, I'm afraid, take every opportunity to practise it,'
said Morley. 'Forgive me.' He nodded to Miss Spranzi. '*Scusi.*'

'*Prego.*'

Miss Harris, clearly unhappy to have lost the limelight,
albeit momentarily, rearranged herself noisily and theatrically in her chair.

'Shall we get on, Mr Morley? I'm sure you're a very busy man. Francesca, would you be so kind as to bring us some tea?'

'Of course.'

'Do sit down, gentlemen.' Miss Harris waved us towards some chairs

'Now, Miss Spranzi did say, but what exactly was it you wanted to see me about, Mr Morley?'

'I'm writing a book, madam, about the county of Norfolk.'

'Well, what a jolly idea.'

'It's the first in a series of *County Guides* that I'm writing.'

'I see. And you intend to write about all of them?'

'That's correct.'

'How extraordinary!' she said, in a way that suggested that the task was not extraordinary at all. 'How terribly ... Wagnerian.'

'Indeed,' said Morley. 'It had not occurred to me before, madam, but I suppose it is what the great man himself might have called a *Gesamtkunstwerk*.'

'Not a term I'm familiar with, Mr Morley.' Miss Harris's face soured: not a woman who liked to be outwitted or outdone.

'It means—'

'You're not a young man, are you, Mr Morley?'

'Alas, madam, no, I'm not.'

'In which case, is it not rather foolhardy an undertaking, if you don't mind me saying so?'

'Possibly. Though I have my young assistant here, who I'm proud to say is full of vim and vigour.'

I had in fact spent most of this conversation staring out of the window, vim- and vigourless, longing for escape from this tiresome woman and her faux-hospitality, but I offered a thin smile at Morley's prompting.

'A sort of swan song then, is it?' said Miss Harris.

'I hope not,' said Morley. 'I regard it more as another of my intellectual adventures.'

'Well, good for you, Mr Morley.' She rearranged her hands in her lap. 'Good. For. You. And how is it that you think I can help you?'

'I wanted to talk to people,' said Morley, 'who in some way represent the county.'

'I see. And you thought of me?'

'Indeed.'

'As a representative? I don't think I would consider myself as representative of anything, Mr Morley. I rather regard myself as *sui generis*.'

'*Sui amans, sine rivali*,' said Morley.

'I'm sorry, what was that?'

'Just agreeing, Miss Harris, that's all. But I'm sure you have many interesting things to tell us about Norfolk. You were born here, I believe?'

'I was.'

'In Blakeney?'

'Indeed.'

'Harris is a local name?'

'Harris is my stage name, Mr Morley.'

'How wonderful! And sporting this *nom de théâtre* you went on to achieve great fame and riches, and now you have returned—'

'In my dotage.'

'In your pomp.'

'I'm really not sure that anyone would be interested in the reminiscences of an old actress like myself, Mr Morley.'

'I fancy you're merely being modest, Miss Harris.'

'It's called good manners, Mr Morley. Or it used to be.'

'Quite so.'

Miss Spranzi arrived back with a silver tea set, and poured us all tea.

'*Mille grazie*,' said Morley.

'Your reputation precedes you, of course, Mr Morley,' said Miss Harris. 'The People's Professor.'

'Not a title I claim for myself,' said Morley.

'But one bestowed upon you.'

'Indeed.'

'An honorific, then.'

'One could call it that.'

'Well, *Professor*, I must confess that I haven't read any of your books.'

This was the phrase, I came to realise, that they all used – the country set, and the aristocracy, and the bohemians and the bourgeois who we met on our journeyings. They always claimed they'd never read Morley's books, though often we could see them right there on their shelves. It was as though they were ashamed of admitting that they shared something with the merely aspirational, as though Morley, in his great quest to spread knowledge among all classes, was a kind of contaminant. It was, I have to admit – or it had been – my own opinion.

'I have never read any of my books myself, madam,' said

Morley, which was his characteristic response to the typical put-down.

'And yet you write them?'

'Indeed.'

'They're not written perhaps by your assistant?'

Morley laughed. 'I employ Mr Sefton here for purely practical purposes, Miss Harris.'

'As I do Miss Spranzi. So perhaps you might explain to us both, what sort of books are yours exactly?'

'They are books intended for the large mass of people, Miss Harris. They would hardly be of interest to someone like yourself.'

'One shouldn't assume, Mr Morley. I have rather a taste, actually, for the commonplace. If one spends one's life on stage, one hardly wants to settle down in one's retirement with George Bernard Shaw, does one?'

'No.'

'I rather enjoy a good Sax Rohmer, actually, or a Nat Gould – you perhaps know his racing novelettes?'

'I do, yes, madam. Very fine.'

'Indeed. And I used to enjoy E.M. Hull. And A.S.M. Hutchinson.'

'Ah, yes.'

'But who now reads A.S.M. Hutchinson, Mr Morley?'

'Who indeed, madam?'

'The last book I read was Oliver Lodge, with his book . . . What was it called?' she asked Miss Spranzi.

'*Raymond, or Life and Death*?' said Miss Spranzi.

'Yes.'

'And was it good?' asked Morley.

'I'm afraid I gave up halfway through. These days I find

my reading is preparation merely for the solving of cross-word puzzles to which – to my shame – I must admit I have become rather addicted.'

'An innocent vice.'

'I certainly hope so.'

∽ ∾

We spoke, or rather Morley and Miss Harris spoke, for some time – interminable time, it seemed – about her career as an actress and singer, and her early childhood in Norfolk. I took dutiful notes, as instructed by Morley. She also told some tales of Norfolk folk and customs.

'You know the story of the Oxfoot Stone?'

'No, I don't think I do,' said Morley.

She leaned back in her chair, closed her eyes, and began to tell the story, punctuated by the Pekinese and with Miss Spranzi by her side, smiling indulgently towards her through-out.

'This was a story told to me by my own grandmother.' She took a deep breath, as though inhaling the memory. 'Many years ago, during a time of great poverty, it was said that there was a great cow that visited the village of Lopham. You know Lopham, Mr Morley?'

'Yes I do.'

'And the great cow of Lopham suffered herself to be milked dry, again and again, day after day, and week after week, by the poor of the parish.'

'Ah yes, the myth of the great mother.'

'Indeed. And then, when they no longer needed the milk, the cow simply disappeared, leaving only her giant hoof-print on the Oxfoot Stone, which lies to this day, I believe, in the village.'

'A wonderful story.'

'Wonderful,' agreed Miss Spranzi.

'An allegory, perhaps?' said Morley.

'A true story, Mr Morley. The stone is still there in Lopham, for all to see.'

More little stories and anecdotes followed, and eventually we rose to leave.

'Thank you so much for your time, Miss Harris. It's absolutely invaluable. And particularly at this time. I'm sure it's come as a terrible shock to you, the death of the reverend.'

'Not a shock exactly,' said Miss Harris, who gazed up towards the ceiling. 'More a surprise.'

'A surprise, then,' said Morley. 'Yes. A fine distinction. A shock perhaps implies great . . . unexpectedness.'

'Yes,' agreed Miss Harris.

'A disturbance,' said Morley.

'Precisely. In one's equilibrium, Mr Morley.'

'And a surprise implies no such overthrow of oneself—'

'Quite,' said Miss Harris.

'And of course a surprise might excite not merely alarm or terror, but pleasure, wonder or excitement. Etymologically speaking, I think you'll find.'

'Indeed?' said Miss Harris, unimpressed.

'But whether a shock or a surprise, it is certainly a tragedy,' said Morley.

'One might say so, Mr Morley, if one were inclined to melodrama.'

'And you're not, madam?'

'I have seen and acted in enough melodrama, Mr Morley, not to have any appetite for it in my private life. And I'm afraid I have very little pity for those who choose to commit the sin against the Holy Ghost.'

'The sin against the Holy Ghost?'

'Suicide, Mr Morley.'

'I had always interpreted the passage to be a reference to those rejecting Christ.'

'Then we shall have to agree to disagree in our interpretation of Scripture, sir.'

'Indeed,' said Morley.

'The Bible speaks clearly against the sin of self-destruction, and those who practise it, I think you'll find, Mr Morley.'

'I'm sure the reverend had his reasons, madam.'

'I'm sure he did.'

'Well. *Audi alteram partem*,' said Morley.

'Which means?'

'There are two sides to every story.'

'Sometimes.' She grinned, showing sharp teeth, like a shark's. 'But sometimes I think you'll find there is only one side to a story.'

'Are you regular churchgoers?' asked Morley. 'Do you mind my asking?'

'I attend regularly, yes,' said Miss Harris.

'And *signorina*?'

'I am a Roman Catholic,' said Miss Spranzi. 'I find the customs and practices of the Church of England rather ... quaint.'

'I'm sure. And I believe the reverend was very ... modern in his outlook?'

'Actually, I found him very *conservatore*,' said Miss Spranzi.

'Conservative,' said Morley.

'Yes.'

'So, you would stay at home while Miss Harris attends morning service, is that right?'

'That's correct.'

'So you were not at the service on Sunday?'

'Actually, yes. I was. I happened to attend the communion service. I like to celebrate Mass.'

'Does the Church of England celebrate Mass?'

'Sometimes we Catholics must take solace where we can find it.'

'You didn't happen to see the reverend after the service?'

'No.'

'I see. And what about the girl?'

'The maid?' said Miss Harris.

'Yes. Did you know her?'

'We knew *of* her, Mr Morley.'

'Knew *of* her?'

'She was his maid, I mean.'

'I see. Such a pity about her, isn't it?'

'Indeed,' agreed Miss Harris.

'And very strange, wasn't it? Her setting fire to herself, down at the front at Blakeney?'

'Very strange.'

'Unless of course she were performing her death as some sort of spectacle. As a piece of theatre. I don't know if that has occurred to you, Miss Harris? With your own theatrical background?'

'It has not occurred to me, no, Mr Morley. And frankly I find the suggestion both distasteful and disrespectful.'

'I do apologise. I suppose I'm just trying to understand what might have driven her to such a terrible act. Her feelings for the reverend, perhaps?'

Miss Harris and Miss Spranzi remained silent at Morley's suggestion, which hung in the air for some time. And then Miss Harris suggested that Miss Spranzi escort us on our way.

'Might I just ask, out of interest, pure curiosity,' said Morley, as we were about to be ushered out of the drawing room, 'what did you make of him, madam?'

'*Make* of who?'

'The reverend?'

'*Make* of him?'

'Yes. What struck you about him?'

Miss Harris paused for a long time and squinted at us, as if the question itself were an impertinence, which perhaps it was. But eventually she answered.

'He wore pullovers.'

'Pullovers?'

'Yes.'

'I see.'

'The most ridiculous thing. I don't know if you've ever seen a priest in a pullover?'

'I don't know if I have, madam, now that you come to mention it.'

'Well, there's a very good reason for that. It's most unseemly.'

'Do you think?'

'I do. Why? Do you not?'

'I'm not sure that I would necessarily describe the wearing of a pullover by a priest as "unseemly".'

'Then you have clearly been infected by the spirit of the times, Mr Morley, if I might say so. A pullover shows a lack of dignity.'

'But apart from the pullover?'

'I shan't be discussing the reverend any further, Mr Morley, thank you.' She gathered her shawl tight around her, and bent forward to stroke the Pekinese. The interview was over.

'No, thank *you*, Miss Harris.'

'I look forward to reading your book, Mr Morley.'

'Thank you.'

'And what was the newspaper you said you wrote for?'

'The *Daily Herald*.'

'It's not a paper we usually take, but I shall make a point of buying a copy and searching for one of your articles. I'd be intrigued.'

'And I would be most honoured.'

'Goodbye then, Mr Morley.'

'Goodbye.'

She did not offer her hand to be kissed. And Morley did not offer to kiss it. He spoke a few more words in Italian to Miss Spranzi, and then we left.

'Well?' said Morley as we walked towards the car. 'What do you think?'

'Interesting,' I said.

'Sharp as a packet of needles, I'd say.'

'She's certainly—'

'Do you think they live as man and wife, Sefton?'

'I couldn't possibly say, sir.'

'I'm not looking for a judgement, Sefton. An observation, merely.'

'It's ... possible, sir, yes.'

'Have you read Sappho, Sefton?'

'I'm not sure that I have, Mr Morley.'

'No? What about Edward Carpenter? *The Intermediate Sex*?'

'No, I can't say I have, sir.'

'Really? Curious work. You might enjoy it. Havelock Ellis? Sexologist of a rather different kidney.'

'I didn't know you spoke Italian, sir,' I said, trying to change the subject. Morley on sex was not a subject I wished to entertain.

'Barely,' said Morley, 'but a little is better than nothing, I suppose. We English do not often trouble ourselves with foreign languages. It's like homosexuality. Something we know about, but don't care to participate in ourselves. Though some slight sprinkling of knowledge does perhaps come in handy.'

'What was it you said to her as we were leaving?'

'I remarked simply that I thought Italy had been nicely tidied up under Mussolini.'

'But you don't really think—'

'Not at all, Sefton. But Miss Spranzi readily agreed: a woman who likes to see things tidied up neatly, I would say, Miss Spranzi. A place for everything – and everyone. And everything – and everyone – in their place. Do you know the expression *albae gallinae filius*, Sefton?'

'No, I don't—'

'Meaning, literally, "son of a white hen". Ring any bells?'

'No. I—'

'An eagle was said to have dropped a white hen in the lap of Livia, wife of Emperor Augustus. Good omen. Supposed to bring luck. Shall we venture on?'

# CHAPTER THIRTEEN

I RETURNED TO THE HOTEL that afternoon – the wrong, wayward feeling of lonely afternoons in small hotels being one of the moods that became depressingly familiar to me during my time with Morley, that mood of something awry, or spoiled; I could never quite put my finger on it. It always reminded me, unhappily, of being a child, the sense of waiting for some unknown thing to happen, that you could not but help expect, excitedly, and with anticipation, and yet at the same time somehow dreaded and knew would be bad: school; dinner; punishment. Not that there was anything particularly unpleasant about the Blakeney Hotel. It had, that afternoon, the fresh smell of a place newly washed and cleaned – all lavender and wax – though underneath it there was that inimitable hotel smell of something having been long cooked, and long ago. Cabbages, perhaps; boiled something, certainly. I longed for rest; for my pills; for something. I found myself caught up instead in endless, unhappy thoughts about Hannah and the hanging priest.

'Would you like some tea, sir?'

I was sitting in the residents' lounge, a fussy, Arts and Crafts sort of a room, full of pointlessly ornate sideboards fitted into pointlessly ornate recesses, and with an absurdly polished piano of glistening walnut obstructing free passage and movement. 'A commonplace piano,' announced Morley one evening, after he'd sat and bashed through some Beethoven bagatelles, 'despite – or perhaps because of – appearances. Never judge a book by its cover, Sefton. Or a piano by its polish.' The room's unrelenting relief ornament, featuring a lot of unnecessary leafage, and its fiddly frieze depicting vague scenes of a bucolic nature, and its plump and peculiarly uncomfortable armchairs upholstered in a swains-and-nymphs-rich fabric, and its far too large polygonal table, which conspired with the piano to prevent ease of access or exit, made it lounge-like in name only: it was the sort of room one was forced to stand back and admire rather than actually to inhabit; rather like Paris. Morley always described such rooms as having been 'executed' in a particular fashion and 'executed in the Parisian fashion' he would say of rooms he particularly disapproved of, 'and too many fancy fitments', he would add. 'Executed in the Parisian fashion, and too many fancy fitments,' I found myself muttering out loud, already having picked up some of Morley's verbal habits. 'Too French and too fancy for a small provincial hotel.'

'Would you like some tea, sir,' repeated the voice. It was the barmaid from the night before.

'Sorry,' I said, 'I was just . . .' It was difficult to say what I was just doing. Dreaming my way out of there.

'That's all right, sir. None of us likes this room much anyway.'

'No. Well.'

'Tea?'

'Yes. That would be . . . lovely, yes, thank you.'

'Not at all, sir. Is everything all right, sir?'

'Yes, yes, thank you. Everything is fine. Absolutely fine. Could not be . . .' I sank deep into the armchair, staring at the concave and convex surfaces of modelled plaster on the wall opposite, following one of the many trails of fronds on the intricately contoured surfaces as it meandered from dark to darker and back again to dark in the cruel play of the weak afternoon sunlight.

She went to get the tea.

~ ~

'Why don't you join me?' I asked when she returned. I suddenly felt the need for the reassurance of female company, something solid and tangible, real – and she was certainly that. There was something coquettish about her: she had those eyes that dilated slightly when you spoke to her, like a cat, or a film star. It was just a bar habit, I suppose, but terribly effective.

'I don't think so, sir, no, thank you. I'm just covering for one of the girls.'

'Oh,' I said, disappointed. 'I'd be glad of the company.'

She smiled, and did her eyes again, and lingered by the chair.

'I don't think so, sir. But can I get you anything else?'

'No, thank you,' I said. 'Though you could tell me your name.'

'Lizzie,' she said.

'Well, Lizzie, perhaps another time.'

'Perhaps,' she said. I thought I saw her bite her lip; I noticed that she wore a gold chain around her neck that hung down ... 'You're not with your friend today then?' she said. 'The old chap with the moustache.'

'Mr Morley? No. He's ... working.'

'Is he famous?'

'Yes. Yes. He's a famous writer, yes.'

'Ah, we thought so. That explains it.'

I didn't know exactly how or what it explained, but I suppose it did.

'Are you all right, sir?'

I realised I was staring at her. This generous, innocent, finely formed young woman seemed suddenly like a hope of escape – from complications, from regret, from Morley, from the strange situation I seemed to have found myself in.

'It's just a headache,' I said.

'My father had the same problem.'

'Really?'

'He suffered very badly from his nerves, after the war, you see.'

'You're too young to remember the war, surely?'

She smiled. 'Yes, sir. But Father's told me all about it. You don't look well, sir, if you don't mind me saying so.'

'I'm fine, really. Just shaken up by this whole business with the reverend. And ... his maid.'

'Oh, everybody is, sir. Everybody in the village.'

'Did you know him well?'

'Yes. And her.'

'Hannah.'

'Yes. She was lovely. Did you meet her?'

'Yes,' I said. 'I did.' I felt myself about to give a little gasp; shock at the memory of what had taken place between me and Hannah. I lowered my eyes. It was as if it were apparent in my face, written on my body.

'Some people in the village were anti-, but I didn't mind.'

'Sorry? Anti- what?'

'The Jews. I don't really mind them. You can't always tell, anyway, can you? And there were rumours, of course.'

'What sort of rumours?'

'About the two of them.'

'I see,' I said. 'Really?' It struck me, through the afternoon haze of my self-absorption and regret, that this was one of Livia's white hens that Morley had spoken of, dropped into my lap. 'Why don't you sit down, here,' I said and patted an adjacent armchair, which she settled into, and as the motes of dust played around us in that sickening, stifling room, she told me about the rumours, about the reverend and Hannah, and about lovers and plots, and the desecration of the face of the Virgin Mary in the church and . . .

'But it's just village tittle-tattle, sir,' she said, at the end of our long, strange conversation. 'That's all. It's just what people say, isn't it?'

'Yes,' I agreed. 'Just what people say.'

Eventually she had to leave to attend to other guests.

I passed the rest of the afternoon alone with my thoughts.

When I sat down that evening with Morley for dinner our conversation moved, as it always did, from topic to topic, and sub-topic to sub-topic, and over great time and distances, as we traversed our way slowly from soup to nuts, occasionally glancing at the views afforded over Blakeney harbour – the Blakeney Hotel, as Morley notes in the *County Guides*, being 'blessed by its situation' – and so it was only as we were approaching our trifle, which we were assured was a speciality of the house, that the moment finally presented itself for me to speak to Morley about what Lizzie had told me.

But just as I was about to speak, a man strode purposefully into the dining room and spoke – equally purposefully – with the head waiter, and then began to make his way – even more purposefully – over to our table. Morley had his back to the man, but I sat facing towards him, and couldn't help but notice that – at over six feet tall, and dressed in a buttery smooth grey suit – he had the disturbed and yet somehow also imperturbable features of someone who'd spent a considerable portion of his youth clambering in and out of boxing rings, and that, as he walked towards us with his profound and ever increasing purposefulness, his face seemed to become forever darker and his fists more clenched: he was, I thought, either a policeman or a thug.

'Policeman?' said Morley, glancing up at me, moments before the man reached our table, as though reading my thoughts.

'Would you mind if I had a word? Mr Morley, isn't it?'

'It is. And you are?'

'I'm the Deputy Detective Chief Inspector for the Norfolk Constabulary.'

'An honour to meet you, sir. And your name is?'

'I'm the Deputy Detective Chief Inspector for the Norfolk Constabulary. That will suffice, thank you, Mr Morley.' The detective's fists were clenched as tight as his jaw was set.

'Of course, Deputy Detective Chief Inspector for the Norfolk Constabulary. We've been expecting you.' Morley rose from his seat to his own not inconsiderable height, shook the detective firmly by the hand, called over a waiter, who brought an extra chair, and quickly settled the detective down, instantly taking charge of the situation. Several diners at nearby tables glanced in our direction.

'This is my assistant, Stephen Sefton,' he said. We shook hands. Or, rather, the detective shook my hand. He had hands like rolling pins.

'I hope I'm not interrupting your meal,' he said.

'Not at all, Deputy Detective Chief Inspector for the Norfolk Constabulary. You're coping with a serious enquiry. We, on the other hand, are merely coping with a trifle. Literally. Perhaps you'd care to join us?'

'No thank you.'

'Very wise. Too much cream, not enough custard, wouldn't you say, Sefton? But coffee, perhaps, Deputy Detective Chief Inspector for the Norfolk Constabulary? Though I don't indulge myself. One tries to avoid too many false exhilarations. You won't accept wine or spiritous drink, I'm sure, if you're on duty.'

'I'll get to the point, Mr Morley, if you don't mind.'

'Of course, Deputy Detective Chief Inspector for the Norfolk Constabulary.' Morley ostentatiously folded his napkin on the table.

'Deputy Detective Chief Inspector is fine,' said the detective.

'Oh, really, we can drop the Norfolk Constabulary?'

'Yes.'

'Well, if you're sure, Deputy Detective Chief Inspector. You have my full and undivided attention.'

'I don't know if you've seen today's papers, Mr Morley?'

'Yes, I think so, Deputy Detective Chief Inspector,' said Morley, who had read and carefully filleted them for information and facts by the time I'd come down for breakfast.

'You write for the papers, isn't that right, Mr Morley? *Daily Herald*, isn't it?'

'That's correct, Deputy Detective Chief Inspector. Though I also write for the *Morning Post*, *The Times*, the *Daily Telegraph*, the *Daily News*, the *Daily Chronicle*, the *Daily Express* and the *Daily Mail*. As well as the *Daily Herald*.'

'A busy man.'

'I'm a terribly disorganised man, actually, Deputy Detective Chief Inspector, truth be told, rather than busy, though I must admit I have always been lucky in finding places to publish.'

'Yes. Well, I'm sure that is the case, Mr Morley, for a man like yourself who's clearly prepared to write for anyone about anything.' The detective's voice was becoming raised and his face slightly flushed. I noticed the head waiter hovering closely at a nearby table, whose diners were staring across at us with a look of some alarm.

'I wouldn't say that exactly,' said Morley, who was breathing through his nose, I noted, in a manner I recognised; it was a technique he said he'd learned on his travels, from a Buddhist monk, and was guaranteed to calm a chap when under verbal or physical assault. 'I'm not terribly good on sport, for example. Or horoscopes – the press now publish the daily influences of the stars as calmly as if it were the weather forecast, don't they? Not something I entirely approve of, I must admit. Are you a reader of the horoscopes at all? *Astra non mentiuntur, sed astrologi bene mentiuntur*, eh?'

The detective glanced at me at this point, clearly looking for a referee, realising that Morley's techniques and rules of conversation were not entirely the same as other men's, and that the thing was getting away from him. I smiled at him benignly, and he threw down a conversational anchor.

'There seems to be some suggestion in the papers, Mr Morley, that the police may require assistance in investigating the suicide of the reverend.'

'Is that right?'

'Yes. Suggestions in an article by you, in fact, Mr Morley.'

'Ah.'

'In today's *Daily Herald*.' The volume was raised once again. More diners glanced across. The head waiter remained hovering.

I hadn't seen the article.

'I didn't mean to give that impression at all, Deputy Detective Chief Inspector.'

'Well, that's what it read like to me, sir.'

'That is really most regrettable, then.'

'We see very little crime around here, Mr Morley.' You could now have heard a proverbial pin drop in the restaurant. Knives and forks had been retired and laid to rest.

'Due in large part no doubt to your careful stewardship, Deputy Detective Chief Inspector. Like Adam in the Garden.'

'I like to think so,' said the detective, unable for a moment to work out whether this was a compliment or not. I wasn't sure myself. It was not, as it turned out; as Morley now made abundantly clear.

'It is a pity then, that like the serpent, sin seems to have entered paradise on its belly, as it were, and one of your most prominent figures in the community has died such a horrible death.'

'Yes. But a suicide is not something that we can—'

'If it is suicide,' said Morley, not unaware, it seemed to me, that he now had as his audience the entire restaurant, its diners and its staff.

'Which it is,' said the detective.

'You say so, Deputy Detective Chief Inspector.'

'I do.'

'Yes. But I wonder . . .' Morley paused, and milked the moment, twirling a moustache-end. 'If there might perhaps be more to it.'

'Do you now, Mr Morley? And I wonder, sir, if you have been reading too many books.'

Morley laughed, something that – despite his continual good humour – he rarely did. The laugh echoed around the restaurant, rattling off the windows, and startled the head waiter into action. He began loudly instructing the other waiting staff in their duties, moving from table to table with words of calm for the diners. A hubbub arose. Our exchange returned to a private conversation. 'It has certainly been said before, Inspector, and I must admit that I'm no stranger to the delights of the written word. Was it Johnson who described himself as a ruminant of reading? Sefton?'

'I don't know, Mr Morley. Sounds like Johnson, certainly,' I said.

'Well, whoever said what, Mr Morley' – the detective

spoke with lowered voice now – 'I would prefer it if you would leave the police work to us professionals, and you keep your theories to yourself, stay out of the papers and stick with your books.'

'Of course.'

'We have a job to do.'

'Indeed. And I have the highest respect for the police profession, may I say,' said Morley. 'Awe, even. Some of my favourite people in the world are policemen.'

'Really.'

'Yes. Monsieur Chevalier Dupin. Eugène Valmont, Inspector Hanaud. Do you know Inspector Hanaud?'

'I can't say I do, Mr Morley.'

'Pity. You'd like him. Very smart. Very intuitive. Much like yourself, Deputy Detective Chief Inspector.'

'Well, perhaps, Mr Morley, given the high regard you claim to hold for our profession, you might show us the respect of leaving our work to us, sir?'

'I certainly shall, Deputy Detective Chief Inspector. I certainly shall.'

'Part of which will be to investigate your own involvement in the discovery of the reverend's body.'

'Of course. In which matter you are assured of our utmost assistance.'

'Good.' The detective seemed satisfied. But Morley was not.

'And can I ask when we might be able to expect to be able to leave Blakeney and go about our business?'

'I can't say at the moment, Mr Morley, I'm afraid.'

'Would it perhaps speed matters along at this stage if I were to offer a little information?'

'What information?'

'Well, what with us having been first on the scene and what have you, I wondered if—'

'If you have information, Mr Morley, relating to this crime, you are obliged to inform us.'

'Well, it's not really information so much as a suggestion, Deputy Detective Chief Inspector.'

'A suggestion?'

'Yes. Or a set of suggestions.'

'Really?' The detective looked as though all and any suggestions of Morley's about anything and of any kind would be thoroughly unwelcome. Of course, this didn't stop Morley.

'I'm sure you have dealt with suicides, during your time as a policeman?'

'Sadly I have, yes, Mr Morley.'

'And in your experience, what would be the main reasons for someone taking their own life?'

'General weariness of life,' said the detective. 'Obviously.'

'Something with which I'm sure we can all identify,' said Morley.

'Some more than others,' said the detective, rather wittily, I thought.

'Indeed. Any other reasons that you've come across?'

'Mental illness.'

'Insanity, you mean?' said Morley.

'Imbecility,' said the inspector.

'Ah, yes.'

'Or idiocy.'

'Mental illness and idiocy being not quite the same thing, though, obviously,' said Morley.

'I speak as I find, Mr Morley.'

'I'm sure you do, Inspector, though neither idiocy nor mental illness applies, presumably, in the case of the Reverend Bowden.'

'Not as far as I'm aware,' said the inspector.

'So I wonder if there might be other reasons that you can think of, why someone commits suicide?'

'I'm not that interested in these larger philosophical questions, Mr Morley, to be honest. I'm a policeman.'

'But a philosopher's profession, surely?'

'I hardly think so, Mr Morley, no.'

'The pursuit of truth and justice? The application of method to mystery? The examination and interrogation of evidence?'

'Anyway,' said the detective. 'The reverend killed himself, and that's unfortunate.'

'But the question of why remains,' insisted Morley.

'The question of why is none of our business, Mr Morley.'

'Really? How curious, coming from an officer of the law. *Omnia causa fiunt.*'

'You keep speaking Italian, Mr Morley, a language I do not understand.'

'My apologies,' said Morley. 'One can hardly expect a deputy detective chief inspector for the Norfolk Constabulary also to be a linguist. I mean simply that everything has a cause, which might tell us about the effect. I'm sure that we can agree on that.'

'Of course.'

'Good. So perhaps you'll indulge me for a moment—'

'I think you'll find that I already have, Mr Morley.'

'Indeed you have, sir. Indeed you have. Very generous.

And for so little in return. Sure I can't interest you in some trifle? Coffee?'

'No, thank you.'

'What was your verdict on the trifle, Sefton?'

'Excellent,' I said.

'Too much cream,' said Morley. 'And we shall have to overlook the sherry. But anyway. Let us imagine, Deputy Detective Chief Inspector, shall we, that we have a little collection of suicides: a dead man, say; a dead woman; another dead man; another dead woman.'

'Yes . . .' It was unclear to the detective, and indeed to me, where Morley was going with this latest analogy. It was getting late. The restaurant was emptying.

'Can you picture them in your mind, Deputy Detective Chief Inspector for the Norfolk Constabulary?'

'Not really, no, Mr Morley.'

'Precisely. But let us imagine now that one of the men is an ex-soldier, say, who has suffered illusions of persecution. He has returned from a war, is unable to resume his previous life, and found himself unable to manage.' Morley glanced meaningfully at me across the table. I looked away. Rearranged my napkin. 'And that one of the women, say, is a religious woman, middle-aged, husband dead, has been suffering from dementing visions. And that the other woman was a servant girl found hanging in a . . . pantry, say, having been found out in adultery with her employer. And that the other man was a . . . farmer? Yes, a farmer, who hanged himself in his barn because of money troubles. Do you begin to get a picture of all these people now? Able to distinguish between them, these suicides? Understand who they are? Why they acted as they did?'

'Yes, of course.'

'Well, there we are, you see, Deputy Detective Chief Inspector. *Multum in parvo. Minima maxima sunt*, and what have you.'

'What?'

'Details. Details, details, details. And as with these others, so with the reverend. Everything we can know about him matters in assisting us to find the cause of his death, and to find the cause of his death is to solve the mystery of his death.'

'Not that there is a mystery,' said the detective, whose fists remained as clenched, and whose jaw as set as when he had first sat with us what seemed a long time ago.

'Ah, well, in that matter we shall perhaps have to agree to disagree.'

The head waiter approached the table.

'Can I offer you gentlemen any tea or coffee? Anything else to eat or drink?'

'No, thank you,' said Morley. 'Deputy Detective Chief Inspector?'

'No, thank you.'

'Sefton?'

'No, thank you.'

'Good. No, thank you,' said Morley to the waiter. 'I think we're almost done here.'

We were indeed almost done, the detective most thoroughly done, though Morley insisted on tormenting him with some further observations as he got up to leave.

'Would you mind if I consulted my notebooks for a moment?' he said. 'I took the liberty of jotting down a few thoughts on the subject of suicide.'

'Well . . .'

'Just a moment. I have so much enjoyed our conversation.' Morley fished one of his German notebooks from his jacket pocket. 'Good. Ah. Yes.' He ran his finger down the page, as if adding up a grocery bill. 'Suicide. Reasons for. Have you ever come across any cases of derangement accompanying religious ecstasy or excitement?'

'Not personally, Mr Morley.'

'And the reverend was not – as far as you know – given to visions and such like? I was just wondering, what with him being a religious man.'

'No.'

'I'm just ticking off my list here, Deputy Detective Chief Inspector. Other reasons for suicide . . . Bodily affliction, perhaps? Illness? Was the reverend suffering from any?'

'Again, I don't know, Mr Morley.'

'Vices.'

'Vices? Such as?'

'Such as drunkenness. Sorrow and grief over others – he was a clergyman after all. He was unmarried. We're sure he was not a homosexual?'

'I hardly think—'

Morley held up a finger and continued reading. 'I'm not suggesting these are the reasons. I am merely suggesting *possible* reasons, Deputy Detective Chief Inspector. Financial distress. Remorse. Shame . . . Oh, I can hardly read my own writing here . . . Sefton, what does that say?'

He handed the notebook over to me. There was nothing written on the page.

I glanced at Morley, bewildered. He stared back.

'I can't quite make it out, Mr Morley, I'm afraid.'

He peered at the blank page. 'Punishment,' he said. 'That's it. What about punishment?'

'What about it?' said the detective.

'Would it perhaps be possible that the reverend was being punished for some unknown crime?'

'By who?'

'By himself, possibly. Though more likely by others.'

'By others?'

'It's just a thought,' said Morley. 'I'll leave it with you.'

❧ ❧

In the end, Morley and the detective parted on good enough terms, the restaurant was calm, and I finally took the opportunity to speak to Morley about the rumours that Lizzie had reported to me: that the reverend and Hannah were lovers; that she was pregnant with his child; that theirs was a suicide pact. Morley listened without interrupting as I spoke.

'Absolute rubbish, Sefton,' he said, when I had finished. 'Really, one shouldn't entertain these fantastical notions. Anyway, time for bed.'

❧ ❧

I spent the rest of the evening drinking in the residents' lounge of the hotel. Lizzie was again serving. I drank perhaps more than I should and asked her more about Hannah and the reverend. She told me a story about Hannah acting as a model for a local artist.

'There're loads of artists here. They come here for the sky, apparently.'

'For the sky?'

'Can't get it anywhere else, is what they say.'

I finished another glass of whisky. 'I'm sure they can't.'

'You being cheeky, mister?'

'Not at all.'

'It's all right, I like it when you are.'

'Perhaps I should do it some more then?'

'Perhaps you should. Or perhaps you should go to bed.'

'That's an interesting suggestion,' I said.

'Is it?'

'Yes, it is.'

'You're not funny, are you?' she said.

'Funny?'

'Queer?'

'No!' I laughed. 'I'm not. What made you think so?'

'Just . . . Your friend's so well turned-out—'

'Exceptionally spruce,' I said. 'It's a phrase of Morley's.'

'And you're very good-looking—'

'Well, I wouldn't say that . . .'

'As you know fine rightly. So, people have been saying things about the pair of you.'

'We'll prove people wrong then, shall we, Lizzie?'

# CHAPTER FOURTEEN

IN THE MORNING, alone, I was woken by bright sunlight streaming in behind white curtains.

It was before six. During what little sleep I had enjoyed I had been troubled by dreams and nightmares. I knew that I had to speak to Morley immediately.

I knocked on his door. He called from inside and I entered.

He was dressed in a shirt, bow tie and waistcoat, a pair of khaki shorts, knee-length socks, his customary brogues, and was vigorously performing a set of exercises. Very vigorously, in fact. So vigorously that his each utterance was first prefaced by and then followed by a pant and a grunt.

'Care to – hff! – join me – hff! – Sefton?'

'No, I think I'll sit this one out, if I may.'

'You don't know – hff! – what you're missing,' he hffed.

'I think I can see, Mr Morley.'

'The important thing – hff! – is regularity – hff! – Sefton. As in all – hff! – things.'

'I'll call back later, Mr Morley.'

'No. No.' He stood still, and began a series of stretching exercises, which seemed to calm his breathing.

'*The Four Bs*, Sefton. I wrote a book, a few years ago. That was the title.' He was breathing deeply. 'Morning routine, key to a healthy and happy day. One: breathing.' He demonstrated by taking several deep breaths. 'Two: bath – cold water, of course. Stimulates the nerves. Three: bowels – open. Good evacuation. And four: breakfast. Fruit. Water. Bowl of oatmeal.'

'I'll certainly consider adopting the routine,' I said.

'Do. Do you the power of good, Sefton. Anyway, how can I help you?'

'I was talking to someone last night.'

'Jolly good. Mixing with the natives. You're learning, Sefton, my little *chota sahib*.'

'Sorry?'

'When I was in India – Rawalpindi, with the Harcourts; do you know the Harcourts? Frontier Force? Terribly nice people.'

'No, I'm afraid not—'

'Got tucked right into the Urdu, the Harcourts. Mrs Harcourt took to wearing the sari. Wonderful woman. Indomitable. Like a mother to me, Sefton. Collected pi dogs. Anyway, I observed that the families who made an effort to get along with the locals – and I mean all the locals, Sefton, the old *bheestie* right the way through to the *rum-johnnie*, you know – were better served than those who didn't. The Scotch in particular were very good at it. Friendly, but firm. Created an atmosphere of remarkable good will. Not that the Harcourts were Scotch. They were from Maidenhead. You've no Scotch in you, Sefton?'

'Not as far as I'm aware, Mr Morley, no.'

'Anyway, good job.'

'Yes. Well, thank you.'

'Who were you talking to?'

'Someone.'

'Female of the species, by any chance?'

'Well . . .'

'I see. Word of advice, Sefton.'

'Yes, Mr Morley.'

'A passing pleasure on a long journey does not always make a permanent addition to the home.'

'I'm sorry, Mr Morley?'

'I think you know what I'm talking about, Sefton. I wouldn't want our every trip to turn into some kind of a . . . stag hunt.'

'A stag hunt, sir?'

'We'll leave it at that, Sefton, shall we? You wanted to see me? The early hour presages some doom or celebration; I'm assuming you're not up picking roses?'

I went on to describe to him what Lizzie had told me about the paintings of Hannah, and the desecration of the image of the Virgin Mary in the church.

'Ah,' said Morley. 'Interesting.'

'That's what I thought. Worth investigating?'

'Possibly. Once we're fully dressed and provisioned. Leave it with me, Sefton, would you?'

∽ ∾

We agreed to meet over breakfast to talk about it. Wide awake, and buzzing with my lack of sleep, and lack of pills and caffeine, I took a walk around the town – the air was fresh, there were men landing their catches – and when I returned Morley was in his usual place in the dining room, poised with a banana on his plate, which he proceeded slowly to peel, as though performing an intricate surgical operation, or playing on a small, novelty musical instrument. Having beguiled and unsheathed the banana from its skin, he proceeded slowly to strip it of its long sinewy strings.

I watched in appalled fascination, drinking coffee, wondering if any other breakfasters – who had already witnessed our lively conversation with the Deputy Detective Chief Inspector for the Norfolk Constabulary the night before – had noticed the performance, which was of course accompanied by the usual and continual flow of loud conversation.

They had.

'Bananas, Sefton. The thing to remember about bananas is that they do not grow on trees.'

'I think they do, actually,' I said.

'Bananas!' said Morley. There was a pause in the restaurant's tinkling of tea cups and crunching of toast. 'Grow on trees?'

'They don't grow on trees?'

'Common misapprehension, Sefton. Looks like a tree, is in fact a perennial herb. Stayed on a plantation when I was travelling once. Sri Lanka. Binks Fairbanks. You don't know him?'

'No.'

'Dies back to its roots every year—'

'Binks Fairbanks?'

'The banana, Sefton, do keep up. And then grows again. Quite extraordinary. Did you know they eat them fried, and as a savoury as well as a fruit dessert?'

'I didn't know, no.'

'Oh yes. A very flexible fruit, our friend the banana.' This seemed to amuse him. 'A fascinating flexible fruit.' It sounded suspiciously to me like a self-description, though I didn't point this out. 'Fine fancy fare. Said the four famished fishermen frying flying fish. Not bad, eh?'

'Hmm.' I took another sip of my coffee, finding it difficult either to agree or disagree with the merits of a tongue-twister, which Morley insisted on rehearsing, loudly, several times. I noticed the head waiter eyeing us suspiciously.

'Good work-out for the lower lip and upper teeth. "The fascinating flexible fruit is fine fancy fare, said the four famished fishermen frying flying fish." Do for our friend Miss Harris and the D'Oyly Carte, wouldn't it? Make a note, Sefton.'

I gingerly checked my jacket pocket, but didn't seem to have the notebook to hand.

'Shame,' said Morley. 'Are you familiar with the practice of girdling, Sefton?'

'I'm not sure that I am, no, Mr Morley.'

'Monks used to have a prayer book tied to them – girdled. You might want to investigate it further. Thus preventing being caught short in future.'

'I certainly shall,' I said, with absolutely no intention of doing so. Morley was of course never in danger of being caught short on the note-taking front, since he kept secreted about his person at all times not only a variety of his German notebooks, but also rubber-banded sets of small index cards, small enough to fit in a waistcoat pocket, 'for emergency purposes', he would say.

'Anyway, botanical classification of the banana,' he continued, picking up his thread. 'Very complex. Had a delicious banana once in Calcutta. Orangey-yellow flesh, incredibly sweet, with a thin skin, almost like tissue paper. Could almost have been a different fruit.' He held up one of the sinewy strings that he had extracted from the banana on his plate, as though an anatomist examining a part of some small animal's intestine. 'You should always pull the strings on a banana, Sefton. It gives you digestive trouble otherwise. They upset your tummy, give you the collywobbles.'

'Really?' I said, sipping my coffee, looking around nervously at the other guests.

'Yes, really. I thought everybody knew that. What are you having?'

'I think I'll just stick to the coffee, actually.'

'Shouldn't skip breakfast, Sefton. The fourth "B", remember. One: breathing. Two: bath. Three, a good healthy evacuation of the bowels . . .'

The people at other tables were indeed all watching us intently again, and the poor head waiter had to set off on a round of conversation and napkin-straightening in an attempt to divert attention.

'Yes, I remember, thank you, Mr Morley.'

'And four. Breakfast! Most important meal of the day, and what have you. Breathing. Bath. Bowels. Breakfast. The four Bs. In that order, Sefton. Bowels *after* the bath, note. Not before. Loosened, you see.'

The head waiter was exercising considerable restraint,

I thought, in not approaching our table and asking us to leave.

'Some fresh hot buttered toast, perhaps?'

'No, thank you.'

'With a bit of bloater paste? Not a bad breakfast. Not good. But not bad.'

'No, really.' My stomach turned at the thought of it.

'Plain boiled egg, just? Porridge. You can't beat breakfast, Sefton. Prosopon of the day and what have you.'

From outside there was the sound of church bells ringing eight – which thankfully saved Morley from explaining the meaning of 'prosopon' to me.

'Ah, good,' he said, rising from the table. 'Come on then. Let's go.'

'To the church?'

'Why?'

'To look at the desecrated image of the Virgin Mary?' I said quietly, not wishing to attract attention.

'We'll not let the Virgin detain us this morning, Sefton.'

This was too much: the head waiter was striding over towards us. Morley himself rose and prepared to leave.

'Good morning!' he said, as the head waiter arrived at our table.

'Gentlemen,' he said. 'I'm afraid I am going to have to ask you to leave.'

'Just on our way!' said Morley, popping a final slice of banana, like a large, thin lozenge, in his mouth. 'Let's up, up and be gone, Sefton. No use sitting here like a couple of pigs with our hands in our pockets, eh?'

'But what about breakfast?' I said. Two cups of coffee had finally started to excite my hunger.

'Breakfast can wait, Sefton. Not good to be always thinking of your stomach, man. We have a book to write. Besides, we have an appointment.'

'With?'

'A Reverend Swain. Bit of background on local religious matters. Come in handy, won't it?'

I hurried after him as he made his way through the tables.

'No time for the Virgin this morning, alas,' he said, ostensibly to me, but in fact to anyone – which was everyone – who cared to listen, over their eggs and bacon. 'Best to leave that sort of matter to the professionals. Deputy Detective Chief Inspector for the Norfolk Constabulary can handle her.'

I smiled at the breakfasters placatingly, and made a hasty exit.

∽∼

And so that morning we resumed our work on the *County Guides* and visited the Reverend Richard Swain, in the neighbouring parish of Morston. 'He's certainly dressing the part, anyway,' said Morley, after our visit. 'I'd certainly cast him in the role, wouldn't you?' Swain was indeed the very image of the clergyman, done out in black cassock and collar, ascetically thin, though simultaneously jowly, and completely bald, except for a couple of pure white angel-wing tufts of hair hovering over his ears and above such a vast expanse of ecclesiastical forehead that the upper part of his face seemed in fact to overhang the lower part, as if the mind were making a bid over the body for predominance. 'Pop a zucchetto on him and rig him out in purple and you'd almost mistake him for a Renaissance Pope, wouldn't you?' remarked Morley. Indeed you would, though the rectory was a rather less than papal residence, being distinguished only by the bright shine of its shiny brown paint on its every lincrusta surface, and the deep sad brownness of the furniture cramming the brown room, with its brown upright piano and brown fireplace, before which the Reverend Swain sat while speaking to us. The place even *smelled* brown; and Morley later named the reverend 'Father Brown'. (Morley was, as is well known, a great admirer of Chesterton, and had debated with him on a number of occasions, though in private he rather deprecated his conversion to Catholicism, which he regarded as a sign of mental and spiritual weakness.)

'Terrible, terrible loss to the Church,' said Swain, who had that curious habit that clergymen sometimes have of leaning the head to one side when talking, in the manner of someone listening rather than speaking, which one presumes is intended to imply empathy and understanding, but which does also rather unfortunately give the appearance of mental incapacity. As he spoke he also fiddled with various pieces of pipe-smoking apparatus arrayed on the desk before him. It was like speaking with an elderly, pipe-smoking, holy orangutan, Morley later remarked.

'Indeed,' said Morley, having solemnly offered the reverend his condolences on our arrival. 'You knew him well?'

'Very well, sir. Yes. Very, very well.' Swain also had a habit of puffing out his chest as he spoke, as though working a set of bellows. 'We were at college together,' he puffed, his hands occupied with removing shag from a pouch and tamping it into a pipe plucked from a rack.

'Really? And where was that, might I ask?'

'Oxford,' said Swain, searching for matches. 'I was studying Theology. He was Mods and Greats.'

'Ah. Of course,' said Morley, as if this explained everything. 'Which college?'

'Balliol.' Matches found, the reverend set the tobacco alight, and with a few strong draws the pipe was set to full steam ahead.

'Balliol College, Oxford,' said Morley. '"The tranquil consciousness of an effortless superiority," is that right?'

'I believe it is, Mr Morley, yes,' said the reverend guardedly, through a haze of smoke.

I must have looked more than usually puzzled, because Morley took a moment to explain.

'Asquith,' he said. 'On Balliol.'

'Ah.'

'You'll have to forgive him, Reverend. Sefton here's a Cambridge man.'

'Forgiven, of course,' said Swain, nodding beneficently towards me. 'And you, Mr Morley? You strike me as more Cambridge than Oxford. Am I right?'

'Alas, I can claim no *alma mater*,' said Morley. 'No mother to nourish me or to give me succour, I'm afraid. I had to raise myself.'

'I see. Not a university man. Pulled yourself up by your bootstraps, then?'

'That's one way of putting it, certainly.' Morley stood up a little straighter at this point, and I could hear the slight crackle of resentment, though it may have been his shoe leather. We had not been invited to sit, and so remained standing before the reverend, like supplicants.

'Well, well done you,' said the reverend, peering up at

Morley. 'Well done you. This country needs more people like you, sir. Wouldn't you say, Cantab?' I assumed he was referring to me. 'Can't all be left to us, can it? All of us, pulling together. Cooperating. It's what made us the nation we are today, is it not?'

'I'm sure it is,' I said.

Puff, puff went the pipe.

'Personally, I'm a great believer in self-improvement. Although I don't entirely approve of the profession of journalism, Mr Morley, I have to say.'

'I'm sorry to hear that, Reverend.'

'Nothing against you personally, you understand.'

'Of course.'

'A man such as yourself has to try to make his way somehow. But we all have choices, Mr Morley, don't we? Hardly a profession for a gentleman – journalism.' He made the word 'journalism' here sound remarkably like a rhyming synonym for 'communism', and was making the fatal mistake of ragging Morley. I did think for a moment of warning him. But then decided to leave him to his fate. Any intervention was pointless: the poor reverend was sweeping towards Niagara Falls in a barrel.

'I might perhaps boast of some small few accomplishments, Reverend,' replied Morley, who was keeping his powder dry, 'but I would certainly never dream of counting myself a gentleman.'

'No. Well.' The Reverend Swain leaned back in his chair, clearly believing himself to have established proper rank. 'Do I rightly detect you're a local?' He wagged a finger.

'That's correct,' said Morley.

'Ah, yes. I have an ear for it, you see,' said the reverend, grinning like the proverbial Cheshire cat. 'A musical ear, you might say. Tuned in, and what have you. And the study of the ancient languages, of course. One acquires a certain sensitivity, through one's education and long study.'

'Of course. And do I rightly detect that you are also Norfolk born, Reverend?'

The long-studying reverend looked shocked. He shrank back in his chair rather. Removed the pipe from his mouth. Certainly to me he sounded thoroughly pure-bred, cut-glass and bell-tinklingly OK. But I was not Morley. And neither was the poor reverend.

'Yes, that's right,' he agreed. 'Or "Do I am, boy," should I say?' He put on a broad Norfolk accent, which caused Morley to grimace. 'Do I am, boy. Do I am. But how could you tell, Mr Morley?'

'Just . . . hints,' said Morley. 'There are always hints, Reverend, aren't there? If one listens carefully.'

'Quite so,' said Swain. 'Quite so.' He adopted a prayerful look and his angel-wing tufts of hair rose slightly, as if in thoughtful praise.

'Though I have to admit,' said Morley, 'that – unlike you – I am not blessed with a musical ear, nor do I have your sensitivity derived from the long study of the ancient languages.'

'A good guess, then, eh?'

'You could say that,' Morley continued, 'though a guess based on my own – admittedly modest and non-varsity – studies and observations over a number of years, that the Norfolk accent tends to be characterised mainly by the lengthening of vowel sounds, the merging of syllables – "going" becomes "gorn" and etcetera – along with more specific phonological variations such as, often, pronounced yod-dropping and h-dropping, as well as larger intonational features such as the characteristic rise at the end of the sentence, all features captured clearly by Dickens, of course, as you will know, in his portrayal of the Yarmouth fishermen, the Peggottys in *David Copperfield*, and perfectly clear and apparent in your own speech, Reverend, if one pays attention, beneath your very fine Oxford veneer.'

'Hmm.' Swain's clerical dignity seemed not only ruffled, but crumpled. He laid his pipe down in an ashtray. 'Hoist by my own petard, Mr Morley.'

'Indeed, Reverend. Or branded on the tongue.'

'Quite.'

'The poor deceased reverend wasn't local, though, was he?'

'No,' agreed the Reverend Swain, more than happy to change the subject. 'He'd come and stay occasionally, while we were at Oxford.'

'And after Oxford?' said Morley.

'Our paths diverged.'

'You lost touch?'

'Entirely. Yes. Absolutely and entirely.'

'Really?'

'Yes.'

'But your paths later converged again?'

'Indeed, sir, and behold and lo! we ended up in adjacent parishes.'

'Quite a coincidence,' said Morley.

'Yes. We make our plans, Mr Morley. But God sometimes has other plans. Don't you find?'

'"Man proposes: God disposes,"' said Morley.

'Indeed. Shakespeare.'

'Virgil, I think you'll find,' said Morley. '*Dis aliter visum?*'

Swain licked his lips. 'Yes. Well done. You really are a veritable mine of ... curious information, Mr Morley, aren't you?' He glanced at me, with an expression seeking, I thought, some conspiratorial disdain. I smiled beneficently back. 'You remind me of a chap I was at school with. Great one for memorising trivia. You know. Cricket scores and what have you. Could recite parts of *Wisden*. Parrotface, we called him; the cruelty of young boys, Mr Morley, eh? He ended up as a music-hall mnemonist, as far as I recall.'

'*Dis aliter visum,*' said Morley.

'Milton?'

'Virgil, actually, Reverend. No longer on the curriculum at Oxford, clearly?'

'I was not a classical scholar, Mr Morley. I studied Theology.'

'Common tellurian, I would have thought, Reverend, especially for a man with the benefit of a long education in the ancient languages.'

The Reverend Swain stopped leaning his head at this point, and looked at Morley square on and direct. 'You're here to ask me about your book, Mr Morley, isn't that correct? *The County Guides*, or whatever they're called.'

'Yes, that's correct.'

'Well, perhaps you'd like to begin. I'm afraid I really don't have long.' He consulted his watch. 'Church business. You understand. One's time is not one's own.'

'Of course,' said Morley. 'Perhaps we should go, and call another time.'

'No,' said the reverend, 'no, no. Best to get it out of the way, now you're here. I can spare you a few minutes.' He began his pipe routine again.

'That's very kind of you.'

'Not at all, not at all,' said the reverend, dismissing Morley's thanks with a papal wave of the hand.

'We shouldn't have imposed upon you at this difficult time.'

'Yes. Well. It is a difficult time.'

'Of course,' said Morley. 'My condolences again. The loss of a friend.'

'Indeed. We were preparing a paper together, actually, on the doctrine of Original Sin.'

'Really?' said Morley. 'A fascinating subject. The inborn legacies of Adam's transgressions.'

'Indeed, yes.'

'Limited atonement versus general atonement. Total depravity versus human ability.'

'Theological debate has moved on rather since John Calvin, I think you'll find, Mr Morley.' The reverend smirked rather at this, I thought.

'I'm sure it has, Reverend, and I am of course only an amateur rather than a professional theologian, though I assume the fundamental question remains.'

'Well, it rather depends which fundamental question you have in mind, Mr Morley.' He gave a thin little laugh. 'There are several fundamental questions, I think you'll find.'

'I was thinking of the gap between who we might be, and who we are, Reverend. Perennially troubling question that, isn't it?'

'I suppose it is, yes.'

'Anyway, the reverend was clearly a learned man, like yourself?'

'He was. We were bound together, I suppose, by our time at Oxford.'

'I see. Though presumably in later life you didn't see exactly eye to eye on all matters theological?'

'Well . . . There were some differences, of course.'

'Such as?'

'He had rather clear-cut ideas about things.'

'Such as?'

'He was . . . very much a sheep and the goats sort of a Christian, Mr Morley.'

'By which you mean?'

'He was of the evangelical persuasion, with socialistic leanings.'

'I see. And you are not?'

'I am, shall we say, otherwise inclined, Mr Morley.'

'Indeed. I guessed as much.' Morley glanced around the room, and I glanced with him, noticing for the first time the many portraits of the saints, and of the death of Thomas Becket, the good deeds done by St Christopher, St George on his horse, the Seven Acts of Mercy, the Death of Our Lord, and a large portrait of the Blessed Virgin.

'He was interested in what he would have called "social issues", Mr Morley. Very influenced by the work of Estlin Carpenter. I don't suppose you've heard of him?' said Swain, hoping to score a few points off Morley. He couldn't know, of course, that Morley had heard of everyone, had *always* read them, and more often than not had met them and was their dearest friend.

'The sociology professor?' said Morley.

'You've heard of him?'

'We have corresponded.'

'Ah, well,' said the Reverend Swain, rather disappointed. 'You'll be familiar with his ideas about religion and social work.'

'Indeed.'

'A big influence on our dear friend the reverend.'

'I'm sure he was a good parish priest?'

'He was indeed, Mr Morley. A ... paragon.'

'Of course. Anyway, we probably shouldn't take up any more of your time, Reverend.'

'Well ... No. Perhaps not. Parish business. Very pressing.'

'I'm sure.'

'Perhaps another time?'

'Indeed, at your convenience.'

Swain rose and walked us towards the door. I noticed that beneath his cassock he wore a pair of cherry-red trousers; they flashed as he moved, as if he were wading through communion wine.

Morley paused at the door. 'I do wonder, just before we go, if you could clear up a theological debate I was having with my young friend on the way here.'

We were not, needless to say, as far as I was aware, having any theological debate of any kind on the way there.

'I'm sure I could do my best, Mr Morley,' said Swain, nodding, clearly keen to return to the comforts of his pipe and his priestly duties.

'Prompted, I suppose, by this troubling matter of the death of the reverend.'

'Troubling indeed.'

'Yes. We usually think of suicide as a voluntary death, isn't that right, Reverend?'

'Yes, of course.'

'But what if it is, in fact, an involuntary death?'

Swain glanced quickly at Morley, I thought, in a manner that suggested extreme anxiety. His angel-tufts of hair twitched.

'I'm not entirely sure I understand, Mr Morley.'

'Well, we were wondering, my companion and I, in our ill-informed way, whether the reverend's suicide would count properly as suicide, theologically speaking, if it were, shall we say, prompted?'

'Prompted?'

'Yes.'

'I'm not sure I understand, Mr Morley.'

'If he were ... invited, or pressured into taking his own life. A bullet in the post, as it were, suggesting an honourable way out. Would that be suicide? We couldn't agree.'

'I'd say it's probably a ... grey area,' said Swain.

'Grey areas being a theologian's speciality, of course,' said Morley.

'Perhaps,' agreed Swain.

'So what do you think?'

'There would probably be a number of possible interpretations,' said Swain.

'We couldn't think of any biblical examples, could we, Sefton?'

'No,' I agreed, even though I had no idea what Morley was talking about.

'Can you think of any, Reverend?'

Swain coughed nervously. 'Biblical suicides that fall into that category, you mean?'

'Indeed.'

'Well, there is most famously of course our friend Judas, perhaps the most interesting example.'

'Ah yes, of course,' said Morley. 'Traditionally depicted, I think I'm right in saying, with his bowels gushing out, is that correct?'

'Yes,' agreed Swain. 'That's correct, although I think you'll find that in the biblical account, having hanged himself, Judas is described merely as having fallen and "burst asunder".'

'Ugh,' I said involuntarily, remembering horrible scenes in Spain.

'A little self-control, please, Sefton,' said Morley.

'Indeed,' said Swain, who was warming to his subject. 'And, furthermore, in Apocryphal and pseudo-Apocryphal writings Judas is said to have been thrown over the parapet of the Temple and dashed into pieces.'

'Any other examples that come to mind?' asked Morley.

'Yes, well. I suppose if we wend our way back into the Old Testament, we have Samson's destruction of the Philistines in the temple of Dagon.'

'Yes. I did wonder about that, though presumably it would count as an act of vengeance, rather than suicide, would it not?' asked Morley.

'Yes,' said Swain. 'Probably. And Ahitophel, of course, hanged himself, after the defeat of Absalom. Zimri, following the capture of the city of Tirzah. And you will recall, Mr Morley, that we are told that when the Philistines and the Israelites clashed on Mount Gilboa, Saul, having fought bravely for as long as he could, fell upon his own sword. His armour-bearer doing likewise.'

'Interesting,' said Morley. 'So we might say that Saul took his life so as not to fall into the hands of his foes?'

'We might indeed, Mr Morley. Yes.'

'And his armour-bearer died out of loyalty.'

'Indeed.'

'Very interesting, Reverend, thank you.'

'Is that all, Mr Morley?'

'I think it is, Reverend, yes. You've cleared up a number of matters that were troubling me.'

'I'm so glad.'

The reverend had his hand firmly on the door handle.

'And just finally,' said Morley, in that last-minute manner of his, 'in relation to this topic – I don't want to keep you any further – I wonder if you recall in Herodotus, his describing the practice among the Thracians of the widow or concubine offering her life when the husband or master dies.'

'I'm not familiar with Herodotus, I'm afraid. Read it at school, of course.'

'A privilege I did not share, alas,' said Morley. 'I have had to come to Herodotus rather late in life.'

'Better late than never, I suppose,' said Swain.

'Yes. And in my rather belated reading of Herodotus I was struck by the similarity between the practice that he describes among the Thracians and the Hindu custom of suttee.'

'I'm afraid I'm not an expert in Hindu custom, Mr Morley.'

'Good to know what the competition are up to, I would have thought?'

'Competition?'

'Hindus? Mohammedans, etcetera?'

'I would hardly describe them as competition to the Christian Church, Mr Morley.'

'No? Well, in Hinduism, the custom of suttee requires that a widow immolate herself with the corpse of her husband, isn't that right? Never heard of it?'

'I'm not familiar with the practice, no. And if you're trying to suggest a connection between the death of the reverend and his ... maid I think you'll find the woman was of the Mosaic persuasion, Mr Morley, rather than a Hindu.'

'Indeed.'

'And little as I know about the customs and practices among the Jews, I am not aware of their womenfolk committing suicide on the death of their husbands. And she and the reverend, of course, were not married.'

'No, of course not. So it remains a mystery then.'

'I'm afraid so.'

'You are in the business of mystery, of course.'

'I am,' said the reverend.

'And I am in the business of demystification,' said Morley. 'Goodbye!'

# CHAPTER FIFTEEN

FOR THE NEXT couple of hours Morley busied himself with his columns and his writing: an article on the theory of colour for *Life* magazine; advice on the removal of oil and grease from silks and woollens for some women's journal; and something on the history of coal-mining for the *Yorkshire Post*. Like a – moustached, teetotal and tweed-clad – Plantagenet ruler he had by now established almost entire control of the Blakeney Hotel and its staff, who were happy ferrying books, and paper and pens, and typewriter ribbons, and envelopes, and sealing wax, and blotters and all his other necessary writing requisites back and forth, as well as providing him with a constant supply of tea, arrowroot biscuits and barley water. He was the sort of man, Morley, like Edward Longshanks, or Charlie Chaplin, who inspired loyalty and devotion.

I spent the rest of the morning smoking, mostly, in the modest hotel gardens, and eventually made an appearance around eleven, just as the sands on Morley's quarter-hour egg-timer were running out. I hovered by his table in the restaurant, waiting to speak until the moment he went to upturn the thing again.

'Mr Morley?'

'Ah, Sefton. Look at that. Perfect timing.' He consulted all his watches, and the table clock. 'Time for us to be off again shortly.'

'Yes.'

'Productive morning?'

'Very,' I said.

'Good, good. Writing up the notes of our meeting with the reverend?'

'Slowly but surely, Mr Morley. Slowly but surely.'

'Super. Getting back on track, eh.'

'I just thought I should check where we're off to next, Mr Morley? I really think we should investigate this matter of the desecration of the Virgin in the—'

'You are obsessed with the desecration of the Virgin, Sefton!' Several of the young hotel staff, who were laying tables for luncheon, glanced in our direction. 'Eyes on the prize, Sefton. *The County Guides* will never be started, never mind completed, if we spend our time on desecrated Virgins.'

'But—'

'No ifs, no buts, no nothing, Sefton. The investigation into the death of the reverend and his poor housemaid is, I'm sure, quite safe in the hands of the deputy detective chief inspector and the good officers of the Norfolk Constabulary. As for you and I, we have serious work to do and we shall in fact this morning be setting off to explore the dark nether-world of smocking, quilting and sexual libertarianism. How about that, Sefton, eh? Tickle your fancy?'

'Erm . . .'

One of the staff hurried off, to fetch the head waiter, I suspected.

'Good. We shall be visiting an artistic "community", Sefton – something for the book. So be prepared, as the Chief Scout himself might say. Gird up your loins and what have you. Never know what we might find.'

'Is it far, Mr Morley?'

'Just up the road, I think. Not far. Miriam set it all up before she went to London. Some sort of a cross between an Arts and Crafts community – chickens and goats and what have you – and artistic bohemians. You know the sort of thing. I came across a similar bunch in Dorset some years ago. Harmless really. Like the Bloomsberries. Best viewed with one's anthropological glasses on, Sefton; imagine they're Solomon Islanders, or Tartars, or some such. Ever been to the Solomon Islands?'

'No, I—'

'They run a little folk-dancing group, apparently, this lot. Make craft items. Communists, possibly. All sounds rather intriguing, doesn't it?'

'Fascinating.'

'Good. I'll meet you in the lobby in . . . thirteen minutes?'

We drove in the Lagonda some miles out of Blakeney, towards Wells-next-the-Sea, and eventually arrived at our destination via a long and winding driveway, crossing a small bridge, and through a twisty, shadowy avenue of trees,

*Norfolk rivers and broads*

the car grunting and heaving rather over the uneven dirt road, and were greeted with a rather garish painted sign proclaiming 'WELCOME TO COLLEGE FARM'.

'And so into ye foreign lands,' yelled Morley from the back of the Lagonda. 'This is the real thing, eh, Sefton? Fieldwork? Life among the savages! If we're lucky we might bag ourselves an Italian Futurist, eh? Look out, Mr Malinowski! We're on the hunt for Marinettis!'

'Yes,' I replied, having, as so often, lost track of the conversation.

The house – a Jacobean-style manor house, 'Note the Flemish gables, Sefton!' said Morley. 'Worth a note!' – backed directly onto mudflats, and was flanked by vast pines, eucalyptus trees, sword-like cactus plants, and several kinds of hanging ivy and mosses. The mood of the place seemed rather medieval. There were doves cooing in a dilapidated dovecote; a small, collapsed tower ('Water tower?' I suggested. 'Ice-house,' corrected Morley); a tennis court, its wires and net rusting and sagging, with all the appearance of a duelling arena; and a gravelled courtyard which was scabbed all over with patches of fireweed, ragwort and nettles. 'The romance of dilapidation!' cried Morley, embarking on a short disquisition on the relationship between Tennyson, Greece, gravestones and the meaning of ruins. 'The trouble with English ruins, of course, is that they lack that lovely sunset pallor of the Mediterranean, and so they look merely washed out and glum.'

We parked the car and knocked at several open doors – 'Best not to intrude,' said Morley, 'don't want to upset the natives in their natural habitat. Had a problem like it once in Tehran. Blundered in, bit of a misunderstanding, got chased by the *farrashas*' – but there seemed to be no one around. Eventually, we followed a sort of rabbit-track around the back of the house, through overgrown camellia and rhododendron bushes, towards a number of flint-fronted farm buildings, from where the breeze coming off the sea carried a strange melodic droning noise towards us.

'Romantic sort of spot, isn't it?' I said.

'Do you think? Really?'

'Yes.'

'"*Romantic*", you say.' Morley rolled the word around. 'Interesting. Hart's tongue ferns. Pennywort. Tumbledown buildings. Rustic, certainly. Verdant, certainly. Gothic might be the appropriate term, I would have thought, to describe the effect. But, we'll grant you your *romantic* if you wish, Sefton. Romantic. Hmm. Interesting. Tells us something about your idea of the romantic, I fancy.'

As we approached one of the outbuildings the noise grew louder.

'What is that?' I asked.

'That,' said Morley, holding a glimmering finger aloft in triumphant recognition – his fingers did often give the appearance of glimmering, an effect of his enthusiasm, one supposed – 'if I am not much mistaken, is the sound of the bandoneón.'

'The what?'

'The traditional instrument of the Argentinian tango orchestra, Sefton. Fascinating. Don't hear that every day in Norfolk, do you? We may have found our tribe of bohemians! Shall we explore?'

We stepped through large, decaying wooden doors into what had once clearly been a building for housing cattle.

There was a dirt floor, and freshly whitewashed walls. Birds' nests perched up in the ancient rafters and beams, which were strung with purple-coloured bunting and chimes made from shells. In the half-light I could make out, in the middle of the room, a dozen or more people dressed in peasant-style clothing – but who did not themselves seem to be *actual* peasants – dancing together in formation, while a man sitting by an old upright piano was squeezing a folk tune from a concertina-like instrument. He had a cigarette balanced on the edge of the piano, which bore the scars of many such nonchalantly balanced cigarettes, as though the room were altogether a gay bar in Montevideo rather than a dark, damp, remote barn in north Norfolk, and he glanced up as we entered, nodded, and continued playing.

'Come to join us, gentlemen?' he called loudly over the droning instrument.

'No, I'm afraid not,' said Morley. 'We just thought we'd watch if we may.'

'Of course. Make yourselves at home!' The man's hair was swept back in what I rather regarded as the Italian fashion, and he was dressed in a heavy, high-necked fisherman's sweater, with a bright red cravat. He had a thin, sculpted beard which gave him the look rather of a jolly Jack tar; Morley referred to him later as Blakeney's Bacchus. After several bars the music came to an end and the man, who was obviously in charge, took a draw on his cigarette and called out instructions for the next set of dances.

'Good! Good! Now, let's change the pace, shall we? We'll have "Gathering Pease-cods", followed by "Rufty Tufty", the "Black Nag" and we'll end with "Sellenger's Round". OK?'

There was an enthusiastic nodding of heads from the people-dressed-up-as-peasants-who-were-not-peasants, who seemed happy to ignore us, and off they went again.

I leaned against the wall and watched the bizarre spectacle.

'Little early in the day for folk dancing, isn't it?' I said to Morley.

'Sshh,' said Morley. 'I'm concentrating. He's good.'

'Who?'

'Nanki-Poo.'

'Who?'

'Gilbert and Sullivan, Sefton. *The Mikado*?'

'I can't say I'm a fan, Mr Morley.'

'Never mind.' He nodded towards the musician. 'Him.'

'What is it, a sort of accordion, the bandy-whatever-you-call-it?'

'No, no, no,' said Morley. 'No. Come, come, Sefton. Accordions have the buttons perpendicular to the bellows, as you know. Concertinas have the buttons parallel. The bandoneón is a member of the concertina family of instruments, as you can see. Fiendishly difficult little box of tricks, actually. Different notes on the push and pull, and different button layouts either side, so you have effectively four different keyboard arrangements to play with.'

'Impressive,' I said.

'Indeed,' agreed Morley. 'And he really is rather good. Worth a footnote, at least, for the book, I would have thought. "The Tango Master at the Edge of the World." Maybe an article in that, Sefton. I'm so glad we came.'

I went to produce my notebook from my jacket pocket.

'No, it's all right,' said Morley. 'I've got it. Worth annotating the dance steps as well, I think.' And he began to draw diagrams and staves in his notebook in his tiny hand. 'Quite, quite fascinating.'

While Morley took his usual meticulous overview, I found myself beguiled by the gallivantings of one of the women in the group, who was throwing herself around with especial abandon.

When the whirling and the jigging eventually stopped, the man at the piano laid down his instrument and came to greet us.

'Welcome, welcome, gentlemen, to our little corner of paradise – guano notwithstanding.' He kicked away a little pile of pigeon-droppings.

'"The island valley of Avilion,"' said Morley.

'Yes,' agreed the man. 'You could call it that.'

'"Where falls not hail, or rain, or any snow. Nor ever wind blows loudly; but it lies deep-meadow'd, happy, fair with orchard-lawns and bowery hollows crown'd with summer sea."'

'Do you know, I couldn't have put it better myself,' said the man, laughing with delight. 'Did you make it up?'

'Tennyson,' said Morley.

'Ah. Of course. But you must be a writer yourself, sir?'

'Of a kind,' said Morley.

'We've not met, though, I don't think?'

'I don't think so, sir, no. Apologies, I should have introduced myself. I'm Swanton Morley. And this is my assistant Stephen Sefton.' We shook hands. 'And you are?'

'A fellow artist, sir. My name is Juan. Juan Chancellor.'

'You are a fine musician, sir.'

Again, the man laughed. 'I am a painter, actually, primarily. But yes, also a musician. And a philosopher. And occasionally a poet, when the Muse deigns to visit.'

'*Invita Minerva*. I wish, I wish,' said Morley. 'I'm afraid I'm too old and too set in my ways to rely on inspiration. I trudge merely in the lower foothills of Discipline and Hard Work.'

'Well, fortunately, here, sir, my Muse is always at hand.'

'Norfolk, you mean?' asked Morley. 'Or your instrument?'

'No!' The man laughed. 'Constance!' He called across to the woman who had been most expressive in her dancing, and who was now deep in conversation with some of the other dancers, who were slowly drifting off. 'Constance, darling! Over here. Come and meet our visitors.'

Constance came over. She was short and plump – or, rather, 'protuberant', as Morley later insisted on saying – and she wore high-heeled sandals of a bohemian kind, and blazing tomato-red trousers, with a black bolero jacket with wide sleeves, and a red silk scarf, and a black bandeau around her head, a look that suggested a gypsy on holiday, while her yellow teeth, which stood out in marked contrast against her scarlet lipstick, suggested that she was also a heavy smoker, a drinker of deep red wine, strong tea, black coffee, and possibly an inveterate chewer of tobacco. She had the look of a woman who might be able to cure styes by passing a wedding ring over your eye. Her own eyes were fresh and sparkling, mischievous – though also somehow shallow, like a fish – as though she had just concealed a precious object for which she knew you were now bound to search, for ever in her thrall. She was, in short, an enchantress.

'Gentlemen, this is my wife, Constance.'

'Charmed,' she said, shaking our hands. 'Charmed.'

'Indeed,' said Morley. 'Have we met before?'

'I don't think we've had the pleasure, no.'

'This is Mr Morley,' said Juan. 'And this is Mr Sefton.'

'Ah yes!' said Constance. 'Your daughter, Mr Morley, wrote to ask if you might visit.'

'Yes.'

'We met once at the Ladies' Imperial Club in London,' said Constance.

'Ah. I see.'

'She's very charming. Miriam, isn't it?'

'Yes. Miriam, that's correct. Thank you,' said Morley.

'She's not with you?' asked Juan.

'No, she's in London at the moment.'

'You must persuade her to visit with you one day,' said Constance. 'I think she'd like it here.'

'I'm sure she would,' said Morley.

'This is the man writing the book that I told you about, Juan.'

'Indeed!' said Juan. 'Marvellous! Marvellous! A celebration of Norfolk, isn't that right?'

'That's right,' said Morley.

'Well, welcome to you, gentlemen, to College Farm. A rough-made thing, but it is our own.'

'Thank you. I wondered about the name, actually,' said Morley. 'College Farm?'

'We call it that,' explained Juan, 'because we want it to be somewhere that people can come to learn. About art, and about music.'

'And about life. And love,' added Constance.

'An admirable aim,' said Morley.

'Thank you. We do our best.'

'I'm sure. And *docendo discimus*.'

Juan and Constance looked blank.

'You learn by teaching,' said Morley.

'Indeed.'

'We were just admiring your husband's playing of the bandoneón,' Morley explained to Constance.

'Ah! You know the instrument?' asked Juan.

'I had the privilege once, while staying in Paris, of hearing the great Eduardo Arolas playing with an orchestra.'

'*El Tigre del bandoneón!*' exclaimed Juan. 'My hero! Mr Morley. You are an exceptionally lucky man. But Arolas is no longer with us, alas.'

'No? I'm sorry to hear that.'

'He died many years ago.'

'And where did you learn, Mr Chancellor?'

'I learned the instrument as a child. I was brought up in Argentina, but educated in England.'

'I see.'

'My father was in the Royal Navy. But he met my mother there, and settled. I have made the return journey, as it were.' He laughed again.

The remaining dancers were making their way elsewhere. Constance went over to say goodbye, embracing them all warmly, men and women, and kissing them on both cheeks, in the continental fashion.

'You have quite a . . . thriving group here,' said Morley.

'Ah, yes, we are very, very lucky.'

'They all live here, on the farm?'

'No, some of them do. Some of them are villagers. And some of them are just passing through.' He waved good-bye to the men who were leaving. 'Michael there, he's an antiquarian. He visits from London occasionally. Stays in Blakeney. Donald is a retired commercial traveller. He stays here with us. David is a lutenist, a great interpreter of the work of Dowland. He comes with his wife. And Ed Dunne, who works in the shop in Blakeney, Podger's – you may have met him? – he sometimes joins us. He has one of the studios, in the outbuildings. He'd be a good person to talk to, for your book. A very promising young artist.'

'Dunne, did you say?'

'That's right.'

'Make a note, Sefton.'

I duly did.

'We'll perhaps get a chance to speak to Mr Dunne about his work another time. But how did you end up here your-selves, if you don't mind me asking?' continued Morley.

'We were living in London, but we decided some years ago now to come to Norfolk and to live life more purely.'

'More purely?'

'Yes. All of us here at College Farm share a desire to create an atmosphere of honesty and of heightened consciousness. It is a new ethic of work and love we are trying to create.'

'Very good,' said Morley. 'A sort of religious community, then? Moral rearmament?'

'No, no!' Juan laughed. 'Here at College Farm we try not to impose upon one another our contradictory ideas, or desires, or ... necessities.'

'I see.'

'We are trying to be free.'

'Free? I see. And how do the local community find that?'

'We have had our disagreements, Mr Morley. But that's only to be expected, surely, when one is attempting to establish a centre of intellectual and artistic activity.'

Constance came back over. 'You'll come up to the house, gentlemen, and join us for lunch, of course?'

The house, splendid as it first appeared, was in fact on the verge of decrepitude, if not indeed collapse. Some of the windows were boarded up, door frames and doors were half rotten. Brambles and briars were making their way from outside to the inside. In the vast, primitive communal kitchen, paintings and books were stacked everywhere, and a dreadful fresco, which either consciously or unconsciously – and one hoped the latter, but feared the former – blurred the boundaries between Botticelli and Picasso, adorned the entire length of one wall, in which mottle-faced and multi-coloured women sprawled across what was presumably a Norfolk landscape, flecked with frenzied windmills and startlingly erect churches.

'These are yours, Mr Chancellor?' asked Morley, indicating a stack of canvases, crudely daubed with lines and dots.

'Yes, indeed. I am their originator.'

'Do I detect the influence of Paul Klee, perhaps?'

'I wouldn't dare to compare myself,' said Juan. 'But yes, maybe, a little. I'm most flattered, Mr Morley.'

'He's very modest,' said Constance to me, having linked

her arm through mine, and led me towards an enormous oak refectory table – a banqueting table, really, twenty feet long. 'He was a Vorticist, you know, for a while. Now he's more interested in Innerism.'

'Innerism. Very good,' I said.

'Many of the paintings are in private collections,' she said. 'One of the sisters of Lord Scarsdale is a great fan of our work here. Do you know Lord Scarsdale?'

'I'm afraid not, madam, no,' I said.

'Exquisite taste,' she said. 'And also the French ambassador to the Court of St James. He has many of Juan's paintings.'

'Known for their good taste, of course, the French,' I said, unable to think of anything else.

'Precisely, Mr Sefton. How very true. Do you like them?' she called over to Morley.

'They are very . . . fetching,' said Morley, though he later confessed to me that he thought the art more suitable for adorning bathroom curtains, if anything. 'Semi-art,' he called it. Then added, 'Demi-semi-art.'

'Well, they're all for sale,' said Constance. 'At the right price.'

'Constance!' said Juan, clearly embarrassed.

'I'm afraid we're not here to buy art today, madam,' said Morley. 'Perhaps another time.'

'Such a pity,' she said. 'Now, lunch? And we'll talk about your book.'

'Thank you. Thank you very much,' said Morley. 'It really is terribly kind of you to entertain us.' He winked at me.

Between them, Juan and Constance produced, first,

bread – 'Our own, of course' – and cheese – 'Our own, of course' – and boiled eggs.

'Your own?' said Morley.

'Of course!' said Juan.

And then Constance produced some soup, in a vast enamel pot from a large, modern fridge.

'And what do we have here?' asked Morley.

'It's a cold soup, Mr Morley, from Spain.'

'Cold soup?' said Morley.

'Yes! We rather like to defy conventions here, Mr Morley.'

'Indeed?' said Morley. '*Gazpacho*, or *ajo blanco*?'

'*Ajo blanco.*' Juan laughed.

'You've tried it before?' asked Constance, obviously disappointed.

'Ah, yes,' said Morley. 'Something similar in Turkey. Nothing quite like the lively, and yet' – and here he sniffed the soup as Constance ladled it into his bowl – 'slightly torpid scent of garlic to rouse one at lunchtime.'

'Torpid!' Juan laughed. 'Very good, Mr Morley! Torpid yet lively garlic! You're quite right, of course.'

'Thank you,' said Morley. 'What else is in the soup, might I ask? I'm afraid I've never been to Andalusia. It is an Andalusian dish, isn't that right?'

'Yes,' said Constance, bitterly. 'Almonds.'

'Your own?'

'Alas, no. And oil. And salt.'

'All the good things,' said Juan.

'Mr Sefton here may also have tried the soup before,' said Morley. 'Have you tried it before, Sefton?'

'You were in Spain?' asked Juan.

'Yes,' I said.

'Recently?'

'Yes.'

'Fighting?'

'Yes.'

'You brave soul,' said Constance, ladling more cold soup into my bowl.

'Ever tried it?' said Morley.

'Never,' I said.

'First time for everything,' said Morley.

'Indeed,' said Juan. 'A first time for everything! *Bon appétit!*'

While we ate, Morley asked questions, and I made occasional notes.

I had of course eaten the soup before, though much colder and much, much saltier, in Spain.

'And what brought you here, Mr Chancellor?'

'I came here for the big skies,' said Juan.

'Yes. It's often said,' said Morley. 'Sixty-eight miles, east to west, and forty-one north to south.'

'Is that so?'

'By my calculation. And ninety miles of coast.'

'It reminded me of Argentina. The sea, and the space and the light.'

'Yes,' said Morley. 'Peculiarly pellucid, isn't it?'

'Very good!' Juan laughed. 'Peculiarly pellucid! I like you, Mr Morley.'

'And you, madam?'

'I'm from Norfolk originally,' said Constance. 'From here. Blakeney.'

'Really? I had supposed you might also be from the Americas.'

'Many people make that mistake,' she said.

'It's her looks,' said Juan. 'When I arrived here I fell in love with her ravishing gypsy looks.'

'And you're an artist also, Mrs Chancellor?'

'I trained as an artist in Oxford, Mr Morley. But I prefer to describe myself now as a maker.'

'A maker? I see. You might want to make a note of that, Sefton.'

'I believe woman is the source of all true making, Mr Morley.'

'Really?' said Morley, lifting his moustache away from his soup spoon.

'Yes. We are the source, are we not? The womb. We unleash the universe from within, Mr Morley.'

'Indeed,' agreed Morley, slurping rather.

'A woman's power is the power of the universe, Mr Morley. We have the power to give life.'

'And to take it?' said Morley provokingly.

'Constance works mostly in fabric,' said Juan, saving his wife from embarrassment, and gesturing towards the end of the room where, beneath a large window, stood a large frame loom. 'Headsquares, scarves, stoles. She has her own signature colour.'

'Her own signature colour?' said Morley. 'Really?'

'Yes.'

'Saponaria,' said Constance.

'Is that a colour?' said Morley.

'Not strictly speaking, no,' admitted Constance. 'But it's from the herb garden. It's an exceptional dye.'

'Ah, purple!' said Morley. There were indeed swatches and tatters of fabric all in a strange, deep purple.

'Saponaria,' repeated Constance. 'It is reminiscent of mulberry.'

'Reminiscent of mulberry,' repeated Morley.

'And toys and ornaments,' added Juan. 'Don't forget your toys and ornaments, darling. She makes the most wonderful ornaments. Do show them, Constance.'

Constance smiled, showing her yellowy teeth, and went over to a tool bench which sported a large vice and a rack of metal- and woodworking tools above it.

She returned to the table and placed something in Morley's hands – a small, smooth, highly polished metal object, which resembled a knuckle-duster, ridged with protuberances.

'It's . . . remarkable,' said Morley. 'I've certainly never seen anything quite like it before.'

'I call them my adult toys,' she said, smiling. 'I make them for all my friends.'

'It's certainly heavy,' he said.

'Yes.'

'And cold.'

'But it warms quickly in the hand, Mr Morley.' She reached out and held her hand tightly around his.

'I see.'

'No, wait.'

Morley struggled rather to remove his hands from her grasp, but she held firm.

'You must wait for it to warm in your hands.'

Morley sat silently for a few moments, Juan and Constance smiling broadly and lovingly at each other.

'There,' she said eventually. 'Isn't that nice and warm now?'

'Yes, lovely.' He went to give it back.

'No, do keep it. Please.'

'No, thank you, I couldn't possibly.'

'No?'

'Really, no, it's terribly kind of you, but—'

'Perhaps your young friend then?' She reached across and seized my hand. 'May I?' she said. 'I am fascinated by hands.'

'Erm . . .'

'I can foretell by the lines in your palm whether you'll find happiness. Would you like to know whether you shall find happiness?'

I agreed that I would rather like to know, though it occurred to me even at the time that it was not something one might find, as one finds a coin, or a missing chess piece.

She grasped my hands firmly and then began stroking them.

'I see here that you will live long and have many children. Is that what you desire?'

'I'm not sure. I don't—'

'Well, perhaps you might find a use for this?' She pressed the small metal object into my hands.

'No, thank you,' I said.

'But I insist. See how smooth it is, Mr Sefton. Can't you imagine finding a use for it?'

'No, really, I couldn't.'

'Ha!' She threw her head back and laughed. Not in a good way. 'It's a gift, Mr Sefton,' she said, holding my hands tightly. 'From me to you. You can hardly refuse a gift, can you? A gift for a hero.' She looked at me in a most challenging fashion.

'Well . . . if you insist.'

'I do.' She released her hands from mine suddenly, leaned

forward, kissed me, and then stepped away. 'Though one might expect a gift in return, of course.'

'How lovely,' said Morley, clearly uncomfortable.

'Now, gentlemen,' she said, with a vast wave of her hand, 'coffee?'

∽ ∾

Over thick, black Turkish-style coffee, Juan and Constance explained in ponderous detail to Morley their vision of creating a William Morris-style community in Norfolk, and how they rented outbuildings to local craftsmen and -women. I took notes and – with their permission – a number of photographs of some of the paintings and objects. Talking about the local community, Morley naturally asked about the death of the reverend.

'A tragedy,' said Juan. 'And the poor beautiful house-keeper.'

'Do you think they died for love?' asked Morley.

'For love?' said Juan. 'How do you mean, Mr Morley?'

'Well, it's rather strange that both of them should die in such unusual circumstances. I wondered if there might have been a suicide pact?'

'Love is pure, Mr Morley.'

'Love is patient. Love is kind,' added Morley. 'But alas, under certain circumstances, it can clearly drive people to-wards committing the most dreadful acts.'

'We know nothing about these people, Mr Morley,' said Constance, hurrying to tidy our plates and dishes away and to place them on a teetering pile of other dirty dishes. 'Our lives are here, at College Farm, pursuing our art.'

'Of course. I wonder if we might visit one of your artists in one of the studios?'

'I don't think so,' said Constance.

'For the book?' said Morley. 'It might be interesting.'

'I'm afraid not, Mr Morley, no,' said Constance. 'Most of the craftsmen and -women have their jobs in the villages, and they only use the studios at weekends or in the evenings.'

'Well, perhaps we could just visit one of the studios?'

'Impossible, I'm afraid, without their permission.'

'That's a pity. Your own studio, perhaps we could visit, Mr Chancellor?'

'I hope we've given you enough to write about here,' said Juan.

'Yes. Yes. Of course you have,' said Morley. 'And we are really most grateful.'

∽ ∼

After some strained farewells, we set off in the Lagonda.

'Well, they seemed like a . . . happy sort of bunch, I suppose,' I said, as we drove away.

Morley sat up front in the car with me.

'Excessive happiness is not good for people, Sefton.'

'Really?'

'No. I have always thought the ideal ratio of happiness to sadness is about 3:1.'

'Happy to sad, or sad to happy?'

'Happy to sad,' said Morley. 'Obviously. Any more than that, frankly, and you're a crank. I like these Arts and Crafts people, Sefton, don't get me wrong. The William Morris-style idealists, who believe we've been on the wrong track since the Middle Ages. Their ideals would all be very well, if everyone were of Morris's calibre, but alas we are not, are we? The work of a man's hands are not always superior to the work of a machine. All very well that they should make their paintings and trinkets and fabrics and such like, but . . . Adult toys? What is an adult toy, Sefton?'

'I'm . . . I don't—'

'Who is going to make us what we need as a modern nation, Sefton? Eh? The good folk of College Farm?'

We drove on. Something was troubling Morley.

'There was something odd about them, Sefton. Do you know the phrase *bene qui latuit bene vixit*?'

'I'm not sure I do, Mr Morley, no.'

'Pity. "He who has lived in obscurity has lived well." The line is from *Tristia*, Ovid's lament about his enforced exile from Rome. You didn't study it at school at all?'

'We may have done, sir, but I think I've forgotten it if so.'

'Never mind. Its meaning is often taken to be a panegyric, if you like, for the simple life.'

'Yes, I can see that that might be so.'

'Trouble is, it's wrong, Sefton. Rather, Ovid is expressing bitterness over the way things have turned out for him. *Bene qui latuit bene vixit*. Keep your head down, might be another way of describing it. Make your hideaway in the country.'

'I see.'

'Pull over, Sefton. We're going to take a look at one of the studios.'

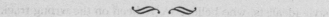

We clambered across woodlands, Morley striding ahead of me, regardless, and found ourselves eventually back down by the mudflats. Crouching down, we made our way towards the outbuildings. One of them – the furthest towards the mudflats – seemed recently to have been set alight. The roof had collapsed. I was reminded horribly of buildings I had seen in Spain; vast canyons of despair seemed to open up instantly to me. I suddenly felt quite liverish. Sick, almost.

'"Everlasting flint,"' said Morley, patting the walls, as we came close.

'Sorry?'

'*Romeo and Juliet*. The roof has collapsed, but the stone remains.'

'Ah.'

'*Mizpah*.'

I was shivering in the cold.

'OK, Sefton?'

'Yes, fine, Mr Morley. Absolutely fine.'

Inside the building, among the blackened beams and the broken pantiles, there were dozens of paintings, some of them scorched, some of them entirely destroyed, some of them with the canvas burned, only the thin lines of frames and supports remaining.

'Look familiar?' said Morley, holding up the charred remains of a sketch, of a woman with heavily lidded eyes, and blonde hair and brooding intensity.

It was a painting of Hannah.

And she was naked.

It was an ugly painting. A painting conceived in a spirit of lust rather than a spirit of awe.

'Great blessed Berninis,' said Morley. 'What do we have here, Sefton?' It was a rhetorical question. 'The female as *objet de culte*, if I am not much mistaken.'

'The desecration of the Virgin?' I said.

'Maybe, Sefton. Maybe.'

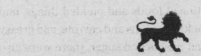

# CHAPTER SIXTEEN

PODGER'S PROVISIONERS – 'Local Produce Procured From Local Providers' – stood in the middle of Blakeney, a veritable sentinel. One village shop, of course, is much like any other, or at least it often appears so from the outside. Outside Podger's were the usual posters claiming that everybody drinks Typhoo, and enjoys Bovril, and smokes Woodbines, and can't resist trying Nescafé Instant Coffee ('Filthy stuff,' said Morley. 'What's wrong with Camp?'). One particularly fetching poster – upon which Morley expatiated at great length, making comparisons with the work of William Blake, Michelangelo and pan-Athenaic amphorae, 'The rhythm and the vigour, Sefton, quite extraordinary!' – showed a grinning, vivid pink pig dragging a cartload of sausages behind him, with, above, the legend, 'Drawing His Own Conclusions'. The window display consisted entirely of half a dozen pyramids of tinned meat accompanied and adorned with packets of Batchelors Peas,'for steeping'.

'They're ziggurats, actually,' said Morley, correcting my pyramid observation, as we stepped inside, to the ting-a-ling of the doorbell.

It was one of those village shops that stocked everything – more general store than grocer's. As well as the usual bacon flitches and shelves of tinned foods and pickled things, and eggs, and sad-looking sacks of onions and carrots, and greasy bins containing flour, and raisins and sugar, there were also displays of bicycle parts, ladies' cosmetics (dozens of eyebrow pencils, I noted), stockings, zip fasteners, collar studs, Brylcreem, alarm clocks, and – half hidden next to a row of either very early or very late Empire Christmas Puddings – a range of contraceptives. And there was of course that characteristic small shop smell: a rich stew of mustiness, mould, tobacco, fish, cats and polish.

A woman stood hunched amid this fragrant *tableau vivant*, behind the long wooden counter, slapping violently at a pat of butter with large patterned paddles. She paused as we entered, quickly wrapped the butter in brown paper on an old cracked bilious yellow oilcloth, tied it with string – which she took from a massive tangle of strings, dangling from a hook, all of which appeared to have been used many times before, washed and hung up to dry – wiped her hands on her apron, glanced at a mirror placed strategically behind the arching wooden display shelves that framed the counter, smoothed her hair, repositioned her glasses, and eventually ready, turned her wide eyes towards us. Or, at least, one of her eyes turned towards us. The other wandered rather.

'Yes?' Her pitiful, pleading expression made me wish we were there only to buy Bisto, some neck of mutton and some socks. Morley, of course, had no such weaknesses or qualms, and got straight to the point.

'Mrs Podger?'

'Yes.'

'We're looking for Ed Dunne.'

'Why? Is he in trouble?'

'No, not at all,' said Morley.

'I told him he needed to be careful. You have to get lights on the bike, I told him. It's the law. He was fined ten shillings the last time, and we can't afford to help out again. It's our deliveries. But it's his bicycle. I told him last time. It's nothing to do with me.'

'It's nothing to do with the bicycle lights, Mrs Podger.'

'Good. You're not the police?'

'No, we're not.'

'There's police everywhere at the moment.'

'I know.'

'We've never had any trouble here before. Nothing. And now there's the reverend, and that woman. And the fire. It's like the end of the world, I said to Mr Podger. The Book of Revelation. It's getting like Cromer. There was a murder in Cromer a few years ago, the body was all cut up, but they never found the man who—'

A man emerged from a back room at this point, hearing Mrs Podger's ramblings. You could see the back room through a yellowing lace-curtained interior window, an office, really, lit by an electric light bulb; the iron safe; the telephone; the ledgers and brochures; the profusion of papers; the Horlicks calendar, 'Against Night Starvation'; the large, loud clock, its pendulum lazily swaying and beating time.

The man wore a tie, glasses, a long white coat of the kind most often worn by butchers, and he was as bald as it is possible to be bald, his head as smooth and as white as a freshly boiled potato. He must have been six foot six: he was not a small man. And he was not a friendly man. He folded his arms and stood, proprietorially, behind a set of brass scales.

'Yes, gentlemen?' He spoke with the same regular plod of the pendulum.

'Mr Podger?'

'Yes.'

'We're looking for Ed Dunne. We were hoping to talk to him about a book we're writing.'

'Are you the writer staying in the hotel?' asked the woman, her hands flapping, either with nerves or excitement, it was difficult to tell.

'Yes, that's correct.'

'We've heard all about you!' she said.

'All good, I trust?' said Morley.

'Well, I heard—' she began.

'Mabel!' said the man. 'That's enough. You need to go and count the seed packets in the office.'

'Now?'

'They won't count themselves, will they?'

Mabel – her hands still flapping – dutifully disappeared.

'Self-counting seed packets, now that would be something, wouldn't it?' said Morley.

'What do you want with Ed?' said Mr Podger.

'We're writing a book about Norfolk, Mr Podger, its character and its characters, and we understand that Ed is a keen craftsman and artist, up at College Farm. And we thought he might be a good person to feature in the book. It would be wonderful for us, and it might be good for him. For his career, I mean.'

'His career?'

'As a craftsman, I mean.'

'I see. And that's all, is it?'

'Yes, that's it.'

'It's nothing to do with the investigation into the reverend's death?'

'No, not at all. Why should it be?'

'I'd heard you were writing for the papers about it.'

'Well, I'm afraid you heard wrong, Mr Podger, sir, with all due respect. I mentioned the sad death of the reverend in one or two of my regular columns, as a matter of public interest, and that was all.'

Mr Podger sniffed. 'I don't like people speaking ill of the reverend.'

'You were perhaps a friend of the reverend, Mr Podger?'

'No.'

'A congregant?'

'No.'

'An acquaintance, then?'

'No.'

'But you had a high opinion of the reverend?'

'He caught my brother once with some partridges. Which he shouldn't have had, by rights. But the reverend didn't let on. He was a good man.'

'That's what I've heard,' said Morley.

Mr Podger looked at us both and seemed to be making some difficult mental calculations. 'You're Swanton Morley, aren't you?'

'Yes, I am. Since birth. That's correct.'

'And who's this?'

'This, sir, is Mr Stephen Sefton, my *homme de confiance*.'

I asked Morley on several occasions during the course of our acquaintance not to use this term, but he persisted.

It almost always got us into trouble. Fortunately, Mr Podger was more interested in Morley than in me.

'I read you in the *Herald*.'

'I am delighted to hear that, Mr Podger. Like you, sir, I need all the customers I can get!'

Mr Podger eyed him closely. 'And you're a man of your word, Swanton Morley? As you make yourself out to be?'

'I am that, sir.'

'So you'll not be asking him about the reverend and his housekeeper?'

'I give you my word, Mr Podger, that I shall not.'

'He's been very upset by it all, you see. He's a very sensitive type, Ed.'

'I quite understand. Would we be able to speak to Mr Dunne, do you think?'

Mr Podger thought about it for a time.

'It'll be good for his career?'

'Exposure, Mr Podger. Advertising. As you know yourself, it all helps.'

'He's down in the storeroom. You can come through here.'

He lifted up the counter, led us through the office, and down some winding steps into an airless, humid underground store, which was lit by a dirty, splotchy bulb, under which Ed Dunne was sitting in complete silence, on one of the big fifty-six-pound butter crates, staring, entirely absorbed, at the pages of a magazine – *Titbits*. He looked as though he might have been sitting there, reading it, for all eternity. Tall, loaded shelves loomed all around in the darkness.

He leapt up as we approached. I thought for one moment

that he might even salute. He was no more than eighteen years old. Underneath his apron he wore a strenuously neat little tie, and a high white collar and a waistcoat, which along with his smooth, centre-parted hair and his full, keen, innocent lips and staring eyes, lent him rather the appearance of the silent comedian Harold Lloyd.

'Mr Podger, sir. Sorry, I was just waiting for the delivery, sir.'

'People to see you, Ed.'

'To see me? If it's about the bicycle, I'm definitely going to get lights as—'

'It's not about the bicycle lights,' said Mr Podger. 'It's Swanton Morley. The People's Professor. He's writing a book. He wants to talk to you.'

'Swanton Morley? *Morley's Thousand Wonderful Things*?'

'That is one of mine, yes,' said Morley, reaching out his hand.

'And *The Children's Little Paper*, and *The Wonder Encyclopaedia*, and *The Treasure House of Wisdom*?'

'Yes. I can lay claim to those also. Pleased to meet you, Mr Dunne. This is my assistant, Stephen Sefton.'

'Why do you want to talk to me, Mr Morley?'

Mabel called from upstairs.

'I'll leave you to it,' said Mr Podger. 'We've a delivery due, Mr Morley. It's already late, and we'll need Ed as soon as it arrives.'

'Of course. We won't be long.'

Mr Podger disappeared up the stairs and back into the shop.

'Who's the cricketer?' said Morley. 'What's his name?'

'Sorry, Mr Morley?' said Ed.

'Australian? Partnered with Woodfull and Bradman.'

'Erm . . .'

'You know, Sefton. Big beefy chap. With the bat . . . Big Bertha. Knocking the balls about. Didn't Mr Podger strike you as an absolute dead ringer?'

Ed was too busy fussing around, dragging over some empty barrels for us to sit on, to take any notice.

'Mr Morley, and Mr . . .'

'Sefton,' I reminded him.

'I'm . . . Sorry. Would you like some tea, gentlemen?'

'Thank you, yes, please.'

He produced three mugs – enamel mugs, stained with age – and poured dark black tea into them from a filthy kettle set on a stove in the corner. He then added spoonfuls of condensed milk from a large tin.

'Cheese?' he said.

'Cheese?' said Morley.

'To go with the tea. I haven't got anything else, I'm afraid. Mr Podger doesn't let me . . . With the mice, you see. Crumbs. You have to be careful.'

'Not for me, thank you,' I said.

'What cheese do you have?' asked Morley.

'Mr Podger lets me have the old toasting cheese for the mousetraps.'

'That's very generous of him, I'm sure. But I think perhaps I'll pass, thank you all the same.'

Ed took a small lump of what looked like solid marble from an old jar of Julysia hair tonic, and popped it in his mouth.

'Now, Ed,' said Morley, 'I wonder if we could ask you a few questions about—'

But at that moment a yell came from up above, a doorway banged open in the ceiling of the basement, and suddenly parcels and barrels and crates came hurtling down a long greasy plank set against the far wall. It was like some infernal mouth had opened and started retching down into the dark.

'Damn!' said Ed. 'Excuse me. I'm afraid I'll have to ... Sorry, Mr Morley, and Mr Sefton ...' And he ran over and started pulling the parcels hither and thither.

'Need a hand?' offered Morley, taking off his jacket, folding it neatly, and instructing me to do the same. Ed, quite rightly, refused our assistance, but Morley insisted, and then Ed refused again, and Morley insisted again, and before I knew it we were hauling goods into piles, with Ed acting as foreman. 'Tobacco here, Mr Morley! Milk powder here! No, here! Tinned pears! Mixed tinned fruits – all tinned fruits here, gentlemen! Huntley and Palmers! Liver salt! Liver salt, here!'

'Purifies and Invigorates!' called Morley, who was a great one for mucking in and who was therefore enjoying himself enormously, and who also, alas, knew the advertising slogan and ditty associated with every brand of goods that came forever tumbling down the plank. Brooke Bond Tea: 'Spend Wisely, Save Wisely!' called Morley, in antiphonal response. Cadbury's Cocoa Essence, up went the cry, 'Absolutely Pure!' Camp Coffee: 'Drink Camp, It's the Best!' After half an hour of this frantic exercise, and Morley's accompanying din, the torrent of parcels and packages suddenly ceased. Morley and I sat down for a moment, while Ed continued to move boxes and packages into their correct positions.

'Underground stevedores, eh?' said Morley. 'That was rather fun, Mr Dunne.'

Ed chuckled, out of genuine amusement, it seemed, rather than politeness while I, on the other hand, remained silent and began to light a restorative cigarette.

'We can't smoke in here,' said Ed. 'Mr Podger doesn't let me.'

'Put it away, Sefton,' said Morley. 'Now, Mr Dunne. I wonder if you could tell us about College Farm?'

'Why? What do you want to know?'

'We're writing a book, you see, as Mr Podger explained, and we're interested in what goes on there.'

'What do you mean, what goes on?'

'I mean, life in an artistic community.'

'I only use a studio at the weekends,' said Dunne, reaching boxes up onto high shelves. 'On Sundays, usually. Sometimes in the evenings, if I'm not working.'

'I see. And is that where you met Hannah?'

'Yes,' said Ed unguardedly.

I glanced quickly at Morley. He was indeed a man quite thoroughly of his word, and he had promised Mr Podger that he would only be asking Ed about his work. So I wondered how he might proceed. He proceeded in the only way available to him.

'My colleague, Mr Sefton, would like to ask you about her,' he said.

I cleared my throat. 'You knew Hannah,' I began.

I, of course, had barely known her, and yet . . . The mention of her made me think of her supple wrists. And her ash-blonde hair. And her mouth on mine. Her breasts pressing tight against me, up against the cold bare flint walls of the church. It was all there lodged in my mind, with everything else: the torsos that were parted from their limbs in my bloodiest of dreams; the visions of Spanish battlefields; cripples on donkeys riding across the landscape; everything in red. As I glanced at Ed I thought perhaps he could see it there too.

'Sefton? Everything all right, Sefton?'

'Yes, everything's fine, Mr Morley. I'm not sure what—'

'Was Mr Chancellor painting her?' asked Morley.

'Yes, he was, sir.'

'And were you jealous?'

'Yes. I was.'

'That's OK, Ed.'

'He shouldn't have been doing it.'

'He shouldn't have been painting her?'

'Yes. And what else they were doing.' Ed did not say anything more. He stared down at the floor.

'What else were they doing, Ed?' persisted Morley.

'She shouldn't have been doing it!'

'What was it?'

'He drove her to it!'

'Who?'

'I'm not going to say!' said Ed. 'I told her I wouldn't!'

Instantly, as Ed's voice was raised, there was a corresponding noise at the top of the stairs. The door to the office banged open, and then shut, and in the half-light I could see the vast outline of Mr Podger, his bald head shining, and in his hands what appeared – and which did indeed transpire – to be a large, home-made cricket bat.

'Ah, Mr Podger,' said Morley, unperturbed. 'We were just asking Ed here—'

'Get out!' yelled Podger. 'You promised me, Morley! Get out of my shop! Do you hear?'

Morley picked up his jacket, as I did mine.

'You seem to be blocking the doorway, actually,' said Morley, not unreasonably, but this proved to be the proverbial red rag to the proverbial raging bull and the final boiling point of Mr Podger's ever-simmering temper.

We both darted across the storeroom as Mr Podger lunged down the stairs, Morley reaching the long, slippery delivery plank before me and beginning to scramble up it towards the light. I made it up onto the bottom of the plank as Mr Podger came bellowing across the room, heaving the cricket bat above his head, with what appeared to be every intention of shattering both my legs. Grabbing both sides of the plank, I braced myself for the moment of contact. Which never came, Ed having reached Podger before me and with the end of a broom handle having restrained his swing, much as a ringmaster might hold off a lion from devouring his keeper. Podger roared. Ed turned quickly to me and nodded for me to make my escape. Which I gratefully did.

∽ ∼

'Are you always at the heel of the hunt?' said Morley, as I caught up with him, striding towards the hotel, and then added, 'W.H. Ponsford.'

'What?'

'That was the name of the chap.'

'Who?'

'Who partnered Woodfull and Bradman. The manner of his swing there, that reminded me ...'

'Well, we were lucky Podger didn't hit us for six there.'

'He was harmless.'

'He might have killed us!'

'Hardly. He wasn't going to touch us. He just wanted to get rid of us. Sometimes you have to tread on a tiger's tail to get what you want, Sefton.'

'Is that right?'

'Yes. Now, finally, we're getting somewhere, Sefton, eh!' he said as we ran towards the hotel.

# CHAPTER SEVENTEEN

'WHAT EXACTLY is a sherry party?' asked Morley. 'I've often wondered.'

'It's like a cocktail party, Mr Morley. Only on good behaviour.'

'Ah. Yes. So I feared.'

We had received our invitation on our return to the Blakeney Hotel. I had to persuade Morley to agree to attend, he was beginning to fret so terribly over the continuing delay to our timetable. We should, according to Morley's plan, have visited most of the churches of Norfolk by now, and investigated its major industries, visited all other places of cultural and historical interest, written up our notes, and been preparing to leave for our next county. Instead, we were stranded in a quayside village in the middle of nowhere, and Morley was becoming restless – a terrible danger, like the dog without its bone, or a man without meaningful work. Morley had to be – as he himself might relate it – *in mobile perpetuum*. If he wasn't, he grew first irritable, and then angry, and then, curiously, utterly listless, like a man falling into a trance or a coma. He was, at this stage in his perpetual cycle, becoming so restless that it was all I could do to talk him down from a plan to start producing our own evening expedition newspaper, based on the model of Scott's *South Polar Times* ('All we need is a printing press,' he claimed. 'Miriam could bring us something up from London, I'm sure'). To distract him, I had taken to playing speed chess with him, but things had got so bad, and he won so consistently, without joy or pleasure, that he was now threatening to get out his knitting – another one of those hobbies that, during our years together, was the cause both of much amusement and much trouble. (He was apt to launch into demonstrations and explanations of the craft – which had been taught to him by the menfolk of Taquile Island on Lake Titicaca, he said – at the most inappropriate of moments. The story of Morley, the dead baby and the mystery of the knitted shawl is perhaps not as widely known to the general public as some other episodes; I shall relate it at another time.) Frankly, the sherry party seemed like a welcome alternative to an evening discussing the history of Peruvian woolly hats.

'But I cannot abide parties, Sefton,' he protested.

'But this is only a sherry party, Mr Morley.'

'Sherry party. Cocktail party. Card party. Shooting party. House party. Musical party. *Salon. Cénacle. Soirée* . . . Same region, soil and clime, Sefton. Waste and wild, the lot of them. Waste and wild.' He sighed a grand, Miltonic sigh. 'And as for the timetable . . . It's slipping, Sefton. We're drifting dangerously off course. We must keep to the timetable.' Panicked and agitated, he could sound worryingly like Ismay on the *Titanic*. 'I don't know if I can get us back, Sefton. It may not be possible.'

Given how far we were now off course, I managed to persuade him that a sherry party would hardly prove disastrous and that, besides, it might give us an opportunity to find out more about the unfortunate death of the reverend, which of course remained the cause of our spirit-sapping detention.

∽ ∾

And so we found ourselves, on a balmy summer's evening, at the Thistle-Smiths', a rather bleak eighteenth-century house on the edge of Blakeney village, set about with mournful, desolate-looking laburnum hedging but stuffed inside both with lively guests and with Mrs Thistle-Smith's extraordinary bonsai collection, displayed in Ming bowls set on tables, shelves and plinths in the entrance hall to the house, and which gave the impression of one entering an enchanted forest inhabited by gibbering giants.

'Imitation Ming bowls, actually,' Morley later corrected me. 'For what I think might be more accurately described not as an "extraordinary" collection – for what, one wonders, might a merely "ordinary" collection of bonsai be, eh? – but rather as a *plethoric* collection of bonsai. Hmm? Plethoric, somnolent bonsai, one might say, if one needed the extra adjective, Sefton.'

In attendance, in addition to the plethoric somnolent bonsai, were the Grices, the Chapmans, the Wells, and many other north Norfolk worthies and dignitaries whose names escaped me.

'Everyone is here!' proclaimed Mrs Thistle-Smith on our arrival, meaning, presumably, everyone in the village with an income, earned or unearned, above about ten pounds per week: a sherry party in north Norfolk being most definitely not a place for the common man. One might as well have been in Mayfair, the only difference being that the rich in the remoter corners of England seem uniquely and peculiarly unburdened when compared to their city counterparts, as though permanently on holiday, the men utterly self-satisfied and comfortable in their moth-eaten, third-generation tweeds, and the women thoroughly relaxed about both their mothballed appearance and their antique charms, though with the exception, I should say, of Mrs Thistle-Smith herself, who was a rather determinedly glamorous, made-up sort of lady, who would not have been out of place as a hostess at one of Miriam's parties down in London, and who was doggedly hanging on both to blonde hair and to fashionable clothes, and who clearly had no intention of allowing her young mob-capped and aproned maids to steal any of her sherry party limelight. Mrs Thistle-Smith was one of those older women who possess – and who are clearly not unaware of possessing – what one might call full candlepower presence, her welcoming smile, her voice, her manner and her powerful wreath of perfume acting like the rays of the sun shining down upon one. One had the feeling with Mrs Thistle-Smith that she had just conjured you into life on her doorstep, and that any previous existence had been merely a kind of limbo, waiting to be summoned forth into her life-giving light. I'm afraid I found her scintillations rather off-putting, but was nonetheless delighted to be able to accept the proffered glass of oloroso, and the promise of an evening's conversation unrelated to cross-stitch, needles and thread.

'Remember, sherry is not a cordial, Sefton,' said Morley, peering at me disapprovingly over his moustache.

'Now, Mr Morley, what can I get you, a dry fino or a sweet amontillado?' said Mrs Thistle-Smith in her finest silk-and-cashmere tones. She quickly and gently brushed a hand against Morley's arm as she spoke, establishing contact. I thought I saw Morley jerk away slightly as she did so. It was not an auspicious start.

'I'll have a glass of water, madam, if I may?'

'Water? Really? Are you not well?'

'No, not well, madam. That's right.' Morley seemed uncharacteristically guarded.

'If you're sure? You wouldn't rather something else? A cocktail, perhaps?'

'No, thank you. Not a cocktail.'

'I know that Mr Thistle-Smith has a nice Cockburn '96 reserved for himself, but I could get one of the girls to fetch it.'

'No. That won't be necessary, madam. Water would be my preferred choice.' His tone was disapproving.

'*Ariston men hudor*,' said Mrs Thistle-Smith.

'Indeed,' agreed Morley. I detected an instant thawing of tone. He loved a Latin – or indeed a Greek – tag. And, as it turned out, he loved a woman who loved a Latin – or indeed a Greek – tag.

'Well, I for one am in complete agreement with you, Mr Morley. There is surely nothing better for man than the taste of water.'

'Exactly,' said Morley, who seemed suddenly to be flushing under Mrs Thistle-Smith's warming attentions. 'I couldn't agree more.'

'I have a great love of water,' said Mrs Thistle-Smith, sherry glass in hand. 'Fountains, springs, mountain pools. So refreshing. So joyous.'

A maid was duly dispatched for water, and we were shown through the house into the garden room, passing on the way a vast excess of paintings, furniture and ornaments which had somehow been hoisted, yanked and crammed into every nook and cranny. One room we passed was filled almost entirely with chairs, huddled together like sheep in a pen – Chippendales and Hepplewhites, Charles the Second chairs with straight backs, little duets and trios and quartets of Victorian slipper chairs, every conceivable type of chair. It really was the most peculiar sight: the house as a storeroom rather than a home. I had recently read F. Scott Fitzgerald's short novel *The Great Gatsby*: the house struck me as the Norfolk equivalent of a West Egg mansion. I mentioned this later to Morley. 'Wrong,' he said. 'East Egg, you mean. Not West Egg. Do pay attention in your reading, Sefton.'

'Are you or Mr Thistle-Smith a collector, perhaps, madam?' asked Morley.

'I am, Mr Morley, for my sins. I don't know what Herr Freud would say about it.'

This seemed further to arouse Morley's interest, his interest already having been well and truly piqued, truth be told, by Mrs Thistle-Smith's welcoming balm. She might as well have revealed that her real name was Flaubert or Turgenev.

'If you don't mind my saying so,' he said, 'the name of Sigmund Freud is not one that one would expect to hear from the lips of the average Norfolk hostess.'

Mrs Thistle-Smith raised a well-tended eyebrow in response and pursed her carefully lipsticked lips.

'Then – if you don't mind me saying so – you can perhaps assume, Mr Morley, that these are not the lips of an average Norfolk hostess.'

'Indeed.'

And so ineffable charm met endless curiosity, and seemed to find each other quite fascinating. The two of them proceeded to spend some time discussing the finer points of collecting and psychoanalysis.

I made my excuses, took another glass of sherry, and mingled.

Small tables had been arrayed around the garden room, without chairs, intended presumably to suggest that one might move casually and informally among one's fellow guests, but suggesting also, alas, the odd, uncertain appearance of a railway station waiting room. The combination of faded velvet brocade, the cool tiles, the golden, misty light of the early evening, and the vague promise of less than fresh viands, reminded me also of a brothel I had visited in Barcelona.

There was the chattering murmur of voices, there were men and women of Dickensian features, there were fanciful flowers displayed in fine porcelain vases, and there were canapés. After one or two more glasses of sherry and a polite conversation with a woman who insisted on telling me about her love for the work of E. Nesbit, I realised that I was hungry, having subsisted largely, despite Morley's deprecations on breakfast, on cigarettes and coffee. Maids were circulating with small plates of food, and I excused myself from my interlocutor and homed in on the nearest tray. Quail's eggs. I was disappointed, the peeling of quail's eggs being a task, I find, requiring efforts much greater than the

*Thomas Thistle-Smith*

rewards, which are both insubstantial and less nourishing even than a railway sandwich.

'I'll do it for you, mister.' A boy in a blue velvet suit had appeared at my elbow. He held out his hand. He was probably no more than twelve or thirteen years old; there was, on his lip, the faintest hint of an incipient moustache, and his voice wobbled on the very furthest, most querulous edge of the soprano. He had thick, dark hair that hung down to his shoulders.

'You'll peel the egg?'

'Yes, sir, I will, sir. I'm an expert, sir.' His face and his manner were, all at once, open, bold, mild and teasing – as though I were merely an entertaining discovery, and he knew well in advance the outcome of our exchange.

'You're a quail-egg-peeling expert?' I asked.

'Yes, sir. That's right, sir.'

'Employed especially for the evening?'

'By my mother, sir. Yes, sir.'

I glanced around but could see no obvious hovering maternal presence. 'Is your mother the cook?'

'No, sir. My mother is the lady of the house, sir.'

'Mrs Thistle-Smith?' I was surprised. Mrs Thistle-Smith seemed a lady long since past her child-rearing years.

'Indeed, sir. I am Thomas Thistle-Smith, sir.' He shook my hand, one eye still firmly on the quail's egg. 'My friends call me Teetees, sir.'

'Teetees?'

'Yes, sir. And my mother always allows me to assist at her parties, sir, if I'm home from school. I'm not allowed to eat them. Only to peel them. I'm a champion quail-egg peeler, sir.'

'Are you, indeed?'

'Yes, sir. If you'd like, sir, I'll challenge you.'

'Challenge me?'

'If you can peel a quail's egg quicker than me I'll give you a shilling, sir.'

'A shilling? And I suppose if you can peel an egg quicker I give you a—'

'Shilling. That's correct, sir.'

'Very well, then.'

I held my quail's egg at the ready. The boy took a quail's egg from a dish.

'Ready,' he said. I braced myself. 'Steady. Go!'

I started fumbling with the blasted thing, but only a second later the boy held his peeled egg aloft, triumphant.

'That's incredible,' I said, for incredible indeed it was.

'Practice makes perfect, sir.'

He held it – tiny, bald, rather grey-looking – out towards me. It looked sad and old rather than shiny and new. I detected hints of pocket lint. I suspected foul play and sleight-of-hand.

'That'll be a shilling then please, sir.'

'A shilling!'

'Yes, sir. It goes towards my school fees, sir.'

'Your school fees? You need to peel a lot of quail's eggs to cover your school fees.'

'Just for the incidentals, sir. There are always incidentals.'

'I'm sure there are.'

I handed over sixpence. He handed over the peeled egg. He looked at the coin. I ate the egg.

'Hold on,' said Teetees, too late. 'This is only a sixpence.'

'Correct,' I said. 'And this is not a freshly peeled egg, is it?'

'Of course it is!'

'Really?'

The boy had exhausted my patience. I was hungry. I had drunk several glasses of sherry, and I had the prospect of a long evening ahead with Morley. I reached forward and forcefully patted the pocket of his blue velvet jacket – and sure enough there came the answering sensation of a handful of tiny pre-peeled eggs squashing together.

'Hey!' he said. 'Hey! They're my eggs!'

'Goodbye,' I said.

He scowled at me, and I scowled back, and he disappeared into the crowd, ready to pester others with his pre-pubescent upper-class begging.

Morley, meanwhile, had been temporarily abandoned by Mrs Thistle-Smith, who was now busy elsewhere in scintillating sherry-party conversation, and he had sought out, or been found by Dr Sharp, who had attended the body of the reverend on our first night in Blakeney. Their voices could be heard faintly over the hubbub, and I felt the distant twitching of Morley's moustache, always a sign of great danger. I hurried over.

'The answer, Morley, if you would care to listen, is birth control,' the doctor was saying. It looked as though I was too late. 'As you know, nature exercises a certain amount of control by effectively sterilising the alcoholic and the diseased, and I am simply saying that there is no good reason why we shouldn't augment her role and prevent some other types of unsuitable breeding. It's hardly unreasonable, man.'

'It's eugenics,' said Morley.

'It's birth control,' said the doctor flatly.

'And who is it who controls the births? Doctors like yourself, presumably?'

'I can think of no others better suited, Mr Morley. Can you? And certainly if individuals are incapable or unwilling to make the right decision—'

'Sorry, doctor. Forgive me. Incapable or unwilling in precisely what sense?'

'Precisely through background, or education or—'

'Race?' said Morley.

'Potentially, yes,' said the doctor.

'Mr Morley?' I said, alerting him to my presence.

'Ah, there. You see, Sefton?' He had – as was his habit – instantly recruited me onto his side of the argument. 'A rather troubling suggestion, wouldn't you agree, doctor?'

'I don't see why,' said the doctor.

'Well, try telling the Aga Khan he can't have any more children, doctor. Eh? Or the Emperor of Nepal. Or the tribal chiefs of Rhodesia and Nyasaland. Or the rabbi of—'

'That is clearly not what I meant, Mr Morley, and I have to say that I am rather disappointed by your failure to take my argument seriously.'

'I'm taking your argument very seriously, doctor.'

'Mr Morley?' I said again, to no avail.

'Good,' said the doctor. 'So you'll understand that I am talking about individuals who cannot provide or account for the consequences of their actions.'

'And you can provide and account for the consequences of all your actions, doctor?'

'I certainly expect no one else to bear the consequences. And I hardly see why we as a nation should bear the responsibility for those born without the capacity to progress or succeed in life.'

I glanced at Morley's face. He looked utterly disgusted, as though having eaten half a dozen rotten quail's eggs.

'I would have thought, doctor,' he said, 'that was an argument beneath the dignity of a man like yourself. But clearly I was wrong.'

The doctor's face reddened. 'I don't see what's wrong with it,' he said.

'Which is precisely what's troubling,' said Morley. 'It is the beginning of the slippery slope, sir.'

'Towards?'

'A deep world of darkness, doctor. A place I would rather we did not go, but where I fear we are plunging headlong.' Morley took a sip of his water to fortify himself. 'What of the mentally unstable in your scheme, doctor? Or, shall we say, the merely psychologically *quirky*? The mentally or physically kinked and twisted. Have them all neutered, should we?'

'Not necessarily,' said the doctor.

'Not necessarily, Sefton, eh? Did you hear that? Very generous of him, isn't it?' He was becoming uncontrollably roused. I had seen the signs before.

'Mr Morley,' I said again. 'Sir, I think we—'

'The epileptic, I take it, you think should automatically be kept from breeding?'

'No. Not necessarily,' said the doctor. 'Certainly not. But possibly, under certain circumstances, yes.'

'And so what of Milton?' said Morley. 'And of Keats?'

'There would be exceptions, Mr Morley.'

'And you would be able to identify these exceptions, *in*

*vitro*? The good epileptic from the bad? The foetus capable of progressing and succeeding in life from the inevitable failure? The wheat and the chaff separated in the belly of a woman? The sheep from the goats, in the womb? It's outrageous, frankly, doctor. Absolutely and utterly—'

'Mr Morley,' I said. 'I think—'

'Again, I'm afraid you've misunderstood my argument, Mr Morley, and twisted it, and taken it too far.'

'The only place to take an argument, surely,' said Morley. I had a hold of his elbow by this stage, and was attempting gently to tug him away. But he was standing firm. 'To test its eventual outcome? It's called the Socratic method, sir, and I would have thought a man of your background might have encountered it during the course of your long and privileged education.'

'Mr Morley! Sir!' I interjected as loudly as I could without disturbing the other guests, though noting that already those around us had begun to take notice of the kerfuffle.

'And what about homosexuals?' continued Morley, horribly. 'Dock their tails too, should we? Hmm?'

The doctor blushed red to the roots of his Brylcreemed hair.

'Hmm?' continued Morley, rather cruelly, I thought, but clearly to the point. '*Medice, cura te ipsum!*'

The doctor had turned away, and I steered Morley fast into what I thought might be calmer waters over by the windows to the garden. Alas, I miscalculated. A schoolmaster, a perfectly agreeable man named Ellison, with a wide, pleasant smile, and the innocent face of a child, introduced himself to us. He was the wrong person in the wrong place at the wrong time.

'A friend of mine attended one of your lectures in London,' he said warmly, after the introductions. 'They said it was *most* entertaining.'

'That's nice, isn't it?' I said, hoping to calm Morley.

'Schoolmaster are you, eh?'

'That's right,' said the poor unwitting, grinning Ellison.

'And would you agree with me then, sir, that the entire problem with our system of education is the problem of our public schools?'

'I'm sorry?'

'No need to be sorry, young man. Where do you teach?'

The teacher mentioned a prep school nearby of high reputation, and even higher prices.

'I see. As you may or may not know, sir, I have spent most of my working life doing my best to offer some skimpy education to those less fortunate than your pupils, those who some among us indeed' – he pointed at the distant figure of the doctor, who was refreshing himself with sherry and cake – 'believe are incapable of progressing or succeeding in life.'

'Yes, Mr Morley, I know your—'

'And it is my belief, in fact, that our public schools are responsible not only – *not only* – for the dulling and stultifying of the young minds with which they are entrusted, doing nothing more than repressing the intellect and the imagination with their pathetic idolatory of athletics and rugby, but are responsible also for the perpetuation of inequalities of opportunity in this country of which we should all be rightly ashamed. Am I right, do you think, in my assessment of the state of our education system?'

'Well, sir . . . I don't know.'

The schoolmaster looked at me, bewildered, evidently

unsure whether he should mount a sturdy defence of his profession. The situation clearly called for decisive action. By chance I was able to grab hold of Mrs Thistle-Smith as she circulated past.

'Mr Morley,' I said, 'was wondering if he might take a look at your garden, Mrs Thistle-Smith?'

'But of course,' she said, sweeping Morley away from me. 'Let's go together, Mr Morley.'

I breathed a sigh of relief, apologised to the poor schoolmaster, and followed Morley and Mrs Thistle-Smith at a discreet distance.

I needed fresh air. Morley needed calming.

The plan worked. Straight away, Mrs Thistle-Smith engaged Morley in hushed conversation. There was the sound of bubbling water in the stream down past the croquet lawn. The evening sun flecked the lawn with emerald greens. The sky was cloudless. I stood by the house, smoking, as they wandered slowly along the borders of the garden. I couldn't make out everything that was said, though snatches drifted towards me.

'. . . and that is a Carmine Pillar I'm growing on the old apple tree . . . a thornless pink Zephirine Drouhin . . . the Japanese Rugosa Single Pink . . . ten feet high.'

'You have a talent,' I think I heard Morley say. Something something something . . . 'Very special.'

It was refreshing, I think she said, to find a man who appreciates . . . something. A garden?

'Sometimes I think my husband would hardly notice . . .' Unintelligible . . . Something.

I watched from a distance as Mrs Thistle-Smith went to light a cigarette. Her match blew out. She went to light it again. I saw Morley move to light it; he kept matches about his person at all times, in case of emergency. As she held up her cigarette to her lips I thought I saw a slight ring of bruising around her wrist, but I may have been imagining it – the distance, the play of light and shade.

'Thank you, Mr Morley, that's . . .' I think she said gallant. Mrs Thistle-Smith drew deeply on her cigarette and they turned slowly and began making their way back towards the house. 'You don't smoke?'

Morley seemed to agree that he did not.

'Which makes your gesture all the more generous.'

'Smoking is . . . a habit I have never acquired,' said Morley, rather disingenuously, I felt, since he was one of the country's leading anti-tobacco campaigners.

'It's a habit that I'm afraid has completely defeated me,' said Mrs Thistle-Smith. 'But they do say it's good for the figure.' She ran her hands lightly over her dress, pausing slightly and turning towards Morley. It was, as Morley himself might have observed – purely from a psychological and anthropological point of view, of course – a signal. From a distance – and it is of course difficult to judge these things from a distance, and it may be that I am interpreting events long ago with the unreliable aid of imagination, but nonetheless – these seemed like the first tentative steps in a complex and dangerous dance.

I feared for a moment for Morley's rectitude and resolved to follow them if they turned and ventured any further away from the house and into the garden. But Mrs Thistle-Smith had clearly not entirely forgotten her duties as hostess, and they continued to retrace their steps towards the house. As they did so they paused for a moment at a clump of flowers

– dictamnus, Morley later told me. And as they stood close together, studying the plant, Morley produced his matches, struck one, held it above the seedheads, which stood out in the evening light like little unhatched eggs, and there was a tiny flash of flames. Oils igniting, Morley later explained. Mrs Thistle-Smith was delighted by this display, and leaned in close to Morley in the flare, holding his arm for a moment. And this time Morley did not flinch in response. They stayed still for a moment.

As they approached the house I could hear Morley quoting Yeats.

"'I will arise and go now, and go to Innisfree, / And a small cabin build there, of clay and wattles made; / Nine bean rows will I have there, a hive for the honey bee, / And live alone in the bee-loud glade.'"

This apparently thrilled Mrs Thistle-Smith even further, who seemed as enchanted by Morley as he clearly was by her. They both spotted me as they drew close. I ground out my cigarette.

'Mr Sefton! We were just talking gardening,' she said. 'It's so lovely to have a man around who appreciates a garden.'

'I'm sure,' I said.

'I used to be able to talk to the reverend, of course,' said Mrs Thistle-Smith. 'Though he was rather keen on heather.'

'Best for grouse, I always think, heather,' said Morley.

'Oh, my point entirely, Mr Morley!' She touched his arm gently again with the back of her hand. 'And so dull! I have a taste for the exotics myself. I have a banana plant down in the walled garden which is doing terribly well. Perhaps you'd like to come and see it sometime?'

'Banana plant! I'd like that very much, Mrs Thistle-Smith,' said Morley. 'Do you specialise in the sub-tropicals?'

'I wish!' she said. 'I think my garden might only ever be remembered for its borders. We are so blessed with our borders here, fifty yards apiece.'

'Really?'

'Yes. Not quite Gertrude Jekyll, but not far off. My mother planted them. We used to play among them when we were children, all of us. Running up and down. Racing, my sisters and my brother. Entirely without a care . . . I adore Gertrude Jekyll. Do you know her, Mr Morley?'

'I know of her work, Mrs Thistle-Smith.'

'Such wonderful ideas!'

'Indeed.'

'You know Gertrude Jeykll, young man?' Mrs Thistle-Smith addressed herself to me, pretending at least that she was interested in my opinion.

'I can't say I do—'

She then turned her attentions straight back to Morley. 'But tell me, Mr Morley, what is your philosophy of gardening?'

'I would not presume to possess such a thing, madam.'

'But you must! I'm sure you do! You are, after all, renowned for your ideas, Mr Morley.'

'In all honesty, Mrs Thistle-Smith,' said Morley, taking a small sigh, and gazing round at the beautiful garden before him, 'I think all a garden really needs are a few magnolias in spring, some red-hot pokers in the summer, and an apple tree to be picked in the autumn. What matters is not so much the garden, but the touch, the care and the vision of the gardener.'

'Ah yes, Mr Morley! How true.' Then she turned and glanced – sadly, I thought – into the garden room, and remembered her responsibilities. 'Now, you really must come and meet my husband.'

'We have met, madam.'

'Yes, of course . . . I should warn you, he can be very . . . forthright in his opinions. He's from Grantham, you see.'

'And nothing good ever came from Grantham?'

'Some things, Mr Morley, I'm sure. But my husband has a healthy collection of *bêtes noires*. And I'm afraid newspaper journalists are one of them.'

'I would be honoured either to confirm or confound his prejudices, madam.'

'I'm sure you will,' she said. 'And then I'll introduce you to the Talbots. Tom is an expert on the flora of the Middle East . . .'

By the doors leading into the garden the professor, in a black velveteen coat, was holding court like a great invalid king, seated on what appeared at first to be a gleaming throne, but which was, in fact, and quite simply, the only chair in the room – 'A *fauteuil*,' Morley later remarked, 'French, possibly, eighteenth century, far too showy' – lit from behind by the evening sun. He had his creamy white panama hat in his lap, like a Persian cat fed too many Yarmouth bloaters for breakfast, and a decanter of sherry on a viciously pie-crust-edged occasional table at his elbow, from which he repeatedly refreshed his glass. Mrs Thistle-Smith led Morley towards him, with me silently in their wake. As the professor turned and saw them approaching I noted the threatening look in his eyes – a very threatening look indeed. The look of a tyrant at a messenger bringing bad news. This was where our evening decidedly took a turn for the worse.

'Darling,' said Mrs Thistle-Smith, gently touching her husband's arm, 'this is Mr Morley, he's staying at the Blakeney Hotel.'

'An honour to meet you again, sir,' said Morley. 'It's a lovely home you have here.'

'An Englishman's home,' replied Mr Thistle-Smith, in his slow, damp voice, that seemed to leak with rancour as his wife's burned with light.

'And an Englishwoman's,' said Morley, rather gallantly, I thought, nodding towards Mrs Thistle-Smith, who smiled in friendly acknowledgement.

'Swanton Morley,' said Professor Thistle-Smith. 'The man who's putting our humble little village on the map.'

'I can hardly lay claim to that distinction, sir.'

'Oh, I think you can, sir. I think you can. *Daily Herald*. Tell me, Morley, do you regard journalism as a trade, or as a profession?'

'I would hardly think it deserved the honour of being regarded as a profession, Mr Thistle-Smith.'

'So, a trade, then.'

'I suppose so.'

'I see. And do you not think we have a tradesman's entrance at this house, sir? Or do you suppose that we welcome our butchers and delivery boys here at all our parties?'

'Darling!' said Mrs Thistle-Smith. 'Mr Morley is our guest. We invited him, remember?'

'You invited him,' said Mr Thistle-Smith.

'I invited everyone!' Mrs Thistle-Smith laughed, trying to make the best of what was already far beyond an awkward situation and was fast becoming a crisis. The little sherry-quaffing crowd around Morley and the professor was growing.

'Anyway,' said Mr Thistle-Smith, his voice dropping even lower, from bass to basso profundo, 'seeing as you're here, Morley, under whatever auspices, can I perhaps ask about your politics?'

'You may, of course, sir, although I might reserve the right to remain silent.'

'Darling, let's not talk about politics,' Mrs Thistle-Smith pleaded with her husband. She was playing nervously with the string of pearls around her neck. 'We agreed.'

Mr Thistle-Smith ignored her.

'You're a Labour man, I take it?' he continued.

'What made you think that, Mr Thistle-Smith?'

'Cut of your jib, Morley.'

'A phrase that derives,' said Morley, pleasantly, blithely, in characteristic explanatory mode, 'if I'm not mistaken, from the triangular sail on a—'

'I know what a bloody jib is, man! I'm not one of your readers in the *Daily Muck*.'

'Darling!' said Mrs Thistle-Smith, as now even more guests began to gather round the two men in anticipation of what was already becoming a bloody battle. Morley seemed oblivious.

'Well, I'll grant you then, I am a Labour man,' said Morley.

'Thought so.' Mr Thistle-Smith sniffed and wrinkled his nose, as if suddenly detecting the unmistakable stench of a working man. 'We don't get many Labour men round here, Morley.'

'I'm sorry to hear that.'

'I'm not.' Mr Thistle-Smith drew great stentorian breaths, as though emerging from deep water. 'And if you don't mind my saying, your first Labour government was a disaster. Except that taxis were allowed in Hyde Park.' A couple of men in the crowd laughed, though why I wasn't sure. 'Which was of some benefit to those of us with . . . business in London.' He looked cruelly towards Mrs Thistle-Smith, whose brightness and stature seemed to be diminishing by the second.

'I see,' said Morley. 'And perhaps I can ask you about your politics, Mr Thistle-Smith? Would you mind?'

'Why would I mind, sir? It's a free country. At least at the moment it is. I am a Tory, born and bred, since you ask, and one of the silent majority proud still to believe in God, King and country.'

'Though I think recent events perhaps suggest that we shouldn't put our faith entirely in the British monarchy,' said Morley teasingly. It was his way. I put my hands over my eyes.

Professor Thistle-Smith was, predictably, appalled.

'Steady on, Morley,' called a man in the crowd.

'You'll want to mind your tongue, I think,' cautioned Professor Thistle-Smith. I was beginning to fear for Morley's safety.

'But how can I know what I say before I see what I say?' said Morley.

I closed my eyes. I was getting a headache. Mr Thistle-Smith looked perplexed.

'The White Rabbit, *Alice in Wonderland*,' said Mrs Thistle-Smith.

'Correct,' said Morley.

'I'm glad my wife can understand your nonsense,' said Mr Thistle-Smith. 'Because it makes no sense to me, man.' He then launched into a passionate declaration of loyalty to the crown, ending with the words, 'This country has relied for a thousand years on a strong connection between the people, their God, and their King.'

'And queens,' said Morley.

'Obviously,' said Professor Thistle-Smith.

'The British monarch being crowned on Jacob's Pillow. The Lion of Judah figuring on the Royal Arms. Potent symbols,' agreed Morley.

'Indeed. Indicating that ours is a Christian nation.'

'I quite agree, sir.'

'Good, and you would agree with me also then that the recent influx of non-believers can't be good for the future of a nation like our own, and is in fact dragging us towards perdition itself.'

'You're referring to the Jews, Mr Thistle-Smith?'

'I am referring, Mr Morley, to any person of any faith who enters this country without sharing or intending to share our common beliefs and habits.'

'And how do you know what common beliefs and habits they share or don't share with us?'

'I know little and care less about the beliefs of other nations, Morley, and have little interest in finding out. But what I do know is that our whole country is being overrun by Freemasons and Jews and perverts and—'

'I hardly think—'

'I've not finished speaking, man. D'you not learn manners where you're from?'

'Clearly not the same manners as you were schooled in, Professor. I do apologise.'

Mrs Thistle-Smith leaned forward and whispered in her husband's ear. As she did so, he shook his head, as if a dog attempting to dislodge a tick.

'We have at least twice as many Jews here as we can possibly absorb, both of the oriental and the aristocratic type and as far as I'm concerned they are both equally unwelcome. England gave the world its three great religions—'

'Really?' said Morley. 'Three? Christianity, Islam and Judaism?'

'The Church of England. Quakerism. And the Salvation Army. Which should be enough for everyone, in my opinion. And if they're not, and we don't do more to prevent this influx of outsiders and unbelievers and to protect our institutions, then I believe we are heading for a social revolution, Mr Morley, with your sort at the vanguard.'

This stung Morley, as it was intended to do.

'My sort?'

'Darling!' said Mrs Thistle-Smith, who was dismissed again with a wave of her husband's hand.

'And which sort would that be?' continued Morley.

'The little man,' said the professor. 'The self-made man.'

Despite the continuing unpleasantness and ferocity of the attack, and the now focused attention of all the other guests in the room, Morley continued to parry and joust.

'The "little man"—' he began.

'One day that's all we'll have, Morley, if you and your like get your way. The bitter. The twisted. Look at the trouble you've been giving us in Spain.'

I was about to open my mouth, but Morley glared at me in warning.

'I'm not sure that—'

'We're heading for a bloody revolution in this country if we're not careful,' continued Mr Thistle-Smith. 'Like the French and the Spanish and—'

'Realistically I think the guillotine is still rather a long way from Trafalgar Square, don't you, Professor?'

But the professor was not listening. He was talking through Morley to the nation at large, and to his gathered guests.

'I'll tell you where this country started going wrong,' he said, pouring himself another schooner of sherry.

'With the General Strike?' said Morley, preparing to defend territory he had clearly defended before. But Professor Thistle-Smith had a longer memory – a class memory.

'No, no, no, sir. We have been slipping and sliding our way towards disaster for years. Decades. Since bloody Gladstone, in fact. Excuse my language, ladies. This country started to go wrong with the Hares and Rabbits Bill, if you ask me. When decent honest farmers aren't allowed to shoot game on their own land the game's up, as far as I'm concerned. Landowners are under attack everywhere in this country. Half of our fine homes and castles have already been turned into hotels and lunatic asylums. God himself only knows where it's going to stop.'

Mrs Thistle-Smith took advantage of a natural pause in her husband's outburst to interject.

'Mr Morley also writes for *The Times*, darling. You like *The Times*.'

Professor Thistle-Smith waved his hand again. 'Who he writes for is a matter of utter disinterest to me, frankly.' He fixed his eyes – rather bloodshot, jaundiced eyes, I fancied, eyes long familiar with the half-lit cellars of a large country house – on Morley. 'Like many of us here in the village, Mr Morley, I am only interested in why you're asking questions about our dear departed reverend, and muck-raking in the gutter press.'

'I have been trying to piece together a picture of the reverend's final hours,' said Morley.

'An enterprise best left to the police, wouldn't you say?'

'The police certainly have their methods, sir. But I, you might say, have a motive.'

'A motive? For the murder?'

'Indeed, no.' Morley seemed unconcerned by the accusation, which caused not a little excitement among those gathered around; there were mumblings and gasps. 'But it is true that I did find the reverend's body, with Mrs Snatchfold, during the course of my researches on my latest literary project—'

'Ah yes, *The County Guides*!' Professor Thistle-Smith laughed.

'Which alas I have been prevented from working on until the police conclude their enquiry.'

'A prisoner here in our little village.'

'Effectively, yes,' said Morley.

'Well, I'm sure my wife will endeavour to make your stay here as pleasant as possible,' said the professor vilely, glancing menacingly towards Mrs Thistle-Smith, a glance that seemed to indicate a gulf of long standing, infinite and unbridgeable.

'Darling!' Mrs Thistle-Smith looked shocked, as did many of the gathered guests.

'What? A man not allowed to speak his mind in his own home?'

'Yes, of course you are, but not if you are upsetting our guests.'

'I think it might be time for us to leave,' said Morley.

'Not a moment too soon,' said the professor.

'And that,' said Morley on our way to the hotel, 'is why I don't go to parties.'

# CHAPTER EIGHTEEN

I RETIRED TO BED, Morley to I know not what; to crochet, possibly; or to learn another language.

I wasn't asleep. I was smoking one last cigarette after another, killing time, and entertaining my usual night thoughts about the horror of it all, and what had gone wrong, and reading a poem in *New Verse*:

> The hill has its death like us; the ravens gather;
> Trees with their corpses lean towards the sky.
> Christ's corn is mildewed and the wine gives out.
> Smoke rises from the pipes whose smokers die.
> And on our heads the crimes of our buried fathers
> Burst in a hurricane and the rebels shout.

Terrible rot. Which seemed about right.

Around midnight there was a tapping on my door. For a moment, I hoped it might have been Lizzie. I extinguished my cigarette, took a look at myself in the vanity mirror, ran my fingers through my hair.

It wasn't Lizzie. It was Morley.

'Come on then, Macumazahn,' he said, whispering. I was shocked. I had never heard him whisper before, and also this was one of the very few of his endless literary and mythological and historical references that I recognised straight away, without any clues or prompting: the name given by the Zulus to Alan Quatermain in *King Solomon's Mines*.

'What?' I said, whispering back.

'We need to get up to the church.'

'Now?'

He glanced at his watch. And then at his other watch.

'Of course now, Sefton. I wouldn't be here otherwise, would I?' His moustache was twitching, in its enigmatic way.

'But—'

'Now. Quickly, Sefton. Come on.'

∽ ∾

I dressed and we strode up to the church in silence, Morley insistently shushing me when I tried to ask any questions.

'*Quin taces*, Sefton, please,' he mumbled. '*Quin taces*.'

I had a vague memory from Latin classes that this meant shut up.

'Shut up,' he said, clarifyingly. So I shut up.

The streets of Blakeney, as on the first morning of our arrival, were deserted. There was a night fog. Up the hill, and we approached the twin towers of St Nicholas.

'How are we then, Sefton?' asked Morley, who had returned to whispering again.

'Fine,' I whispered back. 'Can't see much.'

'Right and proper,' said Morley. 'Diogenes lit a lantern

and walked through Athens by day searching for an honest man and found he not one. And found he not one ... Now,' he said, as we stepped through the church porch and approached the door.

He produced a key, tried it in the lock, and the vast door creaked open.

'Where did you get the key from?'

'*Auro quaeque ianua panditur,*' he whispered. 'A golden key opens any door.'

'You have a golden key?'

'Don't be silly, Sefton. I bribed Constable Ridley for it. Not much point in getting old if you don't also get crafty, eh?'

Just inside the church, in the deep black Bible dark, Morley produced two candles from his jacket pocket and lit them, and so we entered by the soft illumination of candlelight, our feet echoing around the vast empty space.

'Can't see much,' I said.

'Was it not Gideon who won a battle by lamplight, Sefton?' whispered Morley. 'And David who declared that the word of God was a lamp unto his feet? It seems appropriate.'

'Right,' I said, 'and what exactly are we—'

'Sshh,' said Morley. 'Tiptoe walking and hushed tones in church, please.'

'But no one's here, Mr Morley.'

'Does it matter?'

'Well. If no one's here then what's the point of—'

'I take it you are not a believer, Sefton?'

'I can't say that I am, Mr Morley, no. I believe in science.'

'Then God's loss is science's gain,' said Morley. 'This way.'

We groped our way in the dark towards the octagonal font.

'Ah, our friends the Evangelists,' said Morley, striking stone.

I walked into an oak bench and gave a yelp.

'God!'

'Ironic,' said Morley. 'Remind me, which branch of the sciences is it you've studied, Sefton?'

'Well . . . none in particular,' I said. 'All of them. In school.'

'Ah,' said Morley, feeling his way along a row of benches. 'There's our problem, you see. In many ways we are as ignorant and as credulous about science – as utterly in the dark, as it were – as any churchgoer in the Middle Ages.'

'I'm not sure I follow you, Mr Morley.'

'Come on,' he said, misconstruing. 'This way,' and led us across to what I assumed was the south aisle of the church. 'We'll try here first.' He held his candle up aloft, towards the stained-glass windows. 'The churchgoers of the Middle Ages, Sefton, those who flocked to these magnificent buildings, could see but could not understand. Do you follow?'

'Yes, I think so.'

'And science for us today is much the same. Do you understand electricity, for example, Sefton?'

My eyes were now accustomed to the dark. We had paused underneath a window depicting Mary and child surrounded by angels and saints, which was weakly lit by the rays of the moon.

'Electricity?' I said.

'Yes. The wonder of electricity, Sefton. The *miracle* of electricity. Have you ever paused to think, as a switch goes down with a click, and – lo! – the light shines, what miracles of engineering lay behind it?'

'No, I can't say I—'

'Any idea at all, in fact, of how it works? Electricity? Workings of? A brief outline?'

'Well . . .'

'Go on. The Electric Catechism, as it were?'

'Electricity is . . .'

'Yes?'

'It . . . comes in a . . . cable . . .'

'Hmm.'

'With . . . wires . . . to a switch.'

'Hmm.'

'And when you press the switch it . . .'

'Completes the circuit! Not bad, Sefton,' he said, as we moved suddenly on from under the stained-glass window down towards a darker and shadowy area at the far end of the south aisle.

'Thank you,' I said.

'But not good either, eh? No James Jeans are we, Sefton? In fact, you are in many ways, if you don't mind my saying so, as ignorant about electricity as a primitive savage.'

'Well, I'm not sure—'

'The world is as mysterious to you as a headhunter in Borneo, Sefton, or a medieval peasant.'

'Well . . .'

'And so is it not possible, Sefton, that if someone – say, some eminent professor – were to tell you that a man had died from hanging, that you might have no way of judging the truth of his statement?'

'I don't know,' I said. 'Are you suggesting that we shouldn't believe what Professor Thistle-Smith has told us about the reverend?'

'I'm suggesting that we shouldn't take his word for it

*Six Norfolk fonts*

merely because he happens to be a professor, Sefton. *Nam et ipsa scientia potestas est.* Ah!' he said. 'Here we are. The chapel of Our Lady. Time to visit your desecrated Virgin, Sefton.'

By the weak light of Morley's candle I could make out an image of the Virgin, her face having been crudely – and, one suspected, frantically – scraped away, so that all that remained were scars and scratches where the eyes and mouth should have been. I was reminded horribly of some of the churches I had seen in Spain – defaced and degraded.

'Who do you think—' I began.

'I have an idea, Sefton. But ... *Caudae pilos equino paulatim oportet evellere*, eh?'

'Something about a horse?' I said.

'We must pluck the hairs of a horse's tail one by one, Sefton.'

'Right.'

'Let's just retrace our steps, shall we?'

We made our way towards the altar, and up the steps into the room where we had found the reverend. It looked different in the dark: worse; more sinister; like a tomb. Morley seemed unperturbed.

'Now, where was it exactly we found him, the reverend?'

'Here,' I said, pointing up.

'Hanging.'

'Yes.'

'Hanging. Significant, Sefton, do you suppose?'

'Well, it's certainly one way of committing suicide,' I said. 'It's quick and—'

'The Greek Fates, Sefton, you may remember, imagined the life of man hung by a thread spun by Lachesis, while

Clotho held the distaff, and Atropos waited to snip the thread whenever she would.'

'Right,' I said. 'And?'

'Just thinking out loud, Sefton, that's all. Where exactly was he hanging?'

'Here.' I pointed up again towards the pitch-black ceiling.

'From?'

'A beam.'

'Yes. And above a . . . ?'

'Table.'

'Correct. What kind of a table?'

'Just a . . . table. This table,' I said, tapping the table with my hand.

'Yes. But there are tables, and there are tables, Sefton, are there not?'

'I suppose so.'

'There are indeed. There are card tables, and gaming tables, billiard tables, tea tables, marble-topped tables, tables for the sporting of aspidistra—'

'And plethoric bonsai,' I said.

'Indeed, and plethoric bonsai tables, and dining tables, and refectory tables, and credence tables and the great tables of history . . . You know the story, of course, Sefton, that Napoleon was buried in a coffin made from an Englishman's mahogany dining table?'

'I'm not sure that I did know that story, actually, Mr Morley, no.'

'No? Well, make a note, Sefton. The History of Tables. That might make an article, mightn't it?'

'I'm sure it would, Mr Morley, but—'

'Sir Galahad, Sir Lancelot, Sir Percivale, Sir Tristram—'

'The Knights of the—'

'Round Table, precisely, Sefton. Sitting down with King Arthur and Merlin. Those noble phantoms of the dawn.'

'I'm not sure what that has to do with us and the reverend though, Mr Morley.'

'Nothing.'

'Ah.'

'No. Nothing at all. Except that great tables, Sefton, might make us think of "Who loves another's name to stain. He will not dine with me again," might they not?'

'You've lost me again, I'm afraid, Mr Morley.'

'Augustine, Sefton!'

'The saint?'

'The very man. Carved the words onto his table.'

'Really?'

'So legend has it. A message writ on the table, for all the world to see.'

'I see.'

'But that's the point, you did not see, Sefton. You did not observe. And then you did not connect. What if the reverend had left us a message, Sefton, carved onto the table?'

'But he didn't. There was no suicide note ... You don't mean he scratched a message on the table?' I started to lean down closely to examine the table.

'Unlikely, Sefton, don't you think? The final desperate act of a desperate man, carving a message on a table. But what did he leave us? On the table?'

'The Bible?'

'Correct! And his message to us was what?'

'I don't know.'

'Fortunately we made a note of the passage. Do you remember?'

'No, I'm afraid—'

'Judges 16. Which is?'

'I . . . Erm . . .'

'Samson at Gaza, of course.' Morley put on his preaching voice. '"And they called for Samson out of the prison house: and he made them sport: and they set him between the pillars." Did our reverend fancy himself as a Samson, perhaps?'

'Perhaps.'

'And why would our Samson have come here, Sefton, do you think? To Blakeney. Hardly the *caput mundi*, is it? *Caput mortuum*, more like.'

'Perhaps he wanted a quiet life?'

'Perhaps. Perhaps. And possibly . . . No. This brilliant young man from Oxford chooses to come here to Blakeney to fulfil his vocation.'

'It's possible.'

'But unlikely. What if he had been lured here, in love with a woman in the valley of Sorek?'

'Sorry, I . . .'

'Just thinking out loud, Sefton. Oh. And one final thing.'

Morley led us back out of the church, candles aloft, and into the graveyard.

It was, by this time, gone one o'clock in the morning. There was a sharp chill in the air. Morley stood staring around the graveyard, and then spoke, not looking at me, as if addressing the dead.

'Do you know the tale of the Norfolk mermaids?'

I wasn't sure he was speaking to me.

'Sefton? You know the story of the mermaids?'

'No.'

'They are said to be the souls of the damned, that come up from the sea at night and press against the North Door of the Holy Church from which they are for ever shut out.' He gestured behind him. 'Many places have similar legends – the tale of the silkie you may know, from Ireland. Here in Norfolk there is the story of the mermaid who came up and tried to gain entry at the North Door of the church at Cley. She is depicted there to this day. When she was turned away she returned to the sea, where she continues to suck her prey into unseen whirlpools.'

I was tired and cold and I was thinking of Hannah. I was beginning to feel rather uncomfortable.

'But you know of course, Sefton, the story of Shuck the Phantom Hound of the Stiffkey Marshes?'

'I don't, Mr Morley, no.'

'Really? But you should! For the *County Guides*, at least, Sefton. Black Shuck: inspiration for Arthur Conan Doyle – great writer, of course. Terrible thinker. Like a lot of creative types, a mind susceptible to nonsense. Anyway, Black Shuck – from "scucca", I think, from the Old English, for a fiend—'

'Mr Morley, I don't quite—'

'*The Hound of the Baskervilles*, Sefton. Inspiration for.'

'Ah,' I said.

'Nonsense of course. But the story goes there was a storm, and a ship was wrecked up at Salthouse. And all the crew were lost, including the master and his dog, and at night the dog comes howling, looking for his master. If you hear the call of Black Shuck, they say, you're doomed. You don't hear anything do you, Sefton?'

'No,' I whispered.

'Good,' he said. 'Me neither. But many years ago, Sefton, as a young reporter, I was called to report on a case at Cromer. A young woman had come to enjoy the summer, and had been drawn out to sea where she couldn't swim back. The lifeboat was at work elsewhere. And you could hear her scream for an hour before she drowned ...' He gazed again around the foggy churchyard. 'Real terrors, you see, are much worse than the imagined, Sefton.'

'Is there a reason we're out here, Mr Morley?' I asked.

'Yes! Of course. Because we have work to do, Sefton. Work apace, work apace—'

'Honest labour bears a lovely face,' I added.

'Ah, you know the saying?' I knew the saying because Morley said it a dozen times a day. 'So we need corroboration, Sefton. *Testis unus*, *testis nullus*. One witness, no witness. We have the Virgin. We have the Bible. But we need something more.'

'Such as?'

'What we need, Sefton, alas, is the witness of the dead.'

And so between us, shoulder to shoulder, we wandered among the hundreds of gravestones of Blakeney church with our candles until almost dawn: Sam and William Starling, the crew of the *Caroline*, who saved the lives of thirty men; Charles William Grant, Master Mariner; James Spooner; Jane Pinney; Robert Jennings; dozens of In Memory Ofs and Sacred to the Memory Ofs; dozens of Here Lieth Interred the Bodies.

And shortly before dawn, finally, we found what Morley was looking for.

The stone was clear and clean, as though it had been tended only yesterday.

'Olivia Swain, Beloved Sister, Died April 24th 1924, Aged 20,' read Morley.

'A long time ago,' I said.

'Ever lost anyone, Sefton?'

'Yes.'

'Then you'll know. It might as well have been yesterday.'

# CHAPTER NINETEEN

THE MORNING SERVICE at St Nicholas, Blakeney, was conducted by the Reverend Dr Richard Swain, done out in
full regalia: cassock, surplice, robe. 'No expense spared,'
remarked Morley later. And his sermon, apparently, ran the
full gamut, from Daniel in the Lion's Den to the Prodigal Son
to the Conversion of St Paul, a 'good old-fashioned Church
of England sermon', according to Constable Ridley, who
was present, in a good old-fashioned church of England.
Everyone from the village was there – the Thistle-Smiths;
the Chancellors; Miss Harris and Miss Spranzi; the Podgers;
Mrs Snatchfold; half of the staff from the hotel – ranked, as
is according to custom in an English church, from high to
low and front to back, the worthies, best-dressed, up front,
and closest to God.

Morley and I missed the service. We were outside,
Morley explaining his theory to the Deputy Detective Chief
Inspector for the Norfolk Constabulary, while I absented
myself and took a final turn around the graveyard, smoking,
thinking of all that had happened there, coming back round
upon the two men in the final throes of their conversation.

'Methinks not, Deputy Detective Chief Inspector. *E contrario*. I simply do not believe that a man would commit suicide for no reason. *Ex nihilo nihil fit*. And if we find ourselves *a fronte praecipitium a tergo lupi*, so be it!'

The deputy detective chief inspector called me over.

'He's speaking foreign languages again. What did he just say?'

'I don't know,' I said. I was too tired for Morley's word games. 'Mr Morley, could you—'

'Between the devil and the deep blue sea, gentlemen,' said Morley.

'Well, you're right there, Mr Morley,' said the deputy detective chief inspector.

'I think, Inspector, it must be your decision, what action is to be taken.'

'I'm not sure it all adds up, Mr Morley.'

'I know,' said Morley, 'but a few crumbs of information, gathered all together, do add up to a sizeable loaf, do they not?'

'Let's hope you're right, Mr Morley. And you can be on your way.'

We entered the church as the Reverend Swain concluded the service with the blessing: 'The grace of our Lord Jesus Christ, and the love of God, and the fellowship of the Holy Ghost, be with us all evermore.'

There were suspicious glances as Morley and the deputy detective chief inspector made their way up to the pulpit while the congregation chimed in on the final ringing 'Amen'.

'Beautiful pulpit,' said Morley, to no one in particular. 'Late Victorian?'

The deputy detective chief inspector spoke briefly with the Reverend Swain, and then explained to the shocked congregation that Morley had an announcement to make.

Morley took centre stage in his tweeds and brogues and his bow tie, Christ on the cross above him, the congregation before him, and the chequerboard stone floor shining beneath his feet in the morning sunlight.

'Thank you,' he said, for all the world as if he were addressing a meeting of the Workers' Educational Association and was about to deliver nothing more shocking than a talk on the poetry of Wordsworth, or the history of antimacassars, or the characteristics of rock formations around the British Isles. 'It has been my great pleasure this week to spend time here with you in Blakeney, and I would like to thank you for making me feel so welcome.'

Professor Thistle-Smith was set a boiling in his pew.

'The deputy detective chief inspector has been kind enough to invite me this morning to say a few words about the tragic death of the Reverend Bowden. My assistant and I, Mr Sefton, must leave this afternoon in order to resume our literary labours—'

There were groans from some members of the congregation.

'And so I shall be brief in my comments.' He relaxed his shoulders and folded his hands before him, the Twelve Apostles on the pulpit flanking him as he spoke. 'I must be honest with you, ladies and gentlemen, as I have been honest with many of you, that it did occur to me, on discovering the poor reverend's body with Mrs Snatchfold last week, that it was a possibility that he had been murdered.'

There came a groan from Dr Sharp.

'Don't be ridiculous,' said Professor Thistle-Smith.

'There was something odd about the circumstances of his death,' continued Morley. 'Something like an itch that made me want to scratch. Now you may think it the product of a febrile mind—'

'Correct,' said Professor Thistle-Smith.

'But I wondered perhaps if what we had here was a classic locked room murder. Could it have been that the reverend had been poisoned and then strung up, to make his death look like suicide?'

'Absolute rubbish!' said Professor Thistle-Smith.

'Not quite,' said Morley. 'I may be a non-consenting Non-conformist but even I know that according to the rites and rituals of the Church of England, any remaining communion wine must be drunk by the officiating minister, and so it struck me that there was a possibility that someone might have put poison in the chalice—'

'Preposterous!' said Professor Thistle-Smith.

'I agree,' said Morley. 'It seemed unlikely. Could there, then, I wondered, have been someone in the vestry with him, who assaulted him, and hung him up? Choirboys, perhaps?'

The choirboys sitting in the chancel, beyond the rood screen, could be heard to gasp.

'But once gangs of choirboys start committing murder in England, then we really are in trouble,' said Morley. There was absolute silence in the church. 'So I discounted the choirboys.'

'Thank goodness,' said Professor Thistle-Smith.

'Then it did occur to me,' continued Morley, 'that there might have been some kind of hidey-hole in the roof of the vestry, where a murderer might have hidden and sprung out, unexpectedly. And I noted that there is indeed a small entrance hole between the beams of the roof of the vestry. Blakeney was known at one time as the haunt of smugglers. Could the church tower have been a place for smugglers to hide their contraband, I wondered, and now for a murderer to hide himself?'

'Really, do we have to listen to any more of this nonsense?' said Professor Thistle-Smith.

'Let him go on,' said Miss Harris, who was seated in a pew by the Lady Chapel. 'Personally, I am a great admirer of the work of lady detective novelists, Mr Morley. Agatha Christie and Margery Allingham—'

'Ngaio Marsh?'

'Not Ngaio Marsh, no, Mr Morley. But I do hope you are going to thrill us with some elaborate theory about the murder of the reverend.'

'Well, there I'm afraid I shall have to disappoint you, Miss Harris. Because I have simply come here this morning to say that there is no doubt in my mind that the Reverend Bowden . . . hanged himself.'

There was a sigh of relief among the congregation.

'Well then!' said the professor, rising to leave. 'I think we might be excused and you, sir, have been wasting our precious—'

'If you wouldn't mind hearing Mr Morley out, please, Professor,' said the deputy detective chief inspector.

'Sit down!' called Mr Hackford, the bell-ringer, from the back of the church.

'Thank you, Deputy Detective Chief Inspector,' said Morley. 'Assuming he had committed suicide, I then began to wonder about what the poor reverend's suicide note might say.'

'But there was no suicide note,' said Dr Sharp.

'That's correct. So I had to imagine one.'

'Rather ghoulish, Morley, isn't it?' said Juan Chancellor, who sat towards the back of the church, his wife Constance, in a brimless green suede hat, beside him.

'Hear, hear!' said Professor Thistle-Smith.

'An act of imagination, merely, Mr Chancellor, which, as artists – accomplished, versatile artists – I think you and your wife might appreciate. So I tried to compose a suicide note in my mind. "Dear So-and-so—"'

'This is outrageous!' said Professor Thistle-Smith.

Morley continued. '"I didn't want to do this . . . but—"'

'But what?' said Mrs Thistle-Smith, who sat timidly beside her husband.

'That was enough, in fact,' said Morley. 'I needed to imagine little else. The but is the bottom of it, you see.'

'The but?'

'The reason behind most suicides. Everything was fine, *but*, or *except that* . . . X, Y or Z.'

'I'm afraid I don't follow,' said the deputy detective chief inspector.

'You're not alone,' said the Reverend Swain, who had remained silent up until this point, but whose robed presence remained a kind of ecclesiastical threat at the front of the church.

'"I would not be committing suicide *except for the fact that* you had run off with another chap,"' said Morley. 'The *but*, the *except that*, in this instance being a form of direct accusation. Do you see?'

'Yes,' said the deputy detective chief inspector uncertainly.

'Or alternatively, the *but*, the *except that*, might be an apology. "I would not be committing suicide *except for the fact that* I had run off with another woman." Or, indeed, an excuse. "I would not be committing suicide *except for the fact that* I haven't paid my bills on time."'

'None of which circumstances apply to the reverend, I think,' said Dr Sharp.

'Indeed,' said Morley. 'So the question remained: what was his *but*? There had to be one. "I would not be committing suicide *except for the fact that* ...." It seemed very unusual to me, you see, that the reverend should have chosen to take his own life. Perplexing. Everything to live for, and what have you. And then I remembered the passage from the Bible that the reverend had left for us to read. Judges 16. Samson, eyeless in Gaza. "And they called for Samson out of the prison house: and he made them sport: and they set him between the pillars."'

'Lost us again,' said Professor Thistle-Smith.

'Well, let me put it as clearly as I can, Professor. Unlike all of you, I was in the position of coming to know the Reverend Bowden only after his death, and only through the information and facts supplied by those of you here today. A brilliant classical scholar, the Reverend Swain told me.'

'Which he was,' agreed Swain.

'A pullover wearer, Miss Harris told me. A man of great personal charms, according to Mrs Snatchfold. Yet unmarried. And so I began to build up a picture of this man. I imagined those Oxford vacations, all those years ago, when he would come to Blakeney to stay with his friend and fellow student, Swain. I imagined how he might have been welcomed into the Swain family. Welcomed in particular by the four Swain sisters.'

There were glances between the women in the congregation.

'What are you suggesting, Morley?' said the Reverend Swain.

'Not suggesting, Reverend. *Imagining*. Imagining how a young, brilliant Olivia Swain, the youngest sister, might fall in love with such a man, this young Oxford scholar, a friend of her brother's. And how she might have become pregnant with his child, and then how she might have died tragically in childbirth. Your sister died in 1924, Reverend, isn't that correct?'

'Yes,' said Swain, 'it is.'

'So her child would now be . . . what? Thirteen years old,' said Morley.

There were glances again among the choirboys, but most eyes in the congregation fell immediately upon the boy, Thomas, Teetees, the quail-egg peeler who I had met at the Thistle-Smiths' sherry party, and who was seated next to Mrs Thistle-Smith. He was wearing corduroy knickerbockers, a Norfolk jacket, and his long hair was swept back over his collar. He seemed oblivious to people's stares.

Professor Thistle-Smith began to rise up from his seat.

Morley held up a finger, glared at him. 'Think!' he said.

'Let him finish,' said the deputy detective chief inspector.

The professor sat down.

'I imagined then how the Swain family might have felt about the loss of their sister. The disgrace of the pregnancy. And the betrayal, by this so-called friend of their brother. The sense of tragedy. I imagined them going on to their lives

*The Reverend Bowden*

and careers. One of them as an actress, perhaps. One of them married to a professor, raising a son. And one of them an artist.'

'Is this the best you can do, Morley?' said Miss Harris, with characteristic bravura.

'There's more,' said Morley. 'Much more. I imagined, for example, that these sisters might have extracted from the young Bowden a promise to change his ways, to follow the path of their brother, even, into the Church? To devote his life, indeed, to the people of the village they had grown up in, and whom he had so bitterly betrayed? Might they have even had painted an image of their beloved sister Olivia as the Virgin Mary, so that the reverend, as he became, might never forget her presence? "I acknowledge my transgressions, and my sin is ever before me."'

Mrs Thistle-Smith had begun to cry.

'And all, I imagine, had been forgotten. Until the Reverend Bowden employed a new housemaid, young and attractive, and the two of them dream of starting a new life together. Except that the reverend, a good man, is so bound by his conscience, so torn apart and tormented, and thus unwilling to pursue or consummate the relationship, that he is urged finally to self-destruction and commits the ultimate crime against himself.'

There now came a sobbing from all three women: Mrs Thistle-Smith, Miss Harris and Constance Chancellor.

'A suicide pact,' said the deputy detective chief inspector.

'No,' said Morley. 'A pact implies a mutual arrangement between two people who resolve to die at the same time, and in the same place. After the reverend's death, poor Hannah, I think, was merely alone, a Jewess in a foreign country, in a place where she was unwelcome, preyed upon by unscrupulous individuals, and so, facing these insurmountable odds, she too decides to take her own life, though not before destroying the image of the woman she has been judged to usurp . . .'

There was a coughing from Juan Chancellor at the back of the church.

'In a sense,' said Morley, 'I was entirely wrong about Blakeney, and about the death of your reverend. No crime has been committed here. No one is guilty. Except perhaps, in a sense, if I might borrow the language of your Book of Common Prayer, we have all erred, and have strayed from thy ways like lost sheep.'

The professor rose again from his seat. The congregation sat in silence.

'You certainly have a vivid imagination, Mr Morley.'

'Thank you.'

'And now, I think it might be best if you were on your way. Chief Inspector?'

'I think so, yes,' said the deputy detective chief inspector. 'That'll be all, Mr Morley.'

'Good,' said Morley. And he walked down the nave, to the font, and out of the church.

I followed, astonished.

# CHAPTER TWENTY

SUNDAY AFTERNOON. Morley sat down by the harbour, cross-legged, on a rug. He had with him his Cona coffee machine, which he always referred to as a costermonger machine. I'd gone to the hotel to say goodbye to Lizzie, but it was her day off. We were packed and ready to go.

'Ah, Sefton. Tempt you to a cup from the costermonger?'

'Yes, I don't mind if I do, Mr Morley.'

'Bit of an impromptu picnic. Miriam said she'd meet us here at three.' He checked his watches. 'Few minutes to spare. The hotel prepared a few things. Nothing too exciting, I'm afraid. Apple? Patum Peperium sandwich?'

'No, thank you.'

'Not much in the mood for it myself.' He stared out ahead, across the mudflats. 'The flatland of Norfolk, eh, Sefton. Puts us in our place, doesn't it?' The view – flat, uninspiring – did indeed.

'This is where Hannah committed suicide,' I said.

'Yes,' said Morley, stroking his moustache. 'It's really her I feel sorry for. You know the story of the boy martyr,

Sefton, do you? St William? Reputedly murdered by Jews in Norwich. You know the story?'

'I'm afraid not.'

'Unpleasant tale. Young boy, apprentice tanner, mysterious murder. Claims of the blood libel. The sort of thing Herr Hitler is carping on about now.'

'When was this?'

'Oh, twelfth century.'

'Recently, then.'

'Just because it was a long time ago, Sefton, doesn't mean it doesn't matter. That's the lesson of history, surely. Much of what is happening in Germany today one might well impute to the works of Martin Luther.'

'Really?'

'Absolutely. The past explains everything, in the end. This place.' He threw his arms wide towards the village. 'With its narrow streets and its grand houses. The vast church. What you have to remember about Norfolk, Sefton, is that it was once incredibly wealthy. Agriculture paid for the great churches around the Wash. Then in the fifteenth century the wool trade paid for the Perpendicular rebuildings, so there's always been this connection, you see, between the Church and money, and great families.'

'Like the Swains.'

'Indeed. Like the Swains. Also, quietly Catholic, Norfolk. Like a lot of England. The Reformation swept much of it away. But still, behind and within a lot of these churches, if you dig a little deeper, you find this attachment to the Marian, to the medieval. The Mother. Gaia. Goes very deep, Sefton. Have to get it all in the book, somehow.'

'Maybe not,' I said.

'No,' said Morley wearily. 'You're right. Maybe not. Beyond our remit.'

Miriam arrived.

'So, chaps, what do we have for our picnic?'

'Rashers of wind, and fried snowballs—' said Morley.

'And a plate of fried door handles!' said Miriam.

It was one of their well-rehearsed routines.

'Sounds delicious,' I said.

'Apples and a couple of sandwiches,' said Morley.

'Oh dear. Didn't think it'd be up to much,' she said, and began unpacking food from a hamper. 'So I brought a few things I'd been saving up from my last trip to London. Périgord pie, some black cherries in port wine. Chocolate cake from Madame Prunier in St James's. And some smoked sturgeon from the Czarda in Dean Street. And – wait for it.' She pulled a jar of something from the hamper. 'Ta-dah! Some horseradish cream. I know you like it, Father.'

'All rather extravagant, Miriam.'

'Well, I was saving it for a special occasion really, but it's not every day we get to celebrate you solving a crime, Father, is it? The village is murmurous with rumour, you know. You're quite the star.'

'Well . . .' said Morley. 'Hardly a cause for celebration.'

'Perhaps a small celebration, though, don't you think, Sefton?'

'*Dum vivimus viviamus*,' said Morley.

'Indeed,' said Miriam, passing round plates of chocolate

cake and smoked sturgeon. 'I'm absolutely famished, actually. I stayed last night with the Hammertons down in Swaffham, Father.'

'Ah, yes.'

'And you know what they're like. It's all curtains and kippers down there, I'm afraid.'

'Sorry?' I said.

'Fur coat and no—'

'Thank you, Miriam,' said Morley. 'She means a grand but a frugal house, I think, Sefton.'

'Plus-fours but nothing for breakfast. It's just like when you visit the Cliftons, in Aldeburgh.'

'Really?' I said.

'Yes. Just the same. Invite you down for the weekend, and then there's no food in the house, and you have to pay them for the privilege of having you. Which is hardly the spirit, is it, Sefton?'

'Hardly.'

'So, anyway, cheers, chaps!' We clinked coffee cups. 'I want to hear all about your adventure. No detail too small!'

～ ～

We enjoyed our picnic, telling our tale to Miriam, and then we packed the remains of the picnic and prepared to leave.

'What would you call this, Sefton?' said Miriam, as we walked towards the Lagonda.

'Your dress?'

'The colour of the dress, silly.'

'Red?'

'Oh come on, you can do better than that, Sefton.'

'Crimson?'

'Crimson!' She smoothed the creases of the dress against her body. 'Crushed mulberry, I think you'll find, Sefton. And what do you think?'

'Well, you certainly look . . .'

'What?'

'Perfectly dashing,' I said.

'Oh, you are funny, Sefton. You're almost as bad as Father.'

'I'll take that as a compliment,' said Morley.

'*Eiusdem farinae*,' said Miriam.

'Indeed we are,' said Morley. 'He did very well, didn't he, Miriam, on his first outing? Don't you think?'

'He did, Father.'

'We might grant him an *accessit*, what do you think?'

'Oh, I'd give him first prize, Father, without a doubt.'

Miriam settled Morley into the back of the Lagonda, and placed his portable writing desk around him, heaving the typewriter into place.

'I'm assuming you have an article to write, Father?'

'I do, I'm afraid.'

'And what's today's article? "My Favourite Insect and Why"?'

'No,' said Morley. 'It is a short piece in praise of Debussy, actually.'

'Oh, how *au courant*! Before long you'll have caught up with the twentieth century, Father.'

I clambered into the car, up front next to Miriam, and we set off.

Holidaymakers in mackintoshes and gumboots stood

waiting for a bus. There were low, shifting clouds, threatening rain. Fat little rabbits sat lazily at the side of the road.

'Ah, England!' sighed Morley. 'England, my England,' and he started typing, while singing a spirited rendition of Chesterton's 'The Rolling English Road':

Before the Roman came to Rye or out to Severn
    strode,
The rolling English drunkard made the rolling
    English road.
A reeling road, a rolling road, that rambles round the
    shire,
And after him the parson ran, the sexton and the
    squire;
A merry road, a mazy road, and such as we did tread
The night we went to Birmingham by way of Beachy
    Head.

Miriam beeped the horn.

'What do you think, then, Sefton, where to next?'

# ACKNOWLEDGEMENTS

For previous acknowledgements see *The Truth About Babies* (Granta Books, 2002), *Ring Road* (Fourth Estate, 2004), *The Mobile Library: The Case of the Missing Books* (Harper Perennial, 2006), *The Mobile Library: Mr Dixon Disappears* (Harper Perennial, 2006), *The Mobile Library: The Delegates' Choice* (Harper Perennial, 2008), *The Mobile Library: The Bad Book Affair* (Harper Perennial, 2010) and *Paper: An Elegy* (Fourth Estate, 2012). These stand, with exceptions. In addition I would like to thank the following. (The previous terms and conditions apply: some of them are dead; most of them are strangers; the famous are not friends; none of them bears any responsibility.)

Chris Adrian, Jacob Andrews, Neil Armstrong, Johan Philip 'Pilou' Asbæk, Michael Askew, Kim Ayres, Gerald Barry, Amy Baumhoefner, Maurice Blanchot, Hannah Britton, John Buchan, Lewis Buzbee, Frank Carson, Alessandra Chessa, the Child and Adolescent Mental Health Service, E.M. Cioran, Enna Coates, Bill Coles, Richard Coles, Friedl Dicker, John Doherty, Katie Dudwell, Michael Fassbender,

Festival Intercelticu d'Avilés, John Paul Flintoff, Alex Fusco, David Gallacher, Ben Galley, Juliet Gardiner, Nicholas Gardiner, The Great British Bake Off, Sarah Goodman, Walter Gropius, Woody Guthrie, Michael Haneke, Rachel Hard, Robyn Hardman, Daniel Harlow, Devon Hazel, Sheema Hossain, Michel Houellebecq, the Irish Writers' Centre, Johannes Itten, Lars Iyer, Kirsty Judge, Helen Kalpus, Buster Keaton, Tim Key, Paul Klee, Sidse Babett Knudsen, Wyndham Lewis, Craig Leyenaar, Naomi Linehan, Morag Lyall, Rachel P. Maines, Wing Mak, Neil Martin, Georgia Mason, Hugh Massingberd, Helen May, Eleanor McDowall, Frank McNally, Dahler Mehndi, László Moholy-Nagy, Montague Bikes, Ruth Morgan, Johnny Muir, Brain Mullen, Nesco, Kathleen Normington, Ana Oliveira, Richard Owens Opticians, Tommy Peoples, Daniel Piper, Adrian Power, Adam Price, Ross Raisin, Sharon Rankin, Rachel Raymond, Olly Rowse, Steve Rudd, Nathalie Sarraute, Elaine Scarry, Oskar Schlemmer, Maurice Sendak, Elif Shafak, Robert B. Silvers, Emily Simpson, Kimberley Simpson, Josef Škvorecký, Aaron Smith, Anatoly Solonitsyn, Saviana Stenescu, Rudolf Steiner, the staff of Strathearn School, Florence Sunnen, Josh Suntharasivam, Fritz Tschaschnig, Lev Semyonovich Vygotsky, Jo Walker, the Warwick Writing Programme, Waitrose (Kenilworth), Jason Weiss, Emily Wells, John Wesley, the Wigtown Book Festival, Robyn Williamson, Timothy Woodham, Irvin B. Yalom, Behn Zeitlin

## PICTURE CREDITS

## ABOUT THE AUTHOR

IAN SANSOM is a frequent contributor and critic for *The Guardian*, *The Daily Telegraph*, *The London Review of Books*, and *The Spectator* and a regular broadcaster on BBC Radio 3 and Radio 4. He is the author of nine books, including *Paper: An Elegy* and the Mobile Library series.

Visit www.AuthorTracker.com for exclusive information on your favorite HarperCollins authors.